The Chapels on the Hill

Virginia McCullough

VEM Books

Printed in the United States of America
10 9 8 7 6 5 4 3 2

For my mother, Mary Lucille Lindstedt Carlson
(1911-2001)

Acknowledgments

Many judges gave this book an excellent run through the RWA chapter contest circuit, and I'd like to thank all those who offered valuable suggestions. And big thanks go to my first readers, Shirley Cayer, Virginia Athey, Kate Bowman, and my critique partner, Cheryl Nagro, all from my Wisconsin group. I'm extremely grateful for their enthusiasm for the story—and the Northeast Wisconsin setting. I'm just as grateful for their deepening friendship in the dozen years that have quickly passed since I moved to this beautiful state.

I'm also fortunate to belong to a critique/brainstorming group. These women have been writing buddies, advisors, and sources of incredible information, but most of all, they're my long-time good friends. So thanks to Donna Marie Rogers, Stacey Joy Netzel, Lily Silver, and Jamie Kersten for all they've done and continue to do for me—and for the Wisconsin Romance Writers.

Special thanks to a young cellist, Claudia Rufo, and her mother, Kalyn Wulatin, the granddaughter and daughter of good friends of mine. Claudia and Kalyn agreed to speak with me about the cello itself, but also what's involved in being a young musician. I so enjoyed our conversation and their insights helped me envision the characters more clearly.

The Green Bay Botanical Garden served as the inspiration for this book. One of Green Bay's treasures—and a mere ten minutes from my home—the garden has a beautiful holiday light festival and other events that fed my imagination and sparked ideas for this story. The garden's library became far more than a source of information. On many occasions I sat at one of the tables near the bookshelves and watched visitors come and go as I wrote sections of the story and looked at book after book of garden designs. I also regularly wander the gardens and am enriched by the landscape, the views, and the buildings that make it unique. So to the garden and its staff I say: Thanks for being here.

Thanks, too, to all my friends, relatives, writing buddies, and critique partners, along with those involved in production, Brittiany Koren of Written Dreams, and Lara Hunter of Book Technologies. They've supported my efforts, helped me grow, and never uttered discouraging words. I hope I've nurtured your creative spirits the way you've nurtured mine.

Virginia McCullough
January 2014

"What we have once enjoyed deeply we can never lose. All that we love deeply becomes a part of us."

—Helen Keller

Part I

1

October 2001

Aaron Chapel stood alongside his son at the Unity Airline counter, but resisted the urge to take charge of checking in Matt's duffle, or his cello, secure in its travel case. In his sport coat and blue oxford shirt, Matt looked the picture of a young man ready to take the reins of his life. He could certainly handle his own luggage. This new phase of Matt's life, a time punctuated by independent decisions and new directions had come sooner than Aaron ever imagined, but when he traced the events of Matt's life, even this trip seemed inevitable.

Glancing over his shoulder, he spotted Sonia leaning against a pillar opposite the counter. Looking proud, as usual, the happiness of the day had put extra sparkle in her expressive blue eyes. When she realized he'd fixed his gaze on her, she grinned sheepishly, as if caught in the act of looking proud of their son.

"You might say we're a bit early," Aaron joked when he and Matt had rejoined Sonia, "but you can never be too early for a flight." He was about to add "especially now," but thought better of it. He and Sonia had fought against allowing the new threat of terrorism to stop them from living normally. Besides, Matt's trip had been arranged months before.

Seeing Sonia so radiant reminded Aaron of how quickly life can change. Only a year before, they'd lamented Matt's adolescent rebellion, which included an out-of-the-blue statement that he'd quit the cello. Quite a declaration for a boy first declared a prodigy at age five.

Matt eventually reclaimed his passion, but he'd made it clear that from then on, he'd make his own decisions about his future, starting with accepting an invitation to attend a two-week intensive program at Fitzgerald College in central Illinois. Designed for young musicians with extraordinary talent, the program offered Matt the opportunity to work with one of the finest cellists in the world.

Aaron, and Sonia, too, agreed Matt should jump at this opportunity. Although it had been difficult for Aaron to accept—once and for all—that Matt's unfolding career would continue to propel him far away from Lady's River, Wisconsin, he'd finally come to terms with that reality.

Aaron put his arm around Sonia and squeezed her shoulder. "It's a beautiful day. Not a cloud in the sky."

"We couldn't ask for a better day to fly," Sonia said as she nodded to the window.

The three kept up the light banter until it was time to give Matt a final hug and then stand back and watch him go through the security line.

"Call us when you get settled in, okay?" Aaron called.

Matt turned around and smiled. "I said I would, and I won't forget." He took a few more steps, then looked back and raised his hand for one last wave. "Thanks," he said in a voice loud enough to carry over the noise in the airport, "for everything."

Minutes later, he was out of sight.

Aaron and Sonia stood at the glass wall to watch the plane lift off the ground and head into the sky. When Sonia let out a deep sigh, Aaron grabbed her hand and held it all the way back to the car.

* * *

The River Gazette
"A Town Says Goodbye"
By Martha Samuelson, Staff Writer

October 26, 2001 - Nearly two hundred family members and friends of Matthew Scott Chapel gathered on Thursday at the Lady's River Community Center for a memorial service. Matthew, 17, was one of the 48 passengers on Unity Airline's Flight 62 that crashed Sunday, leaving no survivors. The plane, en route to Springfield, Illinois, from Milwaukee, went down in a field near the central Illinois town of Pearson Pond.

Matthew was one of four students from Wisconsin high schools chosen to attend a two-week workshop for gifted young musicians held annually at Fitzgerald College in Springfield. An accomplished musician, he began playing the cello at age five and was quickly labeled a child prodigy. He soon performed as a guest soloist with orchestras across the country.

More than a dozen family members and friends shared their memories of Matthew during the candlelit service. Olivia Morton, an internationally acclaimed cellist and Matthew's teacher, held back tears as she described what the loss meant to the music community. "Matthew possessed a rare and precious gift, a spirit that soared with his music and touched all who were privileged to hear him play."

The Chapel family is well-known in the region as the founders of Chapel's Botanical Garden, one of the largest privately owned facilities of its kind in the U.S. Sonia Chapel, Matthew's mother, has served as the Botanical Garden's CEO since it opened in 1985.

Following the service, Aaron Chapel, Matthew's father and a partner in the Lady's River law firm of Bateman & Wylie, gave a brief statement to reporters outside the community center. "My wife and I wish to thank those who attended today and the hundreds of others who have generously sent their prayers and condolences during this terrible time of loss for our family."

Chapel refused to answer questions about possible lawsuits stemming from the accident. The cause of the crash is still under investigation.

* * *

Chicago, five years later

*H*e had to make a decision and stick to it.

For days, Aaron had shifted back and forth between a firm choice to attend the dedication of the pavilion and an equally strong conviction to skip the event altogether. Nothing worked harder on the knot of tension in his gut than indecision.

He picked up the announcement and scanned it once again. It had Sonia's fingerprints all over it. Well, not literally, but the neat, easy-to-read embossed lettering matched her taste. Aaron no longer followed the Unity Flight Family Group's activities as closely as he once had, but when he'd first heard their plan to build an open-air pavilion on the site of the plane crash he'd known instantly it had been Sonia's idea. The dedication of this final memorial also marked the five-year anniversary of the day they lost Matt forever.

Aaron pushed his chair back from the desk and made his way to the window that spanned the outside wall. On a clear day, he could look down from his twentieth floor office and see the Chicago River below, but that afternoon heavy rain pelted the glass, blocking the view he usually found comforting. He'd lived most of his fifty years in a small town where a river served as the one constant, a reference point for home. Maybe that explained why he'd been drawn to the river in his adopted city, the place where he'd resolved to start over and build a new life.

Absently slapping the announcement into the palm of his other hand, he rationalized that he could use the weather as an excuse not to go to the dedication ceremony. Or, he could beg off because of scheduled weekend depositions.

"Aaron? Am I interrupting?"

At the sound of the familiar low voice, he turned to see Katherine standing at his office door. "No, no, I was just…" He shrugged, but didn't finish.

"Have you decided yet?" she asked, approaching his desk.

He noted apprehension on her softly rounded face. Such a beautiful woman. Her slight frame and large brown eyes made her look vulnerable, but Aaron knew better. He'd leaned on Katherine's quiet strength both in and out of the office. Seeing her standing in front of him now gave him the push he needed.

"When it comes right down to it, I can't stay away."

"I could come with you," she offered, a note of

eagerness in her voice. "I can rearrange a few things here. We have other people to handle tomorrow's depositions."

He quickly waved her off. "Thanks, Katherine, but no, I need to do this alone."

Her face fell in subtle, but unmistakable disappointment. "Are you afraid my presence would upset Sonia? You know, perhaps make it obvious you've moved on."

Aaron frowned. "No, it's not that." Although his sister hadn't spelled it out in detail, she'd said enough to let him know that Sonia, too, had moved on. For all he knew, the man Sonia was involved with would accompany her to the dedication.

"I need to do this for Matt."

Avoiding her eyes, he went back to his desk and made a show of shuffling through a pile of unopened mail. What he'd said was at least partially true, but attending the next day's ceremony wasn't only about Matt. He needed to see Sonia one more time, wish her well and say goodbye. Finally, after five years, he sensed peace hovering nearby, almost within reach. Some people called it closure, but he still choked on that word.

Every cell in his body had once lit up in rage when anyone dared to tell him that one day he'd find closure over Matt's death. Hell, he'd barely accepted the stark fact that he'd never find a person, or a single cause, to blame for the plane going down in that field. The lawyer in him called it *assigning liability*, and for too long, chasing it had been the only thing that made getting out of bed in the morning worth the trouble.

Perhaps seeing Sonia at the dedication would at

least bring a sense of finality to the life they'd shared. Then he'd be ready to give himself completely to Katherine.

"So, you'll call when you get back?" Katherine asked.

"Of course. Let's plan on dinner Sunday night."

"You're on. I'll fix something at my place." She gave him a reassuring smile before closing the door behind her.

Relieved to be alone again, Aaron dropped into his chair and swiveled back and forth. If only he could step out of his tense, rigid body and leave it behind.

Closing his eyes and breathing deeply for several minutes, he willed his muscles to relax. No such luck. Knowing he'd get no more work done that day, he rose quickly, grabbed his coat, and managed to leave his office and escape into the elevator without having to speak to anyone.

* * *

*F*riday's downpour had saturated the fields, releasing damp earthy smells floating on the brisk October breeze. Those scents, along with the sounds of an energetic rendition of "Ode to Joy," played by the Pearson Pond High School Orchestra, reminded Sonia why she preferred open-air concerts to music trapped between the walls of stuffy auditoriums.

From her seat on the stage, she scanned the crowd that filled the pavilion to its capacity of four hundred, with an overflow of attendees sitting on camp chairs on the grounds outside. She shuffled through the index cards on which she'd written the key points of her speech. Rather than having word-for-word text in front of her, she wanted to risk letting her heart do the talking in what would likely be her last public remarks about Matt.

When the orchestra finished and the loud applause died down, Sonia stepped to the podium, pausing to take in the sea of faces in front of her. No sign of Aaron among them, though. She'd so hoped for a chance to talk with him. This pavilion stood as a symbol of the most terrible part of her life, but paradoxically, it also stirred up memories of the sweetest time, the years that Aaron and Matt were her family.

"As most of you know," she began, "Jane and Gary Carpenter once owned this field scarred by tragedy. Eventually, though, time has done its work to heal the land. Gary might have again begun planting corn or soybeans here, eventually erasing all traces of the event that brings us together today."

Feeling a rush of the adrenalin that had propelled her all day, she moved out from behind the barrier of the podium to the edge of the stage. She pointed to her right. Outside the pavilion the last of the wildflowers glistened golden under the afternoon sun. Beyond it, the nature walk snaked through newly planted trees, which one day would provide shade from the summer heat and splash orange and red over the prairie landscape in the fall.

"Take in the beauty here—breathe in the scent of this field that Jane and Gary donated to our Unity Flight Family Group. Now that we've turned the land over to the town of Pearson Pond, this fifty acre park, along with the pavilion we dedicate today, belongs to you, to all of us."

She'd known that line would bring loud applause. The break allowed her a chance to soothe the anxious ache that expanded deep inside her over what came next in her speech. She hoped no one would notice the slight shaking of the mic in her hand.

"We lost forty-eight unique individuals in this field. Flight 62 included husbands and wives, parents and grandparents, neighbors and friends. It's a cliché to say that they came from all walks of life, but it's true. Two engineers and one teacher were lost that day, along with a postal worker and four college students…and on and on. I could tell special stories about each life, no matter how long or short that life was."

She swallowed to clear the catch in her throat and fend off gathering tears. "The son I lost on this field was born with a gift of music, and I can think of no better way to honor his life than by building this pavilion as a venue for theater, dance, the magical sounds of bands and orchestras, and the harmony of soaring voices. We dedicate this facility to the memory of those who died on this spot five years ago, and to the citizens of Pearson Pond who reached out to offer help and a refuge during the days and weeks that followed the tragedy. We know the lives of our loved ones will never be forgotten."

And then, with the crowd on their feet clapping, her two years of work to build the pavilion came to an end. Sonia stepped back and Clark, who had emceed the event, took over. He thanked everyone for coming and invited them to share the buffet set up in white tents in the park.

"Great job, Sonia," Clark said. His eyes were wet, but he smiled as he wrapped his arms around her in a hug. He'd lost his brother on Flight 62, and like her, he'd found a gentle place to live with his ongoing sadness among others who understood his loss. She embraced Gary and Jane next and moved on to others who clustered around her. Then she slowly left the stage cocooned in the warmth of the dozens of people she'd worked with on the family group's projects.

While the others ambled toward the tents, she stayed close to the pavilion to have a few minutes alone. To the west, a bank of pewter clouds rolled across the flat prairie, threatening to darken the brilliant blue of the sky overhead. Her moods sometimes shifted that way, too. Not in sudden swings, but gradually, like clouds sweeping over the land and leaving their dark reminders behind. With the dedication done, she already felt herself sliding toward a letdown, exposing an empty space waiting to be refilled.

Deep in her thoughts, the sound of her name startled her.

So, he'd come after all. She turned to see Aaron approaching, a faint smile turning up the corners of his mouth. She hadn't seen him in almost three years. As he leaned in to lightly kiss her cheek, it might have been yesterday.

"Ah, here you are," she said. "I had a feeling you'd come. You're looking well." That was true, to a point, anyway. His body was trim and fit as ever, but she couldn't miss the change in his face, especially the lines around his deep-set gray eyes. She knew in an instant he hadn't been sleeping well.

He touched her shoulder, but only for a second. "You seem well, too, and as lovely as ever."

"That's kind of you to say. I think we pulled off the ceremony quite nicely." She tapped her lips with her fingertips, but abruptly dropped her hand. Why was she so flustered? This was Aaron standing in front of her, not some stranger or a man she needed to impress. Finally, she said, "I'm having a hard time believing this project is over."

"Yes, I know you've put in long hours on it." He looked towards the pavilion, where the dimming sunlight cast a pale pink shadow on the wooden structure. "It's a beautiful tribute to our son—and to the others. You can be proud of your work, Sonia."

Suddenly, his mouth tightened.

"What is it?" she asked.

"I didn't know how damn awkward this would be for me."

The hundreds of other people in the park faded from her consciousness, leaving only the two of them. "Did you really come to say goodbye to *me*, Aaron?"

His eyes widened in surprise and he laughed softly. "You always did know me better than anyone else."

"Oh, I'm not so intuitive. A while back Dottie told me that you...well...you've met someone." She forced herself to look into his eyes. "She implied, in so many words, that it's pretty serious."

His gaze shifted away for just a second, and then he looked embarrassed. "Trust my sister to spread the news." He cleared his throat. "By the way, Dottie told me the same thing about you."

She nodded, but stared off in the distance. "Yes, it's true. But Ben and I haven't made any real plans yet." She waved toward the pavilion. "I've been so preoccupied here."

"I'm happy for you, Sonia, I really am."

She believed him. "The two of us always believed in second chances," she said. For a second or two she focused on the ground, patchy with damp leaves and flattened yellowed grass. Then she lifted her head to meet his gaze. "I take it you've fallen in love?"

Aaron drew his head back as if shocked by her words. "I don't know if I'd say that. I mean, I didn't expect you…" He threw up his hands.

She didn't hide her amusement. "I'm sorry, Aaron. I didn't intend to fluster you." She'd only wanted to lighten the moment with some friendly teasing. "Don't worry about it. And besides, if you recall, you and I weren't exactly *madly* in love when we got married either."

His wry smile told her he hadn't forgotten.

2

May 1984

𝒜aron closed the door behind him, leaving the four women standing in the hallway. He tried to shake off the image of their suspicious eyes before drawing in a deep breath and unloading what weighed on his mind. "Here's the thing, Sonia. I needed to see you. I want to make sure you understand that we don't *have* to go through with this."

Sitting on the edge of the bed in a robe, she began picking at the lace border of what looked to be the jacket of her suit spread out across the quilt covering his sister's bed.

"I guess you changed your mind?" Still not looking up at him, her voice, usually low and pleasant, was high-pitched and thin.

"No, no, not at all." He took quick steps in her direction, stopping at the end of the antique double bed that dominated the room.

"Then I don't understand why you're here." She glanced at the clock radio on the nightstand. "The ceremony is supposed to start in twenty minutes."

He laughed nervously and shifted his weight from one foot to the other. "I botched my big speech."

She tilted her head and raised her eyebrows. "I'll say."

As much as she'd tried to sound amused, he saw hurt and apprehension in her light blue eyes.

"I'm sorry. Really." He grabbed hold of the footboard with both hands. "I came to offer you a last minute out. I want to be sure *you* don't feel trapped and forced to marry *me*. Whether you and I go through with the wedding or not, I'll take care of you and our baby."

She shot to her feet and faced him with arms folded across her chest. "But like I told you before, I don't want you doing me any favors. I never made marrying me a condition for you to be a father to our child."

Cheerful mid-morning light flooded the small bedroom in his sister's house, but a hush settled over it like a cloak. Having blundered in, he didn't know exactly what to say next. He'd tried to imagine how Sonia might have felt when she first opened her eyes that morning. For his part, he'd been nervous, but kind of excited and eager, too. The one thing that ruined his mood was the thought that she would feel dragged down the proverbial aisle. This particular aisle happened to be in his sister's living room.

When Dottie had first offered it, he and Sonia agreed it made sense as the place for their tiny wedding. But Dottie had a way of feigning good manners and graciousness that masked her real feelings.

"I liked it better when we talked to each other like old friends," Sonia said, breaking the silence. "You know, like the night I agreed to get married, to 'give it a go,' as you put it."

"And I meant it." He walked to the window and stared at the lingering rain drops clinging to the still bare rosebushes outside. The heavy downpour earlier that morning had left the air cold and damp, but the sun had cleared the clouds and lifted the mood of the early May morning.

His deep sigh cut through the close air in the room. "All I wanted was to give you a chance to back out. I don't want to back out myself."

She fluffed up the sides of her short white-blonde hair. "That's a stroke of luck, because neither do I."

He smiled self-consciously, seeing now how stupid he'd been to barge in on Sonia just before the ceremony. But his reason for doing so had seemed sensible enough. "I remember Dottie and her girlfriends going on and on about the fancy weddings they'd have one day. You know, like fairytales. This can't be the kind of wedding day any little girl fantasizes about."

"Hey, I wasn't *any* little girl. I didn't spend my teenage years leafing through brides' magazines, my friend." She raised her hands in the air in mock frustration. "See? We've known each other all our lives, but you don't have any idea who I really am. Think of all we have to learn about each other."

He moved away from the window to close the space between them. "Okay, here's the truth. I've been looking forward to today."

Her eyes widened. "Me, too—almost."

"Almost?"

She pointed to the door, but since her full mouth had broken into a big grin, the twinge of fear in his gut immediately eased.

"We have a collection of relatives and friends crammed into Dottie's living room, which, by the way, looks lovely with the pots of tulips everywhere. I know your sister and your mother are doing their best, but I can feel their disapproval and disappointment." She raised her hands in front of her chest and hunched her shoulders as if protecting herself from attack. "I'm constantly fending off their negative energy—it feels like darts piercing my skin. My own mother isn't doing much better, mind you. *Ha!* We probably should have flown to Vegas."

He smiled at the image of the two of them in one of those tacky Vegas chapels. But the county courthouse might have been better. *Damn it*, he shouldn't have listened to Dottie in the first place. "I'm sorry, Sonia." What else could he say?

Dottie was way off base about Sonia. She even hinted that Sonia had planned to get pregnant. At age thirty, exactly three years older than Aaron, his sister had a way of throwing her weight around, as if she were training to be the family matriarch. Thank God he and Sonia were going to be living in town, not on his family's farm.

She backed up and leaned her weight against the dresser tucked in next to the nightstand. "It's not your fault, Aaron, but I'll be honest. I won't take an easy breath until we're on the road out of Lady's River and headed to the mountains."

She hadn't used the word honeymoon, he noted, a word that implied something that didn't fit their situation. Both he and Sonia had acted like they were planning an ordinary vacation in Asheville, North Carolina. They'd agreed it would offer a change from Wisconsin's spring, which at the moment felt more like the vestiges of winter stubbornly hanging around like a bad cold.

"Okay, I get it. You don't mind marrying me," he said with a laugh, "it's this annoying wedding part that you don't like."

"Right. If I'm nervous at all, it's about getting through the wedding brunch."

The muscles in his neck and shoulders relaxed in relief. "Good. I feel the same way."

He didn't know what else to say, but telling her he'd see her up at the altar didn't sound like a smooth exit line.

She saved him when she pulled at the skirt of her robe. "I can't get married in this, so get out of here." She approached him and playfully shoved him toward the door. He hadn't felt this good all day.

The light-hearted moment ended abruptly once he stepped into the hall, only to be greeted by four frowning women. Leslie, Sonia's matron-of-honor, brushed past him and he heard her ask Sonia if everything was okay. Dottie flashed him a disapproving look worthy of the worst side of her schoolteacher personality and followed Leslie. His own mother avoided his eyes altogether as she fell third in line.

Only Vivian, Sonia's mother, stayed back. "Am I correct in assuming there *will* be a wedding today?"

"Yes, of course."

With a curt nod, she closed the bedroom door behind her. *Just short of slamming it in my face.* He leaned against the tall armoire that filled the narrow hallway and listened to the ripple of voices coming from the living room only a few yards away. The steady buzz of conversation mixed together with the drone of dull classical music in the background. He didn't care much for Sonia's selection of music. But he agreed with her about one thing. The sooner they got this ceremony out of the way, the better.

Their families might have greeted the news with happier faces if he and Sonia had dated each other, even for a short time. He dreaded most having to face his father-in-law-to-be, Bill Van Caster. Putting himself in Bill's shoes, though, made him think the protective dad probably relished the idea of landing a punch square on the nose of the guy who got Sonia pregnant.

On the other hand, they weren't the first couple to get married because a baby was on the way. For a lawyer who could talk confidently about cases and explain the legal lingo to clients, Aaron barely managed to string three words together if the topic at hand was personal. He'd stumbled through the explanation he'd prepared for his mother and sister. Out of loneliness and sadness over their recently broken relationships, he'd explained, he and Sonia had turned to each other for comfort.

No, it wasn't exactly a rebound thing, he'd admitted. Being together that one time had just kind of happened, a choice of words that made his mother wince. Neither family thought much of the way they were starting out, but he and Sonia agreed not to make up a phony romance.

A burst of laughter coming from his sister's bedroom surprised him, also making him wonder what the women found so funny. He'd ask Sonia later, knowing she'd tell him, even if the joke was at his expense. That was the thing about Sonia. She had a way of being honest, almost too blunt at times, but that quality gave him confidence that she'd been truthful about wanting to give their marriage a solid try. They owed the baby that much.

Sure, he'd never imagined marrying a woman he

wasn't in love with. Yet, with Lynne, who'd taken a piece of his heart when she left him, he'd often felt off balance. Even a little crazy with the heady feeling of being in love.

With Sonia he felt more like himself, at least most of the time. Between not knowing each other well, and coping with two sets of disapproving relatives, he sometimes felt awkward around her, too. Maybe the air would clear between them after the ceremony was over. That thought settled his jumpy stomach as he stepped toward the living room, as ready as he'd ever be to walk into his future.

* * *

Sonia propped the pillow behind her back before reaching up to take the champagne glass from Aaron's outstretched hand. She quickly drained it and held out the empty glass for more. "Hmm...not bad. I could almost trick myself into thinking this is real champagne and not ginger ale."

Aaron wrinkled his nose. "Then you have distorted taste buds."

She waved at her tote sitting in the corner. "Get yourself a glass of the real thing. I put champagne and a couple of bottles of cabernet from the winery in my travel bag for you. No reason you can't enjoy a glass of wine just because I can't. Poor me."

"No, really, I'm fine."

Aaron sat on a chair he'd pulled up next to the bed. With his suit jacket off and the knot in his tie loosened, Sonia thought her new husband looked more relaxed now than he had all day. With sandy hair and well-defined, almost sharp features, including a strong chin, even her mother was forced to agree that Sonia had married a handsome guy.

Worn out from the wedding and the long hours on the road, she'd changed into her ivory silk nightgown and matching robe, brand new and more elegant than sexy. She'd felt self-conscious climbing into bed, though, and quickly tucked the sheet up around her waist.

She took another sip of ginger ale, but then a giggle escaped from the back of her throat. "We got into this pickle because of champagne." Sonia groaned, realizing her nerves had gotten the better of her once again. She wished she could suck the words back into her brain and leave them there.

"I'm sorry. We agreed not to rehash all that." She hoped her apology was sufficiently contrite.

At least she and Aaron agreed why they got together in the first place. In early December they'd been seated together at a wedding of an old mutual friend from high school. Weighed down by the pain of their respective broken engagements, she and Aaron had become each other's shoulder to lean on during the reception dinner. A few weeks later, they showed up separately at the same New Year's Eve party hosted by the newlyweds in their cozy starter home—a cottage tucked inside a white picket fence, no less.

One glass of champagne led to another and probably several more, although Sonia couldn't say for sure. She'd accepted Aaron's offer to walk her to her apartment a mile up the road, and then foolishly invited him in. A couple of kisses later, they'd tumbled into bed for some futile "let's comfort each other" sex. In the morning, with hazy memories of whatever had happened between them, she'd said little and he hadn't offered much to fill in the blanks. Being as polite as they could during the awkward silence that spanned between them, they'd trekked back through the snow to retrieve their cars. The only comfort Sonia took from the escapade came from their willingness not to run from each other in embarrassment. They'd shared a New Year's Day brunch at the River's Bend Café and then parted on friendly terms. All in all, though, she hadn't been pleased with the way she'd rung in a new year.

She'd have gone out with Aaron on a real date, if he'd asked. But pride prevented her from reaching out to him. She'd waited several weeks to tell him she was pregnant, and even considered not telling him at all. Later, she attributed that to the irrational fear that he might try to talk her into not having the baby, an unfounded worry as it turned out. Not that his face broke out in joy over the news, but he hadn't appeared ready to lace up his running shoes either.

She scooted down under the sheet to rest her head on the pillow. "It was a nice wedding, Aaron. Seriously, don't pay any attention to my dumb remarks."

He sent a sweet smile her way. "In the end, our families managed to be pleasant, didn't they?"

"Yes, I suppose so. And it was nice of your sister to let us have the wedding at her house. I hope I thanked her enough." *Not likely.*

She tried not to make too much of it, but Dottie's attitude toward her, especially when Aaron wasn't around to serve as a buffer, skittered close to open hostility. One day, Sonia was certain something would happen that would bring good ol' Dottie's real feelings bubbling to the surface.

"Along those same lines, I hope *your* parents warm up to me eventually." His gaze had settled on her middle where she'd absently begun running her hand over the growing roundness of her belly. "Maybe after the baby is born, they'll learn to trust me."

"With any luck, the whole bunch of 'em will come around and accept us being together." Seeing him watching her, she pushed the sheet off and lifted her hand. "Here, come feel for yourself."

She scooted over a few inches to make room for him on the bed. He touched her lightly at first and then spread his fingers so his whole hand covered the baby bump. It had started as a thickness she'd first noticed only a couple of weeks before.

Sonia closed her eyes, noting how pleasantly cool his hand felt through the thin, slippery fabric of her gown.

"I'm getting fat. It's a miracle I still fit into the suit I bought last week."

"You looked beautiful today, Sonia," he said in a low voice, "just like now."

She relaxed under his touch. He had the long slim fingers of a pianist, but didn't have any special interest in music. He hadn't expressed a preference for what he wanted to listen to during their long drive, but neither did he object to the classical tapes she'd brought along.

Maybe it was a good thing to talk about the baby. She hoped it would ease the stiff formality that kept them at arm's length. Looking back, they'd probably made the mistake of staying apart these last few weeks, she in her own place near the winery where she worked, he in his apartment in one of the converted out-buildings on his family's tourist farm. But it would be different living together when they came back from the mountains to their regular lives.

She and Aaron were each tied to the businesses that had put their small town on Wisconsin's tourist map. Last year, she'd designed a sophisticated marketing program for Lady's Slipper Winery, a venture that had done extremely well in its first decade, but needed a branding facelift. Although Aaron had joined a local firm after law school, his mother, along with his sister and brother-in-law, Burt, still ran Chapel's Farm on the Hill, one of the most popular tourist destinations in northeast Wisconsin. And now they were starting a family in their hometown, deepening their local roots even more.

Sonia opened her eyes and saw Aaron studying her face. Her cheeks warmed, making her grateful for the dim light from the bedside lamp at the other side of the king-size bed. "That feels nice," she said, putting her hand on top of his.

He leaned in and brushed his lips against her cheek and then planted small, teasing kisses in the corner of her mouth. She let him linger there until she felt the urgency for a full kiss and turned to meet his lips. The kisses were light at first, but gradually deepened. She tried to relax into the pleasure she felt from his closeness, but their unfamiliarity with each other built a barrier between them. Yet, the sweet kisses…yes…definitely a good start at breaking down the walls.

He pulled away long enough to say that he was going to take a quick shower. "Don't go away," he whispered.

"Not likely."

The bathroom door clicked shut. That was the last sound she heard, because she closed her eyes, intending only to rest a while as she waited for him to come back.

In the middle of the night she stirred in her sleep and felt his arm loosely embracing her as they lay close. It was then she realized she'd fallen asleep while he showered.

Though she felt peaceful and safe with the warmth of Aaron's body enveloping her, she couldn't help recalling times she'd awakened in the night spooned with Troy, her ex. Aaron had probably held Lynne that way in bed, too. Lynne, who had broken his heart. Aaron had blurted that out in a couple of different ways during their more than tipsy night on New Year's Eve.

Of course, she'd unloaded on Aaron, too. She couldn't remember her exact words, but she'd probably repeated Troy's little cliché, "It's time to move on." What a stupid, meaningless phrase. It was just a way for Troy to avoid admitting that he didn't love her anymore. Maybe he never had.

With those old memories hazy in her half-sleep, she willed thoughts of their past lovers out of her mind as she covered Aaron's hand with her own. She faced an uncertain future, too, but she pushed those worries away. Better to focus on that day, even that moment. What had he thought when he came to bed fresh from his shower, only to find her out like a light, dead to the world? But the sound of her new husband's quiet breathing, the heat of his skin beneath her palm, even the faint clean scent of the sheet under her chin combined to deliver a sweet kind of pleasure. A harmony of the senses, she mused, letting herself surrender again to welcoming sleep.

3

$\mathcal{H}$e opened his eyes to the sound of running water, which barely muffled her noisy retching. Morning sickness, he assumed, although Sonia had said it had eased some after the third month.

Glancing at the clock he saw it was only a little after 6:00. Still, he was wide awake and energized, as if he needed to stay on high alert. He quickly got out of bed and grabbed his T-shirt, and then headed into the living room of the suite and poured water to heat in the coffee pot. He couldn't deny his irrational disappointment that after one of the fastest showers he'd ever taken, he'd come back to bed, greeted by Sonia's quiet, rhythmic breathing.

At first he'd felt oddly lonely, as if she'd abandoned him. But she'd looked so peaceful, with her hand resting under her cheek, her lips parted. He'd turned off the light and sat up in bed in the dark for almost an hour.

In the near silence he'd had a chance to think about the reality of his baby growing inside her. Touching Sonia, feeling the new roundness of her, had stirred his desire to be closer to her. Thoughts of Lynne intruded, but he had a feeling Sonia would understand why if he told her. Not that he'd risk talking about it, at least not while they attempted to settle into some kind of workable marriage. But he was confident she'd relate to the feelings that still had the power to throw him off balance.

Of course their wedding day had exhausted her. He'd seen it during their long drive as he searched for topics of conversation. She'd been quiet, and he'd acted like a teenager out on a date, nervous and tongue-tied, his hands clammy.

He heard her padding into the room and glanced up to see her in one of the hotel's thick terrycloth robes, her wet hair curled around her face. She touched her cheek and then the top of her head. "Okay, new husband, this is the real me. No makeup, and as you can see, my hair lacks discipline."

He grinned, grabbing the fabric of the T-shirt he'd pulled on over his shorts. "Well, this is the guy you'll be waking up to every morning." He cocked his head in an effort to be flirtatious. "Besides, you look pretty—and comfortable."

She smiled, then looked down and put her hand over her stomach.

"Are you okay?"

"I think so. My stomach is starting to settle down."

He picked up the oversized hotel menu card. "Shall I order breakfast from room service?"

She waved her hand frantically. "No, no, not yet. I usually eat like a pig in the morning, but lately I can't keep anything down except a few crackers. I won't be able to eat a real meal for a couple of hours."

He put the menu back on the table. *Good one, Aaron. Offering breakfast to a nauseated woman.*

"Go ahead, though, get something for yourself."

He shook his head. "Nah, I'm not that hungry."

And then, silence. *Give it time,* he thought, *they'd*

get used to each other eventually.

She disappeared into the bedroom and he shook out a packet of instant coffee into a mug of hot water. A couple of seconds later, she came back in the room holding a wax paper tube of crackers.

He held up the carafe. "This is hot water. And there's herbal tea here." He picked up a tea bag. "Lemon-ginger?"

"Good. I'll take it, but I do miss my coffee in the morning." She sighed wistfully.

"You had a dreamy look in your eyes when you mentioned coffee," he remarked, grinning at his observation.

"Oh well, as soon as I'm done nursing the baby, I'll get my caffeine back."

He wasn't sure what touched him more, that she planned so far ahead or her lack of complaints about giving up the ordinary things in life like wine with dinner and morning coffee. He guessed he'd known when he'd decided to take a chance on a hasty marriage that Sonia was no whiner. Still, sometimes it felt strange to lack even the slightest idea about what the mother of his child went through every day.

Holding the mug in two hands, she settled at the table with one long bare leg tucked underneath her.

He sat down opposite her and watched as she first inhaled the cloud of steam coming from the cup, and then blew across the top of the mug to cool the tea. Finally, she took a couple of quick sips and sighed with pleasure. Quite a ritual, he mused.

She smiled pleasantly. "So, let's get dressed and get on the road. We can be in Asheville before dark."

"You're feeling up to starting out so soon?"

"You bet. Motion sickness isn't an issue."

"Okay, then, when you get hungry we can stop along the way for breakfast and if you feel like your old self, you can eat like a pig."

Laughing, she got up and rummaged around in her bag and then draped some clothes over her arm. Taking her tea with her, she disappeared into the bedroom. He let out a relieved sigh. Man, sometimes he felt like his whole future rode on each word he chose. But at least his lame banter managed to get a chuckle out of her.

How ironic that their wedding had turned them into a couple of stiff strangers. He and Sonia used to be friends, he reminded himself.

* * *

Aaron continued, as Sonia's mother would say, to walk on eggshells around her. And she was treating him the same way. Nice as he was, Sonia figured he must be repressing the grumpy part of his personality. She'd seen his irritable side erupt when Dottie had asked too many prying questions about their decision to get married. And shortly after the wedding ceremony, he'd brushed his mother's hand away when she'd tried to straighten his tie before the photographer took pictures.

Sonia considered herself a quick study, and she'd keep her hands off Aaron's clothes—at least while he was in them.

During their all-day drive, he'd been overly solicitous. First, he insisted she choose the music they played in the car as he watched for a restaurant he'd read about in the guidebook. Then he double-checked with the waitress to make sure Sonia's French toast came with the dusting of powdered sugar she'd casually said she liked.

They'd no sooner checked into their elegant room at the Grove Park Inn than he asked if she wanted to go into downtown Asheville for dinner or stay at the hotel. Whatever she wanted. "Or, we could order room service," he said.

Enough already. She spun around to face him. "Aaron, please, your kindness is killing me."

"What?"

"I know you're trying to please me, and I'm delighted you're willing to take care of so many details. But this awkward dance has to end sometime—soon, I hope."

His shoulders slumped. "I'm only trying to get off to a good start."

The defeat in his voice made her regret starting the conversation, but it was too late to back out. "Believe me, I appreciate that, but we'll eventually step on each other's toes during this careful little waltz. And I'm beginning to think the sooner the better."

She planted her hands on her hips and tilted her head. "Let's remember we started kindergarten together, for Pete's sake. I remember the day you came to school with new braces on your teeth. You probably have flashbacks of Miss Goody-Two-Shoes winning the spelling bee year after year."

"You *were* kind of spindly back then, but you sure could spell." His voice carried a teasing chuckle.

"You're being nice way beyond the call of duty. I was a shapeless beanpole, already standing many inches above everybody else, except for the tallest kid in the class."

"That would be me," he said, tapping his chest with

his index finger.

She let out a hoot. "See? We aren't strangers, Aaron, but now that we're married, we sound like we just met a couple of days ago."

He kept laughing, so apparently he found her at least mildly amusing. She approached him and put her hands against his chest. "Do you know what I really want?" she asked, looking into his eyes.

He answered with a grin that struck her as downright flirtatious. "Yes, indeed, but I'm afraid to guess."

She went to one of her tote bags and pulled out a bottle of wine and a can of ginger ale. "Here, fix us each a drink while I change. Then let's watch the sun disappear behind those unbelievable mountains outside our window."

Sitting down on the bed, she ran her hand over the elegant mauve and gray satin spread. Then she bounced on it a couple of times. "After that, let's climb into this big lovely bed and see what happens. I know we've been together before, but to be honest, my memory of it is a bit hazy."

His light snicker sounded nervous. "I always knew you'd be direct with me, that you'd avoid all the usual game-playing."

"That's really all we have to start with, isn't it?" She stretched her open hands toward him. "We don't have much history except as kids going through school together."

She felt a sliver of apprehension. When Troy had broken their engagement, he'd come right out and said her frankness had destroyed any aura of mystery about her. She probably ran that risk with Aaron, too. But she didn't know how to be any other way.

"Okay," he said, "I'll fix the drinks. You get comfortable."

A few minutes later, they turned the chairs at the table to face the window and propped their feet on the sill as they watched the dusk dramatically paint the sky with expanding streaks of deep reds. A peaceful silence settled in as the sun dipped below the round undulating mountain tops, leaving the ridge looking like a black cutout against the colorful sky.

"Just think, Aaron, we have five whole days to enjoy mountain sunsets—and this gorgeous room."

"Speaking of gorgeous…" He put his glass on the table and stood. Taking her hand, he pulled her to her feet. He cupped her cheeks in his palms and kissed her, a firm, confident kiss. He smoothed his palms down the sides of her neck and over her shoulders before pulling her closer to him. Without her shoes, he had a few inches on her and she liked that she had to tilt her head back to meet his warm lips.

When they broke the kiss, she relaxed into the circle of his arms. Resting her chin on his shoulder, she ran her fingers lightly up and down his back and listened to him take short, quick breaths as he nuzzled her neck.

He led her to the bed and pulled the covers back. Glad that she'd chosen to wrap only the robe around her, she untied the sash and let the silky fabric slide off her body before climbing into bed.

She tried to relax, but her own self consciousness got in the way of letting Aaron's caresses seduce her into the moment. She rushed the pace, not from passionate urgency, but to get this first time together behind them. The best part was hearing him whisper her name.

Later, as she snuggled into the hollow of his shoulder, listening to his heart beat fast, she accepted that what they lacked in raw passion they made up for in affection and good will. At least she and Aaron hadn't descended into a place so familiar that they took each other for granted. No, they were a long way from that.

Smiling to herself, she decided it was time to confess the one little white lie she'd told him.

4

$\mathcal{H}$e'd drifted into a zone between waking and sleeping when he heard her whisper, "Aaron? Are you awake?"

"Uh, more or less."

She lifted her head off his shoulder and propped herself on her elbow. "I need to tell you something."

He caressed her soft cheek as he opened his eyes. "What's the matter? Are you okay?"

"Oh, yes and no. It's just that you think I'm so honest, but I need to fess up about something. I told you a small lie last week."

The force of the words jolted him to full attention. He sat straight up. "A lie? What are you talking about? Tell me."

"Wait, wait," she said, lightly touching his arm. "I didn't mean to alarm you."

"Well you did," he said, his jaw so tight it hurt. "Just say what you have to say."

"Okay, okay." She leaned across his legs and grabbed the robe off the floor and quickly put it on to cover herself. "Remember last week when we had dinner to talk about the wedding?"

"Of course, I remember," he snapped, conscious of his heart beating hard and fast. "Do you think I'd forget a conversation about the wedding after you'd finally agreed to marry me? I'd been asking you for weeks."

"Hey, no need to get so feisty." She grabbed his hand and held on tight, and he resisted the urge to pull away. "You asked me if I knew the sex of our baby and I said no."

"Right. You told me you wanted to be surprised."

"Well, that was a fib. I had an ultrasound, so I do know. Do you want me to tell you?"

What? She had to ask? "Hell, yes."

Her eyes suddenly sparkled with happiness. "Okay, then. We're having a boy."

"A son?" He and Sonia simultaneously laughed out loud. Then he pulled her closer into his embrace and kissed her forehead.

"I take it you're happy with the news," she said, grinning.

"Of course." Something about this exchange bothered him, though. "But Sonia, I'd have been just as happy if you'd said we were having a girl."

"Really?"

"Yes, my God, yes." Had she really doubted that? Seeing her look away, he sensed she was holding something back. "Why didn't you tell me this when I asked last week?"

She rearranged her body to sit cross-legged. "I'm not sure exactly. But I've been determined that you not feel obligated to me…you know, ever thinking that you had to marry me because of the baby."

"Did you ever wonder if I might feel *more* obligated if I knew we were having a son rather than a daughter?"

"Not exactly, but…oh, maybe a little."

He threw the sheet back, quickly got out of bed, and grabbed his clothes off the chair.

"Are you angry with me?"

He struggled into his pants as he tried to come up with a civil answer. "I don't understand how you could have thought that, even for a second. I asked about the sex of the baby to help make the whole thing real to me. From the first minute you told me about the baby, I've been kicking myself for being so careless and trying to figure out how to do right by the baby—*and you.*"

He flopped into the chair, surprised by how angry he was over being blindsided by her lie, and not even a big one at that.

"I'm sorry, Aaron, I really am."

He pointed to her stomach. "I'm still getting used to the idea that you actually have a baby inside of you—*my* baby. It barely seemed real until last night when…" He didn't finish the sentence, but shook his head and stared at her. She quickly looked down, obviously avoiding his eyes.

"All those weeks you were pregnant and didn't tell me, I had no way of knowing what you were going through." He hit the heels of his hands on the arm of the chair. "Getting sick every morning, choosing a doctor, doing all that stuff that goes with having a baby. You'd already had time to adjust to what was happening."

"I know," she said with a nod.

"And I don't want you to hold my initial reaction against me, you know, the way I acted the night you told me you were pregnant. I was stunned."

She pulled her robe tighter and then nervously rolled and unrolled the end of the sash between her fingers. When she looked up, she smiled sadly. "I'll say it again, Aaron. I'm really sorry."

The sincerity of her voice softened his attitude. "You should be," he said with mock reproach. "I mean it."

"I hope you'll still trust me to be honest with you. I promise I won't make a habit of this kind of thing."

"Okay." What else could he say? He didn't want to start piling up mistakes and keeping score. He'd already been too quick to judge. "I never thought about turning my back on you. I was shocked, a little scared, but I wasn't going to skip town. I only wished you'd told me about the baby sooner."

She nodded and lowered her head again. "I should have trusted you more. To tell you the truth, though, it took a while to be certain what *I* wanted to do." She lifted her head and met his gaze. "I was really bummed at first, and then confused. I'd never been sure I wanted kids at all, but on the other hand, I was afraid you might try to pressure me *not* to have the baby."

His stomach tightened into a knot. "Really? Then you don't know the first thing about me." He cleared his throat. "I'd *never* have tried to talk you out of having our baby."

Not meaning to raise his voice, he'd nevertheless become louder with each word.

"I didn't know how you'd react, but you didn't disappoint me. No matter how we started," she said softly, "or how we end, for that matter, you're a good man. I understand you better now."

He nodded to acknowledge what she'd said. But he hadn't always felt like a good man, especially when Sonia had told him about the result of their careless New Year's Eve. His body reacted first. A wave of nausea hit hard, forcing him to push away the plate of pasta as soon as the waiter put it on the table in front of him. Just the smell of it revved up the churning in his gut. Leaving

Sonia sitting alone, he rushed into the men's room and splashed cold water on his face.

As he braced his arms against the marble sink, he could almost picture his father, dead for more than five years, standing behind him, impatiently tapping his foot as he waited for Aaron to do the so-called right thing.

Back at the table and feeling calmer, he'd interjected the possibility of marriage into their conversation. Sonia waved him off and repeated the old adage about not compounding one mistake with another.

To him, that was the kind of thing parents said to teenagers in trouble. It didn't apply to people old enough to make a good living and take care of a baby. He repeated his suggestion and she finally agreed to think about marrying him, but it had taken weeks to convince her.

One night he'd showed up at her apartment unannounced to argue his case, and finally, two days later, she called him at work and agreed to a quick wedding, telling him she believed marriage was supposed to be forever, but that wouldn't necessarily be true in *their* case. She'd turned into a broken record about that. He'd finally agreed to her terms: if either of them wanted out, they'd share custody of their child and part the same way they'd begun, as friends.

"So, what are we going to name him?" Aaron asked, ready to shift the mood. "Have you thought about it?"

"Not really. I wanted to wait for you." She sat up straight on the bed and wore an eager, happy expression. "How about we talk about names over dinner? A room service dinner."

"Let me guess, you're hungry again."

"Ravenous," she answered with a quick grin. "I feel best this time of day and I inhale everything in sight. I'm eating for two, you know."

"I believe you." He went to the desk and picked up the guest book, glad for a diversion and something to do. He'd be careful not to kill her with kindness, though. He almost laughed out loud. His father used to joke that when it came to women, sometimes it was hard for a guy to win.

Later, after they devoured some of the best lamb chops he'd ever had, they tossed around boys' names, starting with Aaron Junior, which he rejected because he thought a child should have a name all his own, to Zachary, which began to grow on him but didn't win over Sonia. Still undecided, she'd flipped on the radio and found a station playing soft string music. It sounded like elevator music to him, and he was about to ask her to find something livelier. But then she leaned over and kissed him and then kissed him again. By the third kiss, he'd stopped thinking about music altogether.

Later, feeling more relaxed than he had after the first time they'd made love, he'd almost drifted off to sleep when she whispered, "What do you think about Matthew?"

"Is that for someone in your family?"

"No. I like it because it isn't associated with my family. Do you have any Matthew Chapels in yours?"

"Not that I can think of."

"*Good.*"

She spoke with such conviction he couldn't resist asking the obvious question. "And why is that good?"

"It's like a fresh start. No family baggage associated with the name."

He chuckled softly. "Maybe one day I'll figure out how your mind works, but I'm not there yet."

"Ah, but you're willing to go where others have feared to venture."

He rolled on his side and circled his arm around her waist. "So far, the experience hasn't been *too* bad."

"You're not half bad yourself," she said, pulling his arm more snugly around her.

He smiled to himself. *All in all, a good way to end their first full day together.*

* * *

$\mathcal{D}$ottie's call not only disturbed their sense of peaceful isolation, it brought him down from his pleasant high of the previous couple of days. Feeling looser with one another, he and Sonia had made the most of Asheville, an attractive city with upscale shops and galleries and plenty of restaurants. They'd whiled away a couple of rainy afternoons poking around the downtown streets, and one morning he'd played golf with some men staying at the hotel while Sonia relaxed by the indoor pool, engrossed in a grisly murder mystery that kept her reading to the end later that night.

They'd even attempted a tennis match, but with very bad results. How a woman as graceful as Sonia could play such a poor game of tennis mystified him.

"Let's go back to the Biltmore Estate," she suggested as they walked off the court and across the stone terrace to the hotel entrance. "We had our best sightseeing day there."

When they went to their room to change, he saw the light blinking on the phone and listened to Dottie's message. He returned the call before heading out again, but insisted they go ahead with their plan. Still, the call changed the tenor of the day.

"I'm sorry this family stuff broke into our trip," he said later, after they'd found an isolated bench near a quiet reflecting pool just outside the mansion. He heard only a steady din of voices coming from the groups of tourists ambling by on the way to the gardens.

"Don't be silly. This is a huge decision," she said. "The farm has been in your family for over a century, so it can't be easy to consider letting it go."

"I get Dottie's point, though." With his arms resting across the back of the bench, he stretched out his long legs and crossed his ankles. "Right now, the farm still attracts respectable sized crowds every summer, but even my mother admits we're close to capping the potential. They'd rather sell the land when we don't absolutely have to, rather than waiting until we do."

A few days before their wedding, he'd confided some family business to Sonia, believing she had a right to know that his sister and mother had discreetly contacted a real estate broker to send out feelers about selling the land.

Once their farm changed hands, whatever the new owners had planned for it, things would change, and not necessarily for the better. For all he knew, their rolling fields and the woods lining the river bank might end up as a golf course or even worse, paved over for a mall. Aaron knew developers waited patiently in the wings with their chainsaws and backhoes, always ready to clear the stands of birch and ash, oaks and maples to make way for whatever would bring in the most money.

"Are you thinking about what your father would say?"

He closed his eyes and tilted his head back, feeling the cool breeze on his face. "I can barely think of anything else. The tourist farm was supposed to be a way to keep the land in the family, but my dad hoped to preserve those acres, too, for their own sake. Just because it's rich land and has a history."

After a couple of hard years struggling to figure out how to lure tourists and groups of kids on field trips, his father's plan had worked. Both Aaron and Dottie had helped run the business during the summers, but after law school, he'd taken a job with a local firm. That left his sister, a third-grade teacher, to help out during the summer months. Dottie's husband tended the farm animals and handled the maintenance of the farm year round.

"The truth is, I never cared much for the work involved in the business, but the land means a lot to me. Unlike Dottie and Burt, I don't pitch in to help much, so I suppose I don't have a clear cut right to protest."

"It's almost impossible to think of Lady's River without Chapel's Farm on the Hill." Sonia paused and sighed deeply. "Selfishly, I can't help but wonder about the impact that shutting down the farm might have on the winery, not to mention smaller businesses in town."

He already felt edgy, set up to be annoyed by the smallest thing, and she handed him an easy excuse. "Thanks for your concern," he said sarcastically.

"I meant that in a general way," she said. "Don't take it so personally."

"This whole situation *is* personal." He immediately regretted the cold impatience in his voice.

"I was just thinking about the future of our little hometown, that's all." She shifted on the bench to face him. "I don't like seeing you so troubled."

Feeling contrite, he reached for her hand, relishing the comforting softness of her skin. "I know." He smacked his lips together in frustration. "I didn't think ahead and prepare myself for how I'd feel when an in-the-flesh buyer showed up."

Her frown and the puzzled look in her eyes told him she struggled to understand the situation. But hell, he barely understood it himself.

"I know it isn't any of my business, Aaron, but can you tell me why it's an all or nothing proposition?" She raised her open arms in gesture that told him she didn't get what was going on. "It's like there's a missing piece of information here. Your family has over three hundred acres of extremely valuable land. Can't you shut down the farm and sell off a good parcel? Then your mother could live on that money—and for a long time, too."

Tingling energy sped through his body. "Funny you should say that. Something about this situation has bothered me all along."

Over the next few minutes, he laid out his suspicions about Burt, admitting that he'd never liked Dottie's husband. From their first handshake, Aaron had a feeling his future brother-in-law kept some tricks hidden up his sleeve. Over the years, they'd never had a conversation that hadn't included a discussion about the value of the farm. He grudgingly admitted that Burt did a good job keeping up the place, but failed to show any special feeling for the land itself. It had crossed Aaron's mind that Burt went through the motions, but without his heart in the business.

"For a while now I've sensed that Burt might be working on Dottie to unload the farm. Maybe he has plans for her share of the money so he can do something else with his time."

He sighed, relieved to have let Sonia in on his hunch about Burt's conniving.

"I barely know Burt, of course," she said, "but I'd trust your gut on this. Don't assume you're being paranoid."

"Dottie will deny—vehemently deny—that Burt has ulterior motives, but so be it. I don't trust him." Suddenly restless, he stood. "Let's wander around here while I think about what I want to do. If I decide to buck my mother and Dottie, I need to come up with a good reason."

A couple of hours later, they stopped the car on the exit road from the estate and walked down a path that led to a stretch of the French Broad River. With the wind picking up, the water ran lively and loud.

"This reminds me of home," Aaron said, nodding toward the river. "A narrow leg of Lady's River runs through the woods at the far edge of our land. There's a spot with big boulders set back from the riverbank and surrounded by willows on the shore and birches behind them. Dad and I cleared a path to it when I was kid. He called it our secret place."

"Will you show it to me?" Sonia whispered.

He nodded with conviction. "Absolutely. No matter what happens with the land, we'll get down there." He kicked at the thick gray-brown tree roots sloping to the dusty riverbank. "Standing here, all I can think about is how much I want to show that special patch of ground to my own son one day."

Her hand slipped into his. "I know. For what it's worth, Aaron, listening to you, seeing your sadness, I want that for you, too."

"But I have to face facts. I suspect my mother wants to close the business. I can't *prove* Burt has an ulterior motive, so I don't see how I can block a sale the other stakeholders want."

He squeezed her hand and held on to it as they walked back to the car. He didn't feel like talking, and as they left the estate and drove through town he noticed Sonia had fallen uncharacteristically silent, too.

By the time they got back to the hotel, heavy clouds opened up and sent down steady, cold rain. Sonia suggested claiming a spot on one of the leather sofas in front of the stone fireplace in the lobby. "Let's order a drink from the bar and talk."

He tried to read her subtle frown, but it remained a puzzle. He went to the bar and ordered Irish coffee for himself and sparkling water for her. With the drinks in hand, he found her curled up in the corner of a sofa in front of the fireplace, scribbling on the back of what appeared to be a receipt from the gift shop.

"What is it?" he asked, sitting next to her. "You've been lost in your own thoughts ever since we left the Biltmore Estate."

She folded the paper and put it in the pocket of her jacket. "I want to talk about a couple of things. And, I need you to hear me out before you dismiss what I have to say."

Not in the best mood anyway, he bristled at what sounded like a warning. But his curiosity won out. "Okay, I'm listening."

"Then, here goes. First, am I correct in thinking that you really, truly want to find a way to keep the land in your family?"

He resisted the impulse to blurt an answer and took a minute to be certain that his feelings weren't bound up only with missing his dad, and nostalgia over a place tied to a past that was gone forever. Finally, he nodded. "I didn't know how much I wanted that until Dottie called."

A big smile lit up her face. "Then I have an idea, and it's a really good one, too."

His heart picked up speed. Throwing his head back, he groaned. "Spit it out…you're killing me with suspense."

5

November 2006

At one time Sonia enjoyed showcasing—even bragging about—Chapel's Botanical Garden and telling stories, first about the way it had started, and then about its evolution through the years. Aaron used to tease her about her excited anticipation of a FAM, a familiarization tour made up of travel writers and industry pros. But that morning, she'd dragged herself out of bed and coaxed an upbeat tone into her voice as she practiced her presentation in front of her bathroom mirror. Haggard best described what she saw there. She longed to hide out at home, but instead she'd dutifully dabbed concealer under her eyes to cover the blue-red circles.

She felt like an actress—again. After Matt had died, she'd kept up her work at the garden behind a façade, managing to convince most people that she was brave and coping well. Now, on the heels of the dedication down in Pearson Pond, she again felt off balance and frustrated that the sense of closure she'd hoped to find with Aaron still eluded her. They'd said their good-byes quickly, but the memory of his bewildered expression, along with the warmth of his smile, had torn open old wounds.

Forcing those thoughts aside, Sonia ushered the ten

travel writers into the conference room next to her office. She kept up a stream of light banter as the visitors helped themselves to coffee and tea and streusel coffeecake set up in the back of the room. With the garden the first stop of the day, it was up to her to whip up excitement and leave the writers impressed—and ready for more. Later, the group would trek through Anderson Orchards and visit two blocks of Main Street shops and two museums, ending their tour with a catered dinner at Lady's Slipper Winery.

After the group settled around the table, she moved to her computer to start the presentation, beginning with the annual Golden Days festival that had drawn to a close only a few days before. She narrated as the photos of the garden's buildings, decorated with cornstalks and pumpkins for the fall season, appeared on the wall-mounted screen. She followed that with photos of orange maples brilliant against a bright blue autumn sky.

"We coordinate these special fall days with various Oktoberfest events going on at the orchard and winery, and also those in nearby towns. As you can see, Halloween is a lively time at the garden. We have an old-fashioned party with apple bobbing and a costume contest." The writers laughed pleasantly when the images of tiny toddler ghosts and school-age gypsies, pirates, and astronauts appeared on the screen. Sonia smiled inside. Halloween party images always worked like a charm.

Moving back in time, the photo display marked the earlier months of 2006, including "Let's Go Wild," their annual wildflower festival, which started in August and continued through September. Then a series of pictures highlighted the spring forsythia bordering the garden entrance and patches of trillium along the wooded trails. These presentations always included a few late March or early April slides of ice-covered trees glistening like jewels in the sun. Shots taken in late January showed the garden serenely sleeping under a blanket of sparkling snow, and she ended with highlights from last year's Light Up the Holidays festival that drew several thousand visitors to enjoy the light design, not only different, but expanded and more elaborate each year.

She rested her fingertips on the end of the long table and leaned toward the group. "Any questions?"

One reporter asked for details about the joint Halloween venture with Anderson Orchards. Another wanted information about weddings in the garden, giving Sonia the chance to show off their wedding chapel, a small building on a hill.

At that moment, Dottie stuck her head in the doorway and waved.

"Good. You're right on time." Sonia gestured toward her former sister-in-law. "Here she is, Dorothy—Dottie—Chapel Thompson, our official photographer and tour guide, but more important, the bride that launched our wedding chapel."

The next photo on the screen showed a radiant Dottie arm-in-arm with Cal Thompson. Dottie had never been happier—and it showed in her beaming face on the screen. Nobody could resist a radiant bride, so that picture never failed to fill the room with delighted exclamations.

Dottie grinned at the writers. "That was a great day for me and for the garden."

"I'll say." Sonia kept her tone dry in a deliberate effort to sound amused. They'd had this interplay before, and it provided a perfect segue to the tour.

The writers followed Dottie out. From the window, Sonia watched them traipse along the rolling path to the wedding chapel, although it wasn't a chapel in the traditional sense. Over the years, guests booked the glass and stone building for family reunions, birthday parties, and even as a site for romantic candlelight dinners for two. One of the best spots in town to celebrate an anniversary, one article said.

Years before, the promotional slides of the chapel included pictures of Dottie's entire wedding party. Aaron as Cal's best man, she as Dottie's matron-of-honor, and Matt playing a Mozart piece on his cello. What a sweet, happy day.

After Matt died, Sonia removed those photos from the presentation and tried not to think about those missing images as she went through her presentation. The exhilaration of those precious moments in their family made the pain of losing Matt, and then Aaron, still raw, no matter how much time had passed. Sonia also discreetly left out the fact that Cal was Dottie's second husband. No reason to raise the lid on the chest that stored the family's history and spill out all its contents.

Feeling a sudden rush of hot tears pooling in her eyes, she turned away from the window and struggled to get a handle on the wave of bittersweet nostalgia. *Please, no more tears, not today.* She and Dottie needed this FAM. The garden's visitors and revenue weren't down dramatically, at least not yet, but Sonia admitted that the business would continue to stagnate if she didn't come up with a bold new event or a creative garden display to promote—and soon.

Sonia had always been able to arouse some excitement around the garden's activities, but now, even their Web site looked lifeless and dull. She needed to reclaim the garden's reputation as a vital, lively attraction in Lady's River. Sonia had *promised* Dottie that with the Flight 62 dedication behind her, she'd once again throw herself into promoting the garden.

This FAM was supposed to be a kick start on a personal level, too. Sonia had expected to come back from Pearson Pond with her shoulders squared, ready to face the future with renewed energy and hope. She should call Ben and make some plans. He'd wanted to go to the dedication with her and maybe she should have said yes to him after all. Spending time with Aaron disturbed her memories, stirring up random images of the past and feelings that left her lightheaded and unfocused.

Watching Dottie from the window, seeing her stop to point out the path to the wood sculptures, the rose garden, the prairie walk, and the woods beyond, brought images and sounds of the past surging into her consciousness. Dottie might be her closest friend and confidant now, but that was a long time in coming.

She and Aaron used to joke that Dottie's early and ugly hostility toward her was the X-rated part of the history of Chapel's Botanical Garden. Looking back more than two decades, Sonia could still hear Dottie's words, dripping with anger and suspicion. She'd drawn her own personal line in the sand the day Dottie accused her of casting a spell on Aaron—for real.

* * *

May 1984

*I*n a split second, Sonia mused, Aaron could plunk his lawyer's hat over his cap of sandy hair and become his confident professional self. He might hem and haw around when he talked about his feelings, but in attorney mode, he had no trouble grilling her nonstop about her grand, bold idea. He'd done little else during their drive back to Lady's River.

By the time Aaron called Dottie and his mother, Rona, and asked if they could meet that night, even before they dropped off their bags at their apartment, Sonia felt ready for whatever question they threw at her.

Once they arrived, her new mother-in-law ushered them into chairs around the dining room table and asked about their trip. Aaron brushed off the questions by saying it was all fine and the mountains were beautiful. Sonia smiled at the impatience in his voice, knowing his eagerness to get to the issue at hand.

When Dottie and Burt came through the back door, they quickly yanked their chairs out from beneath the table and sat down. Suspicion clouded Dottie's gray eyes. It was almost eerie the way their color perfectly matched Aaron's eyes.

"We wanted an answer by now," Dottie said. "I don't see what we have to talk about anyway. It's all decided."

"Sonia and I have come up with an idea that will give us a chance to hang on to the land," Aaron blurted.

Sonia had prepared herself for the hostile look Dottie shot her way. She willed herself to keep her own expression neutral.

"You and Sonia? Well, well, isn't that interesting?"

Burt nervously thumped the table. "Let's hear it."

51

Sonia could see why Aaron had his doubts about Burt. Angry dark eyes darted back and forth between her and Aaron. Sonia could almost smell the tension, tightly wound and sitting in wait for the right moment to spring into attack.

Aaron nodded to her and she began presenting the basic plan in as few words as possible. But when she said "botanical garden," Burt laughed out loud. Refusing to be rattled, Sonia kept going, laying out her idea to turn the farm into a private botanical garden, a new tourist destination in Lady's River. Wanting to be tactful, she softened the sad truth that the tourist farm had probably outlived its appeal. Today's tourists demanded a bit more sophistication, perhaps a touch of glitz. She struggled to keep a lid on her enthusiasm for her idea. Convincing Aaron's family to accept it was a long shot at best.

Aaron pulled papers out of his jacket pocket and pushed them toward his mother. "We've worked up some preliminary estimates of startup costs," he said. "Remember, we can start small."

The chair creaked when Dottie abruptly flopped back. "You worked up numbers, huh? Must have been a fun honeymoon." With a smug smirk, she turned to Burt. "We had better things to do on our honeymoon than write a damn business plan, didn't we? Of course, these two are practically strangers, but *we* knew each other."

"Dottie, please," Rona said, slipping on her reading glasses. "I'd like to hear any reasonable plan to keep the land in the family."

"Reasonable isn't likely, Mom," Dottie said, sounding remarkably confident. "Al Boggs was adamant that selling the land is the *only* way to secure the money for you to live comfortably."

"Al sells real estate," Aaron pointed out, "so of course he'd say that."

Dottie flipped the back of her hand toward Aaron. "Whatever. But I don't intend to spend my summers digging in the dirt and weeding gardens, and I don't think Mom should have to either."

Sonia saw a good chance to chime in with more details. "Of course not, Dottie. The first thing we'll do is hire a landscape architect. And we'll put a horticulture team together to do the work—it's in the preliminary budget." She glanced at Aaron. "We envision a botanical garden that evolves into a major four-season tourist attraction. We've barely scratched the surface here, but all we're asking is that you hold off on the sale and give us time to confirm that we have a viable concept."

Dottie's eyes flickered with defiance. "What do you know about running an operation like this?" she challenged. "Your family hasn't farmed. I'll bet you've never planted so much as a tulip bulb."

Sonia had anticipated objections and she'd armed herself with logical arguments using the language she'd learned on the way to her MBA. Vision, mission, branding, and marketing she could handle, but this petty stuff threw her for a loop. "Uh, that's not the point, Dottie."

Aaron slapped the table with his open hand. "For God's sake, this plan isn't about taking a trip to the local nursery to buy some flowers to stick in the ground."

"Hey, stop the sniping," Rona said quickly, thrusting her arms to the side, as if separating two scrapping children.

Dottie lowered her voice when she patted her mother's hand. "I don't think Aaron understands how stressful this situation has been for you." Then she turned back to Aaron. "A month ago, she learned that an unplanned baby is on the way, and now you're trying to hoodwink her into hanging on to land that's sapped her strength."

"I'll speak for myself, thank you." Rona didn't lift her head, but continued to study Aaron's figures.

Sonia took note of her new mother-in-law's sharp tone and the impatient glance she cast Dottie and Burt's way.

"One way or another you'll get your money, Mom, and so will you, Dottie." Aaron sounded sure and steady, as if he'd regained command of the situation. "We want to give this a chance, and if it doesn't work, we'll sell the land, no arguments. Meanwhile, you'll share in whatever profits we make."

Dottie shook her head, disdain distorting her features. "Profits? Are you serious?"

Burt put his arm on the back of Dottie's chair, punctuating their solidarity. "You don't know how hard we work to scratch a decent salary out of this place, let alone turn much of a profit."

"That might be," Aaron said quietly, "but Sonia is willing to put up money she inherited from her grandfather as seed money for this new venture."

"No one in the family has to work with me at the garden," Sonia quickly added, "but if we make a go of it, you'll all share in the results."

Aaron unfolded more papers and slid them in a pile to the middle of the table. "Sonia came up with some tentative designs we could start with."

For a minute, all eyes focused on the pencil drawings of garden beds in the fields adjacent to the main buildings, paths through the woods, and the addition of a stone terrace to host outdoor concerts or wine tastings during the summer months. Sonia's heart fell with a thud. The sketches that looked so bold when she'd first roughed them out looked like a kid's scribbling when spread out and scrutinized by skeptical eyes. Still, Aaron had caught her excitement that night in front of the fireplace at the hotel and wanted to give her idea a try.

He'd challenged each premise, of course. But underneath his practical tone, she sensed he understood that her vision could simultaneously fulfill her long-held dream to run her own business and his desire to hang on to his family's legacy.

Struggling to stay focused in the heavy, stifling air in the room, Sonia skimmed away beads of sweat forming at her hairline. "I know this is sudden—"

"You're right about that," Dottie interrupted, rising from the chair. "You've been married to my brother for exactly a week, and now you come in here with some harebrained scheme—"

"It is *not* harebrained." Sonia knew deep in her heart the idea would work. Chapel's Botanical Garden appeared in glorious color and detail in her mind, a fully formed image of the farm transformed. "We can make the garden unique, something beautiful and fine. I *know* we can."

"We?" Dottie glanced at the others around the table. "Wow, it didn't take her long to feel right at home."

Pointing at his sister, Aaron pushed his chair back,

creating a jarring sound as the legs scraped across the floor. He stood and faced off against Dottie. "Sonia heads up the marketing department at Lady's River Winery. She worked hard to get that promotion—and the big raise that came with it. But she's willing to give that up to start this venture. We have a chance to keep the land in our family and I want to take it."

"*I'm* inclined to agree," Rona said with conviction.

"Really?" Aaron's eyes opened wide. He looked astonished by his mother's words.

"What makes you think this is anything but foolishness?" Burt's loud voice shook the room.

Sonia followed her mother-in-law's gaze. Rona stared out the window, as if studying the bird feeder and the blossoming apple trees beyond it. "When we started Chapels Farm on the Hill most everyone we talked to thought a tourist farm was not only a really bizarre idea, but doomed to fail." Rona looked thoughtful for a moment as she wove her fingers through her neatly bobbed gray hair. "But your father ignored those voices and he put in long hours to create something new and innovative. It worked, too, and that's why we still have the land today."

Sonia reveled in her urge to plant a big kiss on Rona's cheek.

"Well, I can see where this is going," Dottie said, bracing her hands on the back of the chair. "But if you go ahead with this risky scheme, Aaron, it will go down as a big mistake. Just like your sham marriage."

"Wait just a damn minute."

"Oh, hold on, Aaron. Let me say my piece and then I'll leave." Dottie gestured toward Sonia. "First, she presents you with a so-called accidental baby and talks you into marrying her. Now you're handing over *our* land to her. Not a bad week's work."

"That's enough," Aaron said. "Getting married was my idea. And I'm not going to stand by and let you insult Sonia."

Rona reached out to capture Dottie's hand in her own, as if attempting to calm her. "Aaron's right, Sonia is part of our family now."

Sonia covered her mouth with her hand, stifling a nervous giggle. Was it possible that once the storm blew over, she and Rona stood a chance of sprouting a friendship?

Dottie pulled her hand from her mother's grip. "Must have been some honeymoon." She pointed to Aaron. "She's *bewitched* you, you poor fool!" Then she looked down at Rona. "Can't you see it? *Your son* is completely under that woman's spell."

The nervous giggle escaped and Sonia groaned inside. To Dottie, it must have sounded like a witch's cackle. But then, she'd always known winning over Dottie would be tough.

6

November 2006

Aaron scrolled through the line of emails, his index finger poised and ready to delete the majority of them. He stopped suddenly, when he saw the subject line of one from a legal organization he belonged to: *ASilverman—dead at 79*.

He pushed away from his desk with such force he sent the chair rolling backward, as if distancing his body from the screen would make the message vanish.

Muttering "oh no, oh no" under his breath, Aaron sat motionless, giving himself a minute to absorb the shock of the news. Then he reached for his cell phone, needing to tell Sonia what happened. Just as quickly he yanked his hand back. *Get your head out of the past once and for all.*

A couple of deep breaths slowed his brain down. He scooted the chair back to the computer and scanned the message. His old professor and mentor, Artie Silverman, had died suddenly in his home in Manhattan. The emailed article described Artie as one of the most respected—and colorful—trial lawyers in the country, with a career spanning more than fifty years. Aaron could easily imagine the retrospectives the cable news channels would quickly produce to highlight Artie's career. Sonia would learn about his death on TV or in the newspaper, like everyone else. She didn't need to hear it from him.

Thinking of Artie and the old cluttered brownstone he'd called both office and home, Aaron stared out his apartment window and found the view wanting. Even sad. Others might admire the metal and glass high-rises, but their straight lines and sharp angles bored him. Only the slivers of sky between the buildings made him linger and long for more.

Letting his mind meander through memories of Artie, he smiled at the newspaper photo of his mentor reproduced in the email. Towering and barrel-chested, Artie had become known for his flapping wide ties and mop of gray hair always in need of a trim. How many careers had Artie help shape?

During law school, Aaron had the good luck to be accepted into one of his seminars. Artie's big gestures and loud delivery exuded passion for the law in every lecture. Aaron left the seminar with new-found enthusiasm for his profession fueling his goal to be a trial lawyer—no sitting behind a desk for him. Aaron's passion had never diminished, either, not in twenty-five years of taking on tough cases and eventually becoming a trial strategy consultant.

Glancing at his watch, he saw he had three hours before he was due to meet Katherine. He couldn't beg off their plans, no matter how much he wanted to. She'd chaired the committee in charge of a gala for pediatric cancer research, and she'd made it clear she counted on him to be at her side—in his tux—on her big night. After the number of volunteer hours Katherine had put in over the previous months, Aaron owed her his support. And his attention. She'd had little enough of it these last couple of weeks. He had no right to unload his grief over losing Artie and ruin her triumphant evening.

Too jumpy to stay put, Aaron grabbed his jacket and keys and took the elevator from his tenth floor apartment to the street and headed to Michigan Avenue. His feet led him toward the bridge, where he'd quickly lose himself in the crowds on the plazas in front of the buildings on both sides of the river.

Memories of Artie's booming voice, as bold as the legal positions he argued, raced through Aaron's mind. The world was a lesser place without Artie's warm heart. How odd, too, that Sonia had mentioned Artie during their last conversation in Pearson Pond. Aaron had joined her at a table in the buffet tent and during the few minutes they'd spent alone, he'd told her about a case involving major safety violations in a chemical plant in Texas. Smiling, she'd lightly tapped his hand and asked, "Is it a Silverman?"

He'd nodded, unable to trust himself to speak. That old phrase once had so much meaning between them and still rolled easily off her tongue.

Now, as he wandered along Chicago's river walk, other images from the past left him longing to go back to the early days with Sonia and Matt, the time in his life he'd come to understand what it meant to be content. If only he'd savored it.

He'd been surprised to eventually find his heart so full of love and passion for Sonia. On their wedding day and honeymoon, with its awkward moments, he hadn't dared to envision the bond that would blossom between them.

With the gusty wind blowing off the lake, the raw air felt angry, even punishing. He'd left his apartment to escape the silent solitude, but then he tried to tune out the noise of people talking and laughing as they passed him by. He winced at the sound of the buses braking to a stop. The smell of exhaust fumes assaulted his nose. At that moment, all he could think about was the day he took Sonia to his dad's secret spot on the bank of Lady's River.

* * *

September 1984

Aaron led the way from the farm road through the weeds and tangled vines until they reached the narrow path leading deep into the woods and ending at the river. The leaves on the birches and maples had begun to turn, but the trees still clung to their branches, providing a cover that allowed little sunlight in. After the recent dry spell, the carpet of decaying leaves and pine needles crunched under their feet.

"Aaron, wait. I need a second."

He pivoted and saw Sonia standing still, holding her round belly with both hands.

"Are you okay? Should we turn back?"

"Not on your life. It's taken us all summer to get out here, and if we wait any longer we'll have to haul the baby with us." She glanced down at her stomach and laughed. "Haul him in our arms, I mean. I'd like to see the secret spot for the first time when we don't have any distractions."

"It isn't much farther."

She blew out air with loud exaggeration as she ran her hands over her stomach. "You know, I'm usually up for a long walk, but this is taking a lot out of me."

"Is he kicking?"

"Nope. He's been kind of a lazy butt the last couple of days. The doctor said he'd need to rest up before he decides it's time to make his grand entrance. And first babies often dawdle, too, and don't get moving until after their due date."

"Lazy butt? Dawdle?" he teased, turning to forge ahead. "You have the funniest way of putting things."

Even traipsing on the path more slowly now, it took only a few minutes for the trees lining both sides of the river to come into view.

"Oh, look at the lovely willows." She pointed to a spot a few feet from where they stood. "Don't you love how the branches caress the water as it flows by?"

"Now you're a poet?" he quipped. But he saw what she meant. In the light breeze, the drooping willows gently brushed the water's surface.

"Wow—this is a great hiding place." She lifted her arms as if embracing all she saw. "When we clear the walking paths for the garden we'll bypass this section. We'll design a path to go between the fields of prairie grasses and wildflowers instead. That way, this spot will always be a private family place. I'll bet your dad would approve."

Aaron pointed back to a grassy area near some birches deeper in the woods. "My folks used to come down here in May to see the yellow lady's slipper. My dad used to act like only a select group of people knew where to look. Next spring, we'll come back and find them for ourselves."

"Sounds wonderful. And we'll have the baby with us."

The river curved and widened up ahead and flowed past a few houses with boat docks. That afternoon, though, they had the river all to themselves.

Aaron spread the blanket on the ground in front of the biggest of the three boulders near the riverbank. He sat down and then patted the spot beside him.

"I can get my body down there," she said, frowning at the ground, "but getting back on my feet might be another story."

"Don't worry," he said, flexing his biceps. "I'll use my mighty muscles to get you up."

"Okay, but no laughing allowed."

She got down on her hands and knees and then flopped on her hip before squirming into a sitting position. She rested her back against the boulder, bent her knees, and pulled them as close to her body as her bulging middle allowed. Normally, she walked with long, sure strides, not so much graceful as confident. But these last few weeks, she lumbered—she called it waddling. Aaron was careful not to use that word, but was privately amused by its accuracy.

"I woke up this morning feeling kind of odd— peculiar," she said, patting her stomach. "Not bad, not good, just different. But I feel okay now. Every day of pregnancy is an adventure."

"You don't complain much," Aaron said with genuine admiration.

"Ah, I've fooled you. You don't hear me muttering under my breath all day as I waddle from room to room or propel myself out of the chair to fix a cup of one of my bland herbal teas."

He picked up her hand and laced his fingers with hers. "No, I suppose I don't."

"I hate to break this mood," she said, "but every once in a while, one of us needs to bring up our dear, sweet families. Have you talked with Dottie at all?"

"No." That was the simple answer, the truth. "What about your father, Sonia? Any word from him?"

When she lowered her head, he regretted bringing up her dad. More than anything, her father's continued cold stance toward her had inflicted a deep, festering wound.

"Not a peep out of him. But my mother and I talk almost every day. She checks in to see how I'm feeling, and always tells me that my dad sends his best. Great, big deal."

He almost said he was sorry, but he swallowed the words back. They'd covered that ground over and over. She felt bad about Dottie, and he was sorry about her dad's rejection. *So what?* Nothing changed, except that he and Sonia grew closer as they shored up their united front.

"To be honest, I'm losing patience with them," she said.

He squeezed her hand to show camaraderie. "That makes two of us. By the way, I've got some important news, professionally speaking, that is. I'm not sure why I've kept it to myself. I suppose I've been waiting for the right time to tell you."

"How 'bout now?" She gestured in an arc that encompassed the trees, the sky, and the river. "What better setting for good news."

He explained that he'd been asked to help the founder of the firm, Chuck Bateman, with a meaty case involving a safety flaw in a lawn mower manufactured in a town not far from Lady's River. "Fourteen injured people came to us, and we expect others to join as co-plaintiffs. But, the downside is that people around here are bound to fear that the plant will close and workers will lose their jobs."

"Will the company settle? Wouldn't that be better in the long run?"

"Probably. The owners are local guys, and they'd like to avoid the bad publicity. The crazy thing is, they have a fix for the machine they *could* implement, but they keep delaying. A quick settlement would help a lot. I did research for a similar case last year, and now I've got a chance to work with Chuck on the strategy for this one. And there's much more at stake here." As the excitement built in his voice, he saw her blue eyes deepen with interest and curiosity.

"Your enthusiasm for this case is written all over your face," she said. "But I'm puzzled. Why didn't you mention it before now?"

He didn't have an adequate answer. "Unfortunately, it's going to be demanding and I may have to work some evenings and weekends, or at least bring work home. And with the baby coming and you working on the plans for the garden…" He stopped in mid-sentence. It was obvious the timing of this positive development for him wouldn't be good for Sonia.

Until recently, she'd thrown herself into research for the garden. During the sticky, slow August days, he'd come home from work to find her on the couch with her bare feet propped up on pillows stacked on the coffee table. She'd surrounded herself with file folders and a pile of specialized books on things like herb gardens or cultivating the hardiest roses in their climate zone. She also studied a sheaf of papers filled with demographic data useful for the marketing plan.

But the last couple of weeks or so, she'd slowed

down even more and put the garden and business books aside in favor of those blood-soaked thrillers she enjoyed, and equally puzzling, historical epics with half-naked people on the covers. She called them her beach reads, even without the vacation or the beach.

"Let's not worry about your schedule now. We'll figure it out," she said in the confident tone he'd come to expect. She started every undertaking with the attitude that sooner or later, all obstacles could be overcome. Sometimes her thinking struck him as naïve, child-like optimism, but today he found it reassuring.

"I'm excited about this chance because of Artie Silverman, a professor of mine in law school."

"What? You had a class with *him*? You've got to be kidding? He's not just a lawyer, he's a legend, a celebrity."

Aaron snickered. "I know. I'm shamelessly namedropping." He told her about Artie's seminar and helping with research for a case. Aaron had been on the team of law students that uncovered and analyzed safety data a drug company had suppressed for twenty years. After the legendary lawyer had won the liability case at trial, he made a trip back to the law school to celebrate with the students who'd worked with him. Before he went back to his practice in New York, he'd urged his former team to stay in touch.

"I'd never seen anything close to Artie's flamboyant energy before. Nothing reserved about him. And he made a believer out of me. From that point on, I knew what kind of law I wanted to practice. Whenever I see a case like this, one that uncovers fraud and stops practices that could harm people, I call it a 'Silverman'. Now I have a chance to prove myself in a Silverman of my own."

"Wow. I'm so glad you told me. I think I understand why this means so much to you." She flashed him a broad smile. "I hear the excitement in your voice—and I like it."

"I had a feeling you would," he said. "From what I can tell, you throw your whole self into whatever you do, too."

"I'm glad we have that in common." Staring at the river, she added, "I remember you as the kind of kid who always stood up to the bullies in school."

"Oh, you bet. My dad would have disowned me if I hadn't. He was big on honor, which, to him, meant confronting the mean guys." Aaron closed his eyes and the image of his father's serious face flashed before him. For the next few minutes, only the sounds of chipmunks and squirrels scampering through the dry leaves broke the hush that settled over them.

"You're so quiet," he finally said, squeezing her hand again. "What are you thinking about?"

"Well, first I was thinking about being pleased for you, but then my mind took off on one of its flights and landed on the topic of our birthing classes. I hope you remember some of the breathing rigmarole, because right now, my mind is mush."

"You're tired, that's all."

"We'll see. But I'd hate to think that having a baby could make me stupid."

"No chance of that," he said, amused again by her quirky train of thought.

She squirmed around on the ground, first stretching her legs, then trying in vain to curl them under her. "Oh, dear."

"What?"

"Remember what I said before…about feeling peculiar?"

"Tell me you don't mean now."

She rolled into a kneeling position. "I'm not having contractions if that's what you mean, at least not yet, but I have a feeling that something is going to happen soon. We need to go home."

When she raised her arms toward him he cupped her elbows and gently pulled her to her feet.

Sounding genuinely curious, she said, "I wonder if whales feel this swollen and huge when they're about to deliver their calves."

He laughed. "Who knows? Maybe they gripe to each about feeling like beached humans."

He hadn't thought his one-liner was all that funny, but she chuckled all the way back to the car.

* * *

The River Gazette
September 19, 1984

Spotlight on Lady's River People

Our town's population increased by one when Sonia Van Caster Chapel, wife of local attorney, Aaron Chapel, gave birth to their son, Matthew Scott, at Townsend Community Hospital in Lady's River. Matthew, the couple's first child, weighed in at a hearty 7.2 pounds and measured 22 inches. We wish the newest member of our community all the best.

Mandy & Amy

7

February 1985

*I*f what Sonia said was true, and the honeymoon *was* over, then Aaron conceded it was mostly his fault. Not exactly a fight, Aaron thought. More like sniping at each other. Even sitting at his desk trying to draft a brief, he couldn't shake off the words that had passed between them earlier.

On their wedding day she'd reminded him that they had a lot to learn about each other. For the most part, he'd enjoyed the discoveries. Had he fallen in love? Not exactly, but he appreciated being around Sonia and watching her devotion to Matt and her willingness to devise a way to save his family's land. Sometimes he felt more content with the small everyday rituals in his life than he ever had before.

That morning, though, the petty side of him provided the justification for walking out of the house without a word. He sighed as he shuffled through the pages of the half-written brief.

Okay, he'd acted like a rude jerk. But how could a woman as organized and focused as Sonia, not to mention one with an excellent sense of smell, have so much trouble noticing, once again, the plume of smoke coming from the toaster? She insisted on cramming extra-thick slices of bread into it and then wondered why they got stuck and burned. This was a woman who wrote grocery lists in an order that matched the layout of the supermarket. But maybe the real question was why her odd contradictions hadn't rubbed him the wrong way before.

True enough, in the early months of their marriage he'd found it amusing—even charming in a way—when she tended the toaster or pancakes on the griddle with one hand while the other was busy leafing through a magazine or jotting items on that day's to-do list. She often got lost somewhere in between and then chided herself when breakfast went awry.

But that morning, the scene in the kitchen that greeted him had included the sound of Matt in full protest over being kept in the baby seat on the table. Matt usually liked his bird's eye view of the two of them going about their routine, but even Sonia rocking the chair and singing choruses from a string of her favorite old Beatles' songs hadn't distracted him.

He'd brushed past her in the small kitchen to unplug the toaster and retrieve the charred bread. "Do you think just once we could get through a morning without you threatening to burn the place down?"

"Sorry." She pointed to the coffee pot. "It's ready."

"I'll get coffee on the way to work," he'd snapped.

"Don't be silly. Have a cup before you leave."

He hadn't looked at her when he tersely muttered, "No, thanks."

She'd planted her hands on her hips with a no-nonsense motion. "Well, I see the honeymoon's definitely over."

"Huh?"

"My faults are no longer cute and amusing." She'd

turned her attention back to Matt.

He'd grabbed his coat and left without saying goodbye.

No more accusations of killing her with kindness. Those days were over for good. He also knew what Sonia meant by the honeymoon. For them, it wasn't about marital bliss, but about building a friendship on mutual respect and getting to know each other. Still, all couples fought over little stuff, didn't they? It wasn't as if they'd argued over something important. It was toast, for Pete's sake!

Struggling to concentrate on the brief, Aaron's guilty thoughts refused to disappear. For one thing, he hadn't made funny faces at the baby like he usually did before he left for the day. He hadn't offered to help quiet him either. Meanwhile, he pictured Sonia's morning of caring for Matt and carving out time to work on plans for the garden.

He ran his hands through his hair and sighed. How many times was he going to stare at the same page of the rough draft of a brief that needed hours of work to shape up? No use even pretending to work.

After telling his secretary that he'd forgotten a file, he headed for the car and steered it towards home.

The apartment was so quiet as he entered he assumed Sonia had fallen asleep after getting Matt down for his morning nap. But when he walked through the kitchen Aaron saw her sitting at the dining room table wrapped in a towel, with another tucked turban style on her head. Piles of papers fanned out on either side of an open book.

She glanced up. "Oh, hi. I didn't expect to see you." One bare crossed leg started swinging, so he knew she wasn't as relaxed as she'd attempted to sound. She hadn't smiled back at him, either.

The sight of her in the towel beckoned him to move in closer. "Just out of the shower?"

"Uh huh. Some of my best ideas come to me there, and I had a thought about a separate lily display. I needed to catch it before it slipped my mind." She patted the page of the book in front of her. "I had no idea how many varieties of lilies exist in this world."

He stood behind her and looked over her shoulder, resting his hand on the back of her chair.

She ran her fingers across a photo of an ivory lily. "I love these creamy ones. I bet the petals feel like velvet. I was thinking we could have these and other lilies in beds along the stone terrace—when we build it, that is." She tapped on the picture. "This variety is called White Perfection."

"Really?" Her shapely pale shoulders and long graceful neck looked like perfection to him. "I'm sorry about this morning."

She didn't turn to look up at him, but said, "I know."

"You do?"

"Yeah, like I'm sorry I get so distracted and make a mess of something as simple as toast."

He shrugged. "You're juggling a lot. And I shouldn't have walked out like that."

"It's okay. Stuff like that wears thin. What's amusing absent-mindedness one day looks like carelessness the next. Besides, we're together because of mutual carelessness. Burning the toast almost every day probably reminds you of that."

No, it hadn't. He wished she'd stop, once and for

all, bringing up that one night.

"Sonia, I know you're not careless." He bent close and brushed his lips across her shoulder. "Hmm, speaking of velvet, at the moment, I can concentrate on only one perfect lily. You."

"You can stalk out of the house and leave me behind if you choose, but I didn't like the way you left without even waving goodbye to Matt. I know he's only a baby, but still…"

"I know," he said, keeping his mouth close to her ear. "I felt bad about that, too. I can't promise I won't ever be in a bad mood again, but I promise you I won't ignore Matt like I did this morning."

She took in a breath, then tilted her head, which let him plant soft kisses up and down her neck. Then he unwrapped the towel from her head and inhaled the faint almond scent clinging to her damp hair. "Where's the baby?"

"Sleeping," she whispered, reaching up to touch his arm.

"You're so beautiful," he murmured, barely lifting his mouth off her skin.

With every graze of his lips, her fingers tightened a little more around his arm. Accepting the invitation, he pulled her to her feet and picked her up and carried her to their bedroom. She kept her eyes closed as he laid her on the bed and loosened the ends of the towel tucked above her breasts. He brushed his mouth across every inch of her, inhaling the warmth of her skin. Stopping only long enough to get out of his clothes, he savored the velvety softness of her hips and thighs, tuning out everything except her low moans and cries of pleasure.

Later, with their hearts still pounding, he held her

head close to his chest. He quickly reached down to pull the blanket over them to capture the warmth between them. Aaron didn't speak, afraid words would break the tenderness that lingered in the silence. They stayed entwined until they heard Matt's cry. Instantly, she turned away and began to slip out of bed, but he touched her shoulder to hold her back. "I'll get him."

His red-faced son took the insistent cries down a notch when Aaron lifted him from the crib. "Don't worry little guy," he whispered, "I'll take you to your mommy so you can have your lunch." Matt protested again when Aaron put him down on the changing table, but Aaron worked quickly to unsnap the sleeper and take off the wet diaper.

"Wanna know a secret?" he whispered. "I really like your mommy. And one day soon, when the time is right, I'm going to tell her—in words."

Matt wailed again. "You're not impressed by my news, huh," he said, grinning at the baby. Once the dry diaper was snug, Matt became less frantic. Aaron wrapped him in a blanket and lifted his son to his shoulder and headed back to the bedroom. "But for now," he whispered, "we'll keep it between us. Okay?"

He put Matt into Sonia's waiting arms and a second later, the slurping sounds of nursing began. After he draped a throw around her bare shoulders, he gathered his clothes off the floor and dressed quickly. He leaned down and kissed Sonia's forehead, but with her free hand she grabbed his neck and pulled him back, kissing him hard on the mouth. They didn't speak, but he kept his eyes on her until he'd closed the door behind him.

* * *

Sonia had sized up Aaron as a call-the-plumber kind of guy, much like her father, whom she'd never seen perform a manly crawl under a sink to locate the source of leaks. But one Saturday morning, she looked on as Aaron, armed with a wrench he'd discovered in a seldom used toolbox, disappeared into the cabinet under the kitchen sink.

The top half of him was out of her view from where she sat next to the highchair, trying to catch strained pears before they dribbled out of Matt's mouth, down his chin, and into the soft folds of his neck. With the sound of him babbling between bites combined with the banging of wrench-meeting-pipe, Sonia laughed at her realization that she felt grown up and very married. And what's more, she liked it. Even the occasional grunts and groans coming from the direction of the sink added to her sense that all was right with her world.

When Aaron finally reappeared, he stood and said he needed to run to the hardware store for an elbow joint and a washer. He grabbed his jacket off the hook by the kitchen door, but instead of leaving, he kept his hand on the doorknob for a few seconds.

"Let's buy a house," he blurted. "If I'm going to fix plumbing, I'd just as soon that we own it."

He didn't wait for a response, but quickly opened the door and disappeared.

Sonia let out a hoot. "He sounds like a husband, doesn't he?" she said, making circles with her index finger, moving closer and closer until finally planting it on the tip of Matt's button nose. "We're going to get a house for the three of us to live in together."

With their first anniversary only a few weeks off, she and Aaron had only started settling into a real relationship. But what a turning point to remember. How discouraging it had been that morning a few weeks ago when she'd watched Aaron leave the apartment without even saying goodbye to her, or worse, to Matt. But he'd come back, allowing her to trust him with her passion.

Before Matt was born, Sonia feared they'd have to resign themselves to sex that was just okay and not all that satisfying. That fear had disappeared for good. Instead of the honeymoon being over, it had just begun.

"As it turns out, my precious Matt, your daddy is a pretty good guy." She grabbed the sponge from the sink and swiped it across the highchair tray to clear away the remains of lunch. "And, I guess he's not tired of me yet. What do you think of that?"

Matt gurgled and then rewarded her with a funny grin.

Before she'd agreed to marry Aaron, she'd hashed out the pros and cons with her closest friend, Leslie. Aaron had continued putting the pressure on, but she'd questioned whether his sense of honor toward her was reason enough to say yes to a wedding. Finally, though, Leslie had pointed out that she could turn the tables and marry him as the honorable thing. She'd laughed at Leslie's suggestion, but later joked with Aaron that she was ready to make an honest man out of him.

Secretly, Sonia had been willing to settle for an accommodation based on a sense of duty to their child. Ironically, she'd set her sights way too low.

More and more every day, Sonia craved Aaron's touch and the sound of his voice whispering her name when he held her close in the night. Just thinking about him brought heat to her cheeks.

But then she rested her gaze on Matt and the

disconcerting guilt returned. She couldn't forget the careless way they'd created this new, sweet life. Aaron disliked her bringing it up, but memories of the night they conceived Matt still left her feeling shallow. Sometimes, even on the days she felt nearly perfect joy, a judgmental voice declared her undeserving of such happiness. The way she and Aaron became a couple invited in the shadows and darkened her moods.

She spoke a string of nonsense words to Matt to distract herself from negative thoughts as she wiped his mouth. Laughing at the baby's attempts to babble back, she picked him up and danced him out of the kitchen and into his room. "Let's get you dressed," she said, picking up the baby jeans. She captured his chubby legs kicking away and pulled the jeans over them, quite expertly, too. The sweatshirt was next, and then she sat in the rocking chair and folded his hands into her own and clapped them together in a beginner's rendition of pat-a-cake.

She heard the kitchen door close and then the sound of Aaron's steps in the hall.

"Grab your coat," he said as he came through the door. "We're going for a drive. I've got something to show you."

"What is it?"

"It's a surprise." He lifted Matt off her lap and sat him up on the changing table. "Let's get you into your jacket and hat, little man. We've got places to go and people to see."

Sonia watched Matt staring into his daddy's face, reaching for his nose while Aaron got the other arm through the jacket sleeve. What a cute duo. Sonia felt a surge of energy flow through her, light and free and up for anything Aaron had in store.

* * *

*H*e pulled up to a house at the end of a street that dead-ended at a narrow creek and a stretch of woods—the only positive feature. The dilapidated Tudor brick and stucco house looked forlorn in its yard, a jungle of decaying shrubs and vines. A barely visible For Sale sign sprouted from the patchy snow behind a tall wrought iron fence.

He didn't waste time trying to think up a preamble to justify his admittedly impulsive idea. "Let's buy this house."

She frowned, but in a surprised, thoughtful sort of way. At least she hadn't laughed out loud at what, on its face, stood out as a completely ridiculous idea.

"But we haven't seen the inside, and we don't know if we can afford it. Besides, it looks like it could use some major work."

He let out a loud laugh at her understatement. While cleaning up the yard would be a cinch, the cracks in the stucco and peeling paint on the door and window frames offered evidence of long-term neglect. "That leaves us free to do whatever we want to the place."

She shifted Matt from one hip to the other. "Okay, why this house? What am I missing?"

"I thought you'd never ask." He grinned and waved toward the woods. "The land on the other side of the creek is a long narrow stretch that's a piece of the western edge of the farm. So if we buy this house, we'll be living adjacent to the garden."

Aaron wished he had a camera to capture Sonia's look of happy surprise.

"So, if your family ends up having to sell after all," she said, "you could hold back some of the woods along the creek and we'd own land around this house."

"Exactly." He pointed to a break in the trees. "But looking on the bright side, let's assume we won't have to sell the land. You planned to extend the walking trails out here anyway. We'll put in a footbridge over the creek and you can walk to your office at the garden. Just think, if we buy this house we'll live right next to the garden grounds."

Her eyes glistened with tears. "What a wonderful idea."

"And I don't doubt that the garden will be a great success," he said quickly. Unsure of what had brought on her tears, he didn't want her thinking he doubted her hard work would pay off.

Aaron had admired how carefully and systematically she'd proceeded through all the beginning conceptual stages, with his mother doing her part by explaining the way they'd attracted visitors to the farm and how each employee contributed to the whole picture. In her business-like manner, Sonia sent regular status updates to Dottie and Burt, too, even though his sister and her husband had pulled away entirely.

He'd barely talked with Dottie since that ugly exchange during their meeting in their mother's dining room almost a year before. The holidays had been excruciating, with Matt providing the only common ground for the hour or so of overlapping visits to Rona.

"Maybe, just maybe, the three of us will live in this house," Sonia said to Matt in the happy sing-song voice she used to tell him everyday things. "Yes, indeed. But we'll make it pretty first, and you'll have a new room, yes you will."

"So, I take it Matt approves?" There it was, a stitch in his chest that happened more and more these days. He touched the spot, as if he could make these moments of near perfection durable and part of him.

"As far as I can tell," she said with a quick grin.

Aaron jogged down the block to the corner gas station and called the number on the sign from the pay phone. He knew the owner of the agency, but he didn't know Vera Smart, the agent listed. She answered her phone on the second ring, and sounding eager to show them the place, she offered to swing by within the hour.

True to her word, Vera pulled up thirty minutes later. Unfortunately, Matt had tired of the adventure. Sonia wore a path around the side of the house and then back to the front, all the while jiggling him and exclaiming over the size of the place, but he fussed on. But hey, she told Matt, don't cry, that rickety old porch wasn't so bad, and surely the stairs could be fixed, and a coat or two of paint would do wonders. As she babbled to Matt about all the wonderful repairs they'd make, the more Aaron realized that the idea of renovating the shabby shell of a house looked like a catastrophe in the making. Maybe he'd carried spontaneity too far.

But Vera, professional in a power-of-positive-thinking sort of way, reassured them that getting their hands on the house would be a breeze. The owner now lived in a nursing home and his closest relative, an elderly sister, wanted to unload the property as quickly as possible. When Vera unlocked the door and pushed it open, the hinges protested with a squeak loud enough to make Aaron wince.

"What a disaster," Aaron said, when he and Sonia stood side by side in the living room. "This was probably not one of my best ideas. I'm sorry I dragged you here."

Sonia didn't agree or disagree, but shifted Matt to her other hip. When he squealed even louder she held him under his arms and handed him over. "Maybe he'll be happier with his daddy."

Aaron swung Matt over his head and made ridiculous noises and goofy faces to distract him while Sonia, frowning in deep thought, wandered into the kitchen.

The next thing he heard was Vera's remark that the price was so low "because it needs some updates."

Still in the other room, he smiled to himself, knowing exactly how Sonia would respond. She didn't disappoint.

"*I'll* say."

"We hadn't expected to show the house just yet," Vera explained defensively, "even though we put up the sign. We planned to get the place cleaned up and do a few repairs first."

Aaron didn't hear what Sonia said next because Matt wailed and squirmed in his arms.

"Sonia? I'm not having any luck with him," he hollered into the kitchen.

She didn't look pleased when she grudgingly took him back. "What makes you think I will?"

He couldn't think of an answer. Much as he hated to admit it, he often felt like a bumbler with the baby. Half the time, he couldn't explain why Matt fussed or what made him stop. What's more, he didn't completely buy Sonia's assurances that no one in human history had ever figured it out.

"You're tired, aren't you?" she cooed to Matt before turning to him. "We better go."

While Sonia settled Matt in his car seat, Aaron thanked Vera and apologized for wasting her time. Then he slid into the car while Sonia sat in the back with Matt, patting his legs and humming some droning song about a short, stout teapot as he drove. By the time they arrived home, Matt was sound asleep.

"Let's go back and have another look," Sonia said, sounding oddly eager.

"Now?" he asked, looking at her through the rearview mirror.

"Matt's conked out, so we can sit on the porch and reconsider. The place is a hellhole now, but who knows what we could do with it? It sits adjacent to your family's land, so that alone makes it worth another look."

Since he'd begun to wish he'd never seen the house, her suggestion annoyed him, and "hellhole" accurately described the place. But then he thought about the land. At worst, they could tear down the house and sit on the lot until they were ready to build. Besides, it wouldn't kill him to go along with her and drive back.

"Okay, maybe I can figure out a way to get inside the dump."

* * *

Sonia waited on the porch until Aaron yelled that he'd found a window on the side of the house he could force open. After he'd let himself in, he opened the squeaky front door. She carried Matt inside, still asleep in his car seat, and gingerly lowered it to the floor by the oak window seat in the living room. Lots of bay windows, she observed, and all the woodwork was oak, though darkened with time. At least no one had painted over it. Score one point for the house. Saying he was going to check out the basement, Aaron disappeared down the stairs off the kitchen.

She took a deep breath and looked more closely at the wide front yard with two old maples on one side and a couple of tall blue spruces on the other. She'd already seen the cedars bordering the back yard. True, time had not been kind to the inside. The dirty cracked walls needed new plaster as well as fresh paint—and she wouldn't choose the pinky beige that currently covered the walls. She shook her head in wonder that anyone would voluntarily pick such an ugly color to look at day in and day out. But the old wreck had the diamond windows typical of Tudors and lots of built-ins and cubbyholes.

Despite everything the place needed, and she couldn't help herself from jotting a dozen or more initial jobs on her mental notepad, she'd always been partial to Tudors. Something else played in her mind, and her heart, too. She sat on the window seat and immediately felt at home. She could picture herself coming down the oak staircase in the morning and through the side door from the garage at night. She slid Aaron and Matt into the vision and felt content.

Then she saw something that brought on a quick laugh.

She quickly went to the top of the basement stairs and called out to Aaron. "Hey, come on up. We've got company."

"I'll be up in a minute."

"I think you better come now."

"What is it?" he asked curtly when he reached the top stair.

She threw up her hands in exasperation as she walked into the living room. "You can be so prickly sometimes. I thought *you'd* prefer to deal with the police."

He followed her to the window. Two Lady's River officers were coming up the walk with flashlights swinging. "What the hell," she said, "go ahead and tell them we're buying this palace."

Amused by the way he shook his head in disbelief, she watched from the window as Aaron went out to meet the officers. Handshakes all around, followed quickly by grins and nods. She guessed he knew the guys, since the two officers probably represented about ten percent of the total Lady's River police force. She smiled as she watched him gesture and point back to the house.

Aaron stayed put on the walk until the officers got back in their cruiser and pulled away.

"So, do we own this project now?" she asked when he came back inside. She could only laugh at what they were getting themselves into.

"More or less. I said we were making a preliminary offer. Not exactly true, but it should keep us and the baby out of jail for breaking and entering."

Grinning, she wandered to the fireplace and ran her fingertips across the mantle, not surprised when she came up with grime on her hand.

He braced his arm on the wall. "The basement looks sound, by the way, and dry. We need to do some foundation repairs, but the furnace might be the newest item in the place."

"That's good. I wondered what you were doing down there," she said, running the toe of her shoe across the hearth to see if any bricks were loose. "So, maybe the place looks worse than it is."

He studied the cracks in the ceiling. "I'll bet a lot of people would tear the house down and start over. That seems to be the trend nowadays." He twisted his mouth in disapproval. "I suppose we *could* do that, too."

"I don't know—it's a lovely old home if you can look beyond the superficial mess." With a quick laugh she turned in a circle. "I can't believe we're seriously considering buying it and we've barely left this room. Let's go exploring."

Together, they discovered a huge old-fashioned pantry, and two bathrooms in hideous shape on the first floor. Between a family room off the kitchen and a formal dining room, plus a den, they could probably live on the first floor while they renovated the upstairs.

Aaron picked up the baby carrier, where Matt still slept soundly. They climbed the stairs and ambled through the rooms on the second floor and then the attic. Even the upstairs had built-in hutches and window seats everywhere. The ugly paint and layers of grime made the rooms dreary, but the windows were large and plentiful. Sonia could almost feel the cooling cross breeze traveling through the upstairs on summer days.

Space wasn't an issue. With plenty of rooms downstairs and four bedrooms on the second floor, the attic could be finished off, too.

Aaron grinned flirtatiously. "We could have a ton of kids."

She rolled her eyes at him, and then looked down at

their still sleeping baby. "So, little one, I guess your mommy and daddy are going to make the Wreck of the Tudor our very own."

* * *

Somewhere in the twilight zone of consciousness, he heard her ask if he was asleep. Did she ask that every night just as he was drifting off? Maybe it just seemed like it. Sometimes he found it mildly annoying, but that night he didn't mind. "I'm still awake. What's on your mind?"

"I was thinking about how we're tying ourselves together more and more."

His stomach lurched. "What of it?"

She lifted her head and propped herself on her elbow, an angle that let him see the outline of her face in the dark. "I mean between the baby and the garden and now the, let's just call it what it is, a big old rundown house—"

"That you aptly named the Wreck of the Tudor," he interrupted. He'd laughed out loud when she'd first said it and knew the name would stick.

"I guess what I'm trying to say is that if we decide to disentangle ourselves down the road, it's going to get complicated."

He groaned as he reached up to flip on the light. "You were thinking about *that* just now? After spending most of our day impulsively buying a home of our own?"

"I didn't mean it in a negative way." She sat up and reached for the robe she'd hung on the spindle of the bed.

She'd done it again, he noted. Every time he

sounded annoyed by one of her off-the-wall remarks, which inevitably started a touchy conversation, she reached for something to cover herself. If a robe or a shirt wasn't handy, then she grabbed a sheet.

"Honestly, Aaron, you get so feisty so fast."

"Well, you have an odd way of putting things. Sometimes I wonder if…" He stopped while he tried to put his thoughts into words. "Be honest. Are you unhappy with me? Is your cheerful attitude an act?"

"No, no, that's not it at all." She shifted and curled her legs under her and sat back on her heels. "Over these past months, I've come to a realization. I really, *really* like you."

He snorted in surprise. "Oh, yeah? Well, I *really* like you, too. So there."

A dreamy look crossed her face. "I've been thinking about this for a while now, but it all came together for me when I saw you crawl under the sink this morning."

"What? And they say *women* are the romantic sex."

"I mean, I felt so married. Then you left to do your hardware store thing. The next thing you know we're standing in the middle of an empty, dirty living room painted a hideous non-color." She laughed lightly. "And then we were snapping at each other over the baby fussing."

He drew back his head. "C'mon, that wasn't snapping. We were merely expressing impatience."

She laughed. "Okay, have it your way. But knowing that we would sink every penny we'll ever hope to earn into that house, it hit me that I really feel married to you."

"If that's as good as I'm going to get," he said in the best dry tone he could muster, "I'll take it."

"So, when did you figure out that you really like me?"

He snickered sheepishly and wished he could think up something clever or original.

"What's so funny?"

"I'm thinking about the day I came in and saw you with a towel wrapped around your luscious body." He reached out and ran his index finger across her knee. "Hey, it's not crawling under a sink, but it's the best I can do."

Even in the dim light, he saw her cheeks redden.

"You're blushing," he whispered.

She lowered her eyes. "I know."

"You have to admit, my moment of romantic realization sure beats yours."

She reached over him to turn off the light. "When you're right, you're right." She kissed him lightly on the mouth. "I guess I'll have to redeem myself."

He tightened his embrace to keep her in place on top of him. "That's going to take a very long time, but you can start right now."

She laughed and it struck him again just how much he looked forward to hearing that sound.

Part II

8

June 1986

The River Gazette
"Garden Launch Washout"
By Martha Samuelson, Staff Writer

June 9, 1986 - *Heavy rain hindered events scheduled for the grand opening weekend of Chapel's Botanical Garden, the facility designed to replace the family-owned Chapel's Farm on the Hill. The garden's General Manager, Sonia Chapel, remained upbeat despite the small turnout and the need to move the festivities inside the farm buildings, many of which are still undergoing renovation.*

Mrs. Chapel thanked her former employer, Alex Stahl, owner of the Lady's Slipper Winery, for hosting the wine tasting event, and she also acknowledged the Northeast College Chamber Quartet, which provided entertainment throughout the weekend.

The steady downpour didn't prevent State Representative, Leila Ginsburg from attending and offering words of encouragement about the future of this new attraction. "I expect the garden to be an excellent recreational and educational resource for both local residents and tourists."

Aaron Chapel remembered the late Roger

Chapel, remarking that his father would approve of the way the garden continues to celebrate the natural landscape of Northeast Wisconsin. He also remembered his wife's father, the late William Van Caster, a prominent Lady's River businessman, who passed away suddenly in December of 1985.

"This is just a beginning," Sonia Chapel said, when asked for details about the colorful models of the future garden on display in the reception building. "We invite visitors to share our vision, and be sure to watch for the future special events we're planning. Meanwhile, we hope our neighbors will visit often and take a stroll on our new walking trails, or enjoy a picnic by the pond and watch us bloom."

* * *

The River Gazette
June 10, 1986

Spotlight on Lady's River People

Conspicuous by their absence, Dorothy Chapel Webster and her husband, Burt, were no-shows at Saturday's muddy grand opening of Chapel's Botanical Garden. The family has remained mum on their absence, other than saying that the couple had other plans. But rumor has it that the missing pair hid out inside their home, located on the farm/garden grounds. While we can't say for sure, we suspect that not all the Chapels see this new garden as a paradise in the making. We'll keep you posted.

Mandy & Amy

* * *

November 2006

*E*ven the scent of the wood burning in the fireplace couldn't overpower the aromas of garlic and thyme mingling with the rich, fruity notes of red wine that floated through the air in the restaurant. A converted farmhouse located off the county highway into Lady's River, The French Kitchen featured hearty country beef and chicken soups and stews, rich desserts, and an impressive variety of wines.

Sonia closed her eyes and inhaled deeply, comforted by the mixture of fragrances. What a contrast to the noisy, harsh rattling of the windows as the wind whipped the rain into a nearly horizontal stream stinging the glass.

She reached for her wine glass first, and then flopped back in the chair, letting her shoulders droop into an exaggerated slump. "This was such a good idea, Ben. I can finally stop rushing around."

Smiling at the thoughtful man studying her from across the table, she didn't like seeing his troubled frown. Hoping to change his expression, she injected a cheerful tone in her voice. "Smells good in here, doesn't it?"

He nodded. "I thought we needed a chance to get away from things. Fall is such a busy time, especially for you." He held up his glass as if to toast. "So, here we are."

She tipped her glass toward him, then glanced around the room, unhappy that the edginess that had plagued her all day hadn't yet dissipated.

"This kind of downpour always reminds me of the weekend we had our more or less disastrous grand opening of the garden," she said, realizing that it was better to talk about what was on her mind rather than suppressing her nostalgia. "Different season, but those two June days were so cold and raw it might as well have been November—that's what everyone who showed up said."

Ben smiled in acknowledgment, but Sonia knew he couldn't see the whole picture. A relative newcomer to town, Ben didn't fully understand the role that Chapel's Botanical Gardens had played in Lady's River over the past few years, or for that matter, the importance of the tourist farm in its day.

Ben also hadn't understood why she'd insisted on going to the dedication at Pearson Pond by herself. She'd tactfully explained that the weekend would be draining, and if he'd been at her side, she'd have felt obligated to feign a cheerful mood that didn't match her heavy heart. Ben felt otherwise, saying that he only wanted to support her and didn't have illusions about what the weekend meant to her.

On the other hand, Ben's quiet presence had been exactly what she'd needed this past year or so. A native of Minnesota, he'd sought a change of scene after his wife had died unexpectedly. After phasing out a retail business, he'd returned to his original profession and accepted a job teaching sixth grade in Lady's River.

Sonia had met him when he'd brought his class to the garden and had enjoyed their conversation. She eagerly accepted his invitation to have dinner with him the following weekend. She'd confided to both Dottie and her old friend, Leslie, that it was a relief to spend time with a person who didn't know every detail of her history. Besides, Ben appreciated her weird sense of humor. A few dates later, she'd laughingly confided to

Leslie that she might be falling in love.

Lately, though, she'd begun to sense she disappointed Ben too often, or maybe she'd pulled him up and brought him along on her emotional rollercoaster ride. She picked up the menu to distract herself and to stop over-analyzing their relationship. "So, everything is good here, isn't it?"

Ben glanced over his reading glasses and smiled politely. "And they know us here. Well, they used to. It's been a while."

"That's about to change," she said, lightly snapping the menu for emphasis. "Let's make a deal to get out here for dinner more often."

Perhaps if she fell into a rhythm of doing ordinary things like going out to dinner and picking up her romance with Ben, she'd feel like herself again.

"I've been waiting for the right time to make some plans, starting with the holidays," he said. "I know you've been distracted, but I sometimes get the feeling you're avoiding me."

"No, that's not it." She sipped her wine while she mentally rehearsed what she wanted to say. "I've felt off balance. It's the kind of state you get into when something is finished and you realize that you've poured all your energy into it—then boom," she said, swiping her palms together, "all of a sudden it's over."

He rested his forearms on the table. If she'd leaned in, he'd probably fold his hands over hers. But she held back.

"Are you drained? Is that what you're trying to say, Sonia?"

"I suppose that's a good way to describe it. I feel like I'm at a way station and need to stop and give myself time to recover. Maybe it's like stopping at an oasis in the desert. I need to rest and replenish."

"I see," he said with a disappointed sigh. "I thought we were that for each other, a safe haven where we leave distractions at the door. Perhaps leaving the past behind, too."

"We are, and I'm so enjoying this moment right now." She nervously tapped her fingertips on the side of the wineglass. "It's raw and wet outside, but here we are, snug and dry and enjoying a quiet evening."

Now how could anyone argue with that? But what a whopper. She sounded as if she'd read the lines off a script. Sure, going out to dinner at their favorite place was great, but she also felt pulled toward home, where she could hide out in the den, and curl up in the corner of her familiar couch with a throw around her shoulders. She could watch a movie or pick up her place in the mystery she was reading. Maybe, after all was said and done, she needed to replenish at the oasis alone.

To change the subject, she asked about Lonnie, Ben's grown daughter, and Kim, Ben's only grandchild. She could always make his eyes light up when she asked about them. That's when he suggested they fly down to Florida to celebrate New Year's Eve with Lonnie and her family.

Thrown off balance once again, she muttered that they should talk about the trip soon, sounding, she quickly realized, like a businesswoman committing to discussing plans for a conference call.

Later, in the parking lot, she gave Ben a warm kiss goodbye before they drove off in their separate cars. It was an okay night, but she had no desire to extend it. Dinner was all she could handle.

Relieved to close her door behind her, she tossed her coat on the back of the couch, stopping to stare at the fireplace. It was still early and maybe she'd enjoy a fire. That would break her routine.

Ha! Rut was more like it.

Until she'd seen Aaron again, she avoided all thoughts about the sinking standards of her lifestyle. Now the worn out carpeting under her feet felt like an indictment of the way she'd been living. Sometimes the Tudor even smelled stale and old, as if the life of the house she'd worked hard to revitalize had leaked out through the walls and windows in the last few years.

Making her way to the kitchen, she picked up the teakettle and filled it with water for chamomile tea, but changed her mind and poured a half a glass of cabernet. Instead of going directly to the den, she walked under the arched entryway to the dining room. The first time she'd done that in months. She turned on the light and rotated the dimmer switch to brighten the room where years before she'd gathered around the table for big dinners with friends and family, sometimes on holidays, sometimes just because she liked a good dinner party.

One particular holiday stood out, though, and not in a good way. That year, she and Aaron planned to have both families over for Christmas dinner in their newly renovated dining room. Sonia had hoped the holiday would serve as a catalyst to finally mend some fences, especially because she and Aaron had found surprising happiness with each other. Plus, working with Rona as her partner, she had scheduled the garden launch for the following spring.

Secretly, she'd hoped to rebuild her relationship with her dad, who clung to his stubborn disapproval of her pregnancy, even after Matt was born. He'd practically shouted his objections to her investing money in the garden, too. But Sonia stiffened her spine and vowed to show him what she was made of.

Then, only a few days before the holiday, her father died suddenly.

Sonia turned away from the dining room, but not before the passing thought that it needed some sprucing up. Not wanting to think about that now, she went into the den and stretched out on the couch, suddenly overwhelmed with the memory of bitter tears shed over her father's death. Sounding like a plaintive young girl, she'd moaned to Aaron about her father not seeing Matt grow up and that he wouldn't know about the garden launch either. Aaron had held her and listened to her give voice to her grief. It had taken another couple of years before she matured enough to see that Bill Van Caster, the father she'd adored, had let *her* down, not the other way around.

Damn it, these trains of thought led nowhere good. She picked up her book off the coffee table, and then turned on the TV, keeping the sound so low she could barely make out the words of the newscast. In the years since Aaron had left, complete silence in the room made her uneasy, even when she wanted nothing more than to lose herself in a novel and block out everything else.

Glancing around, though, she had to admit that the den looked shabby. If she lived here long enough, the place would turn back into the Wreck of the Tudor.

Pushing that dreary thought away, Sonia sat up long enough to take a few sips of wine. Then she settled back down and found her place in the book. She stared at the print on the page and struggled to concentrate, but her eyes grew heavy. Seconds later, she let the book slip from her hands and land on the floor with a dull thud.

* * *

Waking with a start, Sonia sat up and squinted at the clock on the desk. It was nearly six o'clock. On the TV screen, a cheery woman in a bright red pantsuit swept her hand across a weather map that promised another gray day ahead.

Sonia rubbed her aching temples with her fingertips. She'd done it again, slept on the couch until morning. Not that it happened every night, she thought defensively, but often enough to become a bad habit she needed to break.

It had started after she and Aaron, each lost in their grief—and separate obsessions—had all but stopped talking.

With thoughts of Aaron still lodged in her mind, she showered quickly, then pulled on jeans and rubber boots and a heavy wool sweater. She dashed out of the house and across the footbridge to the path, still muddy from the previous day's downpour. To the east, the morning light barely peeked through the bare branches of the trees lining the horizon, still heavy with clouds. More rain was in store. If she'd spent the night with Ben, as he'd suggested, they'd have donned their jackets and taken mugs of hot coffee out to his deck to watch the sun break through the darkness over Lake Michigan. They'd spent many pleasant mornings that way, but not lately, and that was her doing, not his.

When she reached her office, she flipped on the light, but kept the blinds closed. The day would distract her soon enough. She pulled open the top drawer of her desk and reached to the back, feeling around past her daybook and notepads until her fingers touched the envelope. Each time she took out the letter, she noted Aaron's return address on East Ontario Street. It still felt strange to picture him living in a boxy apartment in a high-rise. She took out the folded paper and smoothed the creases. Then she reread his words to her.

April 20, 2004

Dear Sonia,

It was for the best that I left without more conversation between us. Words had done all they could and in the end, they weren't good enough. So, I understand why you spent the weekend with Leslie. Although my move to Chicago finalized things between us, we'd already been emotionally separated for a long time. I expect you agree.

If I don't get these thoughts off my chest now, I might find a reason not to write this letter at all. First, I want to make sure you understand how grateful I'll always be for what you did to keep my family's land. It's your land now, too. Nothing in the divorce will change that, and I will never forget the way you stood up to Dottie—and your father—and held on to your vision for the garden. Odd as it seems, when I look back on those early weeks and months of our marriage, I realize how proud I was of you.

I probably don't need to say this, but I will anyway. I no longer harbor the nonsensical belief that Matt would be with us today if you hadn't nurtured his gift with such passion. Or, maybe I should simply say that I don't blame the cello for some indirect path to Matt's death. When I look back, I know you did the right thing to guide him. Eventually, he'd have needed to be free to set his own course, but if it had been left to me, I might not have recognized Matt's talent at all. As you correctly pointed out, I am tone deaf in the literal sense. It will always hurt to know that I missed in

Matt's music what virtually everyone else heard. But you made a believer out of me. And on the morning he left us, he'd become a young man eager to expand his life in music.

I can't say I feel at home here in this city, so different from our hometown. With all it has to offer, I still find myself mostly drawn to the river and the lake. But now that I've left Lady's River, I can't see myself ever returning. Ironically, you're closer to Dottie and her stepchildren than I am, and with my mother gone, I expect to put the town and I suppose, even the garden, behind me. You, however, will never fade into the distant past.

My biggest regret is that after first clinging to each other in our pain, we eventually faced in opposite directions. Dottie once put it that way and it's as apt a description as any.

But, the truth is, I will always "really, really like you."

Of course, I wish you the best.
Aaron

Sonia held the letter to her chest and let the tears run down her cheeks. She'd known before she shuffled through her desk for the letter that she'd cry, but she couldn't stop herself from reading it again. When the letter had arrived two and a half years before, she'd completely unraveled, sobbing so hard she'd rushed out of her office and into the open spaces of the garden. That day, she'd wandered every mile of the walking paths feeling furious with her soon-to-be ex-husband on the one hand and heartbroken over him on the other. Yet, she sensed relief in his letter, and her little secret was that she, too, felt tension drain from her when he'd gone away.

She'd waited a few weeks to reply, and by that time she'd found a semblance of inner peace. At least with Aaron gone, she'd no longer needed to apologize for the time she spent with the Unity Flight Family Group or feel guilty that the grieving men and women felt like her new family.

Refolding the letter and holding it in her palm, Sonia debated, as always, what to do with it. Maybe the time had come to throw it away. It would be so simple. She glanced at the wastebasket next to her desk. Just let it go, drop it in.

No, not yet.

She slid the letter into the envelope and then tucked it in the back corner of the drawer.

She swiveled in the chair and stood to open the blinds, forcing herself to allow the day to start. Her straight ahead view took in the sloping gardens that led to the fields of now brown prairie grasses beyond, but when she looked to her right, she saw the front of what used to be Rona's house. Now Dottie lived there with Cal and his three kids, grown into young adults.

From her window she saw the taillights of Cal's car as he drove off, probably to teach an early class at Northeast College. Seeing Cal brought back memories of years past, the time of her life that passed so quickly. Every day had felt full—at times, too full, or so she'd thought—with the garden and Matt's music. In one of those years, the Chapel family grew in one great leap when Cal and his kids came into their lives. But, long before that, Sonia had to deal with Dottie herself.

9

August 1989

Sonia shuffled through the stack of job applications, trying to narrow the field of candidates. She'd joked with Aaron that she needed an expert to take over the *real* public relations, not just the publicity and promotion, areas she'd thrown herself into with great enthusiasm—what Aaron called gusto. The garden needed someone to handle kids on the growing number of school tours and those organized for senior citizens, too, especially during the peak of fall color. The first of the fall trips was only a couple of weeks off.

Rona remarked that with more and more busses parked in the gravel lot, it was beginning to feel like the days when Chapel's Farm on the Hill had hit its stride. But Rona also made it clear she wasn't interested in tramping through the garden with adults or kids in tow. She preferred her niche in reception and helping the part-timers run the small gift shop Rona helped convert from the old farm themes to a fresh garden-related atmosphere. Besides, Sonia noticed that Rona, once wiry and quick, often pulled up the stool behind the reception counter and rested one hip on it. More and more she let the younger staff stock the gift store shelves rather than insisting on doing it herself.

Neither naturalist nor teacher by a long shot,

Sonia's own tours got passing grades, but she was the first to admit she didn't have the knowledge plus the flair necessary to make them memorable. That was okay. From her early days of planning, she'd never intended to don all the hats needed to keep their garden blooming.

Sifting through the applications and résumés, she pulled out one from a retired science teacher and another two from recent graduates of the horticulture program at the community college. She envisioned someone with the attitude of a naturalist and familiar with the terrain of their corner of Wisconsin. The person had to be fit enough to take several treks through the gardens each day, too. She shuffled through the pile again and pulled out the top six candidates.

A knock on the door broke her concentration, especially since the garden didn't open for an hour. Probably Rona checking in. "C'mon in."

She looked up to see Dottie standing in the doorway.

"Oh, hi," Sonia said. "I...uh...didn't expect to see you."

"No, I don't suppose you did. Can I come in?"

Flustered, Sonia waved to the chair across from her desk. "Sure. Have a seat."

Because she rarely saw Dottie, she didn't have much to say. Over the years, they'd finally settled into distant civility, especially during holiday celebrations with Rona. But she and Aaron continued overlapping their visits to limit the time they all spent in the same room.

The previous fall, Aaron had told her that Burt had left Dottie. Rona mentioned it, too, but hadn't provided any details. Sonia had swallowed back a mouthful of questions and respected her mother-in-law's desire to avoid talking about the demise of Dottie's marriage behind her back. Aaron also offered little insight into what happened to prompt Burt to take off. Then in early June, Dottie left on a six-week camping trip out west with a couple of women friends. Sonia hadn't known she was back.

"So, how was your trip?" Sonia asked pleasantly.

"It was good for me to get away. I'd never been west of the Mississippi River. I had time to think about things." She studied her folded hands. "It was a healing trip."

Since she didn't elaborate, the silence grew awkward, leading Sonia to speak up. "I've never acknowledged how painful it must have been to break up with Burt." At the time, she'd felt uncharitable satisfaction in learning that Aaron's hunch about Burt had proved correct. But she'd felt no joy that Dottie had been hurt in the process.

Dottie smiled sadly. "Look, I'll just say what I have to say. You and I don't see each other often, and I'd like that to change. I'm here to take the first step—a big one."

"Really?" At long last, an apology?

Dottie straightened in the chair. "I'm here to apply for the job you advertised."

Sonia choked back a nervous giggle. "You're kidding, right? You want to work *here*? With *me*?"

"Your mouth is hanging open," Dottie said with a laugh. "Like my dad used to say, you better close it before the flies get in."

"My dad used to say that, too," Sonia said. Damned

if *she* didn't feel self-conscious, with butterflies tap dancing in her stomach. Nothing had prepared her for Dottie showing up. To be fair, though, Dottie looked flushed and embarrassed, too.

"I know this seems to come out of left field, so let me explain."

With her curiosity aroused, Sonia relaxed back in the chair to hear Dottie out.

Looking directly at Sonia, Dottie said, "First, let's deal with the past. I'm sorry about how badly I reacted when you and Aaron came up with the idea for the garden. I mean that. I was nasty and accusing, and it was all uncalled for." She leaned forward and rested her arms on the desk. "And don't feel as if you have to respond. I don't expect you to warm up to me just because I've apologized. But I've watched what you've done, every year adding events and features. Rona calls you bold and innovative—you're just like my dad."

"Thanks, but not everything worked," Sonia interjected. She could handle only so much praise from this woman she barely knew. "What made me think we could design an entire weekend event around some whimsical allure of dandelions? And make no mistake, Rona warned me off the dandelion wine theme," she said, giving the desk a light slap, "but I didn't listen."

Dottie's hearty laugh told Sonia that she'd heard all about the handful of visitors who'd straggled in to get their free sample of dandelion wine and to look at display boards depicting dandelions in folklore. What a dud. The outdoor Easter egg hunts hadn't fared much better. Spring weather in Wisconsin proved too unpredictable, and hunting for eggs in snow, sleet, mud, or downpours held little appeal. Sonia had wiped the egg hunt off the calendar.

"Oh well, win some, lose some," Sonia quipped.

"From what I can see, you're winning most of the time."

Sonia nodded to acknowledge the kind words. "That's why I need someone to take over the adult tour groups and handle the school trips. The person will help Rona in reception and help me supervise the horticulture team and the maintenance crew, work with me on special events, basically be flexible enough to do what's needed."

"I think I'm just the person to do all that."

"But it's a fulltime job. I need someone year round. Doesn't school start in a couple of weeks?"

Dottie shook her head. "Not if I get the job here. I've been a teacher a long time, and during my trip I realized I need a change. Besides, I'd like to be part of the family business again."

The fluttering in her gut intensified. She was glad it didn't show on the outside. While not exactly afraid, she couldn't say yes just to make Rona happy—and probably Aaron, too. She needed time to sort out how she really felt about her sister-in-law's idea.

As if reading her mind, Dottie said, "I'm aware that I'd be working for you. Just like my mother."

Sonia raised her hand. "Whoa. I don't think of your mother as exactly working for me. Frankly, she chooses where she wants to be involved."

Dottie smiled. "That might be. But she likes having the responsibility lifted off her shoulders." She rose and walked to the window. "It's really come together."

Sonia joined her and took in what Dottie saw through the glass that ran the length of the building.

When Sonia had renovated the main offices, she'd modernized by expanding the windows, which allowed panoramic views of the garden from all the meeting rooms and offices. That day, the garden, awash in color, came alive in the summer breeze.

A couple of early visitors ambled past the Adirondack chairs artfully placed on the terrace around the traditional terracotta planters overflowing with petunias, impatiens, and geraniums. Molly, their landscape architect, had designed sections and garden rooms, each with its own theme and color combinations. The curving paths between were bordered with daisies and black-eyed Susans, zinnias, and cone flowers. Rows of hollyhocks, dahlias, and phlox hid the red brick garden wall.

From the beginning, she wanted winding paths and arbors and cut away spaces for benches and sculptures. She'd added showy outdoor chess tables and benches, like those she'd seen at the lakefront in Chicago.

As she'd expanded the garden, it provided something for everyone—a feast for the senses. During summer evenings, the fragrance of honeysuckle and night blooming jasmine filled the air, encouraging visitors to linger a little longer. Moonlight offered white petunias and impatiens a chance to show off in the dark. The evening events they'd tried, especially the wine tasting and music on the terrace, had proved more popular than she'd ever imagined.

"It's beautiful this time of year, isn't it?" Sonia said. "Next year, we're starting a wild flower festival. I'm thinking of calling it "Wild Days" or something like that. We'll have some evening events, too." She laughed. "To be announced. I have to come up with ideas first."

She stopped herself, realizing that she was talking to Dottie as if she'd already hired her. But her jittery stomach told a different story. She didn't trust Dottie. It was easy to talk pleasantly about the garden and accept compliments, but Sonia had never excelled at faking her feelings. Sooner or later, wouldn't Dottie's bossy side slide through the cracks of the friendly façade? What would happen then? When it came to the garden, Sonia felt like a mother bear with a cub, always on high alert to protect it from predators.

"Anyway, I thought a wild flower festival would make a smooth transition to the Golden Days harvest celebration and Halloween."

Still staring at the garden, Dottie nodded with approval. "Sounds like a good idea to me."

Despite her apprehension about working with her sister-in-law, Sonia acknowledged that Dottie had changed. Anyone could see it. For one thing, her chin-length light brown hair softly framed her face, a big change from her previous short cut, a really badly done cut, too. Sonia had often suspected that Dottie had handed the scissors over to Burt and let him hack away. She'd updated her clothes, too, and the slim-legged jeans flattered her curvy figure. More than anything else, Dottie's gray eyes had softened, all traces of hostility gone.

Dottie turned and headed for the door. "I don't expect you to make up your mind today. I realize that you'll want to think about this, and you're under no obligation to go along with my idea. But, no matter what, I do plan to be part of the family again."

"Of course. Aaron and I want Matt to know his

aunt."

Dottie stared into space, as if gathering her thoughts. "Burt was a controlling man. I didn't realize the extent of his hold on me until he left. The land was one thing he couldn't keep in his grasp and he gave up trying."

A painful admission, Sonia acknowledged with a nod. She felt compelled to clarify an issue and make sure it never hung between them again.

"From the beginning, Dottie, I've been clear about who owns this land. True, I've ushered in a new era of how these precious acres are used, but ultimately, you, Rona, and Aaron determine the destiny of your family's legacy."

Dottie smiled, but opened the door and left quickly without responding.

Sonia felt lightheaded, the air around her buzzing with energy. Looking at her desk, she almost chased after Dottie so she could put her to work. She glanced at her calendar, noting all the filled-in spaces. Excited by the thoughts frantically bouncing around in her mind, Sonia tried to focus on how Dottie could help right away. She could order the box lunches for the tours and supervise the setup of the picnic shelters. Sonia would be only too happy to relinquish the details of those tours—and the need to be on hand and make sure everything went smoothly.

Sonia's body seemed lighter already, simply at the thought of sharing the load. With more hours free, she could do what she did best, design promotion campaigns and create themed festivals to draw new visitors, plus team up with the winery and the orchard and host more joint events.

Still, resistance tempered her excitement, like a steel band holding her in check. For one thing, she needed to talk to Aaron. Would he think this was a great idea? She had a difficult time erasing Dottie's initial reaction to her—the anger flashing in her eyes and the contemptuous looks she cast Sonia's way when she and Aaron were first married. And was it possible that Dottie still harbored the belief that Sonia got pregnant on purpose?

The dilemma stayed with her all day, and that night, after settling Matt in for the night, she grabbed a book and sat up in bed reading. She was impatient as she waited for Aaron's call from his hotel in Omaha, where he'd been working on a case all week. When it finally came, she eagerly told him about her day.

"I wonder if she understands that she'd be working for you, not taking over the place," he said.

"Thanks for understanding my skepticism." So, her jitters weren't so irrational. After outlining her concerns, she asked the question that had never gone away. "Do you think Dottie still believes I tricked you into marrying me?"

Her heart thumped harder as the seconds passed.

"To tell you the truth, I doubt she ever believed that. I think Burt planted that idea."

"She admitted to me that he was a controlling man, but she didn't offer details."

"After he left," Aaron said, "I came right out and asked her if he'd been more than controlling…it was hard to talk about it."

She curled one leg under her and sat upright. "You mean you asked if he'd been *abusive*?"

"Uh huh. But she said no. He demanded her loyalty

and pulled her into his plans, and she fell into the habit of going along." Aaron sighed. "Sad to say, she feared losing him."

"Whew. You had me worried for a minute."

"I couldn't tell you this before. After Burt left, Dottie came to my office to talk, and she told me about Burt in confidence. I had to keep it to myself, and couldn't even tell you. I'm sorry, Sonia."

"I understand." She'd always been conscious that as an attorney, Aaron knew things about people, even some mutual acquaintances in town, which he wasn't at liberty to share. His sister deserved the same promise of confidentiality. "But what do *you* think about bringing Dottie in? Should we go ahead and see what happens?"

"Ultimately, it's your call. But, from what you told me, it sounds as if she's got the qualifications you're looking for." He chuckled. "Besides, if you keep her busy doing tours and working with my mother, then you probably won't see her all that much."

"Hmm…don't think I haven't considered that." She breathed in deeply. "Okay, I'm going to take the plunge."

"You'd about made up your mind anyway, hadn't you?" he teased.

"You're on to me, as usual. But I wanted to discuss it with you first, just in case you felt strongly against it. On to other things. When are you coming home? I miss you. *We* miss you."

"Friday. Then we won't have to come back until next month."

"Why don't I put a lunch together at the garden with your mother and Dottie? Everything is lush and green right now, and maybe when he's home from preschool, you and Matt can get down to the river. Hey, if I hire Dottie, I could get down to the river more often, too."

"See? You're already seeing the advantages of having my sister around."

In her heart, Sonia knew Aaron wanted an end to the family tensions. Aaron wouldn't have interfered, but he probably hoped she'd hire Dottie.

When they ended their conversation, she threw the sheet back and went down to the kitchen to get Dottie's number off the emergency list by the phone. Odd, she'd never called Dottie, not even once, so she didn't know the number. She got Dottie's machine and waited impatiently to hear the beep. "This is Sonia," she said. "Why don't you come to my office around ten tomorrow morning? Um, I'd like to start making some plans."

Short and sweet, if a bit nervous and choppy. But even if she didn't like Dottie, she'd be an asset to the business. At least now she knew Dottie wanted to see the garden succeed. That's as far down the road Sonia's heart would let her travel.

* * *

The River Gazette
September 6, 1989

Spotlight on Lady's River People

Chapel's Botanical Garden is even more beautiful this Labor Day...we can report expanded gardens in full bloom, more benches and picnic tables, and Rona Chapel told us of plans to keep the weekend snack bar open through Christmas. And who was that we spotted leading a group through the garden? Looks like Dorothy—Dottie—Chapel (we hear she dropped her ex's name) is back in the fold of the family business. One of the teachers Dottie worked with at Roosevelt Elementary tells us that the garden's gain is the school's loss.

Mandy & Amy

10

May 1990

$\mathcal{A}$ frown etched a deep furrow between Aaron's eyes. "The cello? How could that be? He's five-years-old, Sonia."

"I know." She shrugged to show him that the situation wasn't clear to her either. "Apparently, age doesn't have anything to do with it. According to Karen Baldwin, our son isn't simply talented. He has an *unusual* gift. Very rare, she said."

"But look at him. He's just a tyke." Aaron pointed out the window of the breakfast porch to the patio. Matt, snug and dry in his yellow rain slicker and boots, was happily leaping into puddles, his arms like little windmills making circles in the air. "He's jumping for joy—literally."

"And why the cello?" Aaron added. "Couldn't he pound on a piano the way all kids like to do? Or, maybe he could beat a drum—preferably in the basement. Wouldn't that get it out of his system?"

"Out of his system?" She'd accepted that the man she'd married had no appreciation of music, but this was ridiculous. "You're not getting this. We need to find Matt his own teacher—and a good one, too. They have instruments at school for all the kids to fool around with. And a music teacher helps the kids learn to use them.

But Matt took a special interest in the kid-size cello they have. Karen and the music teacher, Ann, could spot his talent, his gift. He has an ear for music that kids—and even most adults—don't."

"Oh, come on, that sounds very odd."

She understood how incredible it seemed to Aaron that a child of his could have a musical gift. But what magic words would get the man to catch on? "I hope you don't take this the wrong way, Aaron, but you don't *hear* music the way many people do. It took me a while to figure that out, but it's true."

She didn't want to be mean about it, but Aaron barely understood the concept of a melody. He'd never been one to hum along to music, and she couldn't remember a single time when Matt was a baby or a toddler that he'd spontaneously hummed a song or sung a lullaby.

For herself, she'd listened carefully to Karen, who had paid such close attention to the way Matt gravitated to the cello. But even earlier, she'd heard Matt play a couple of times during her volunteer mornings at the school. She'd been startled by the pure tone he coaxed out of the miniature cello, an eighth size, which Karen said he was rapidly outgrowing. The teacher had quipped that with two tall parents, Matt looked older, almost professional with his cello between his knees and a bow in his hand. Sadly, Sonia didn't know how to describe to Aaron the quality of what she'd heard with her own ears.

Still watching Matt from the window, she said, "This is something we need to do for him. It's possible that with a true gift, music will be his calling. As it is, all he wants to do at school is play the cello or sound out songs on the piano, and he's very good at it—no pounding involved. I've watched him carefully plunk the keys and come up with a melody without reading music. And he runs to get the cello when it's time for the class music lesson."

Aaron put his arm around her shoulder and gave it a squeeze while they watched their kindergartener play. "Okay. I'm certainly not going to stand in the way. I think I read somewhere that kids involved in music do well in their academic subjects, too. So it can't hurt him." He laughed and kissed her cheek. "But look at him splashing in the puddles. It's hard to imagine him serious and focused on music, at least not for long."

"I suppose." She tried to appear agreeable, but something told her that Matt's mysterious pull to the cello was no lark.

He glanced at his watch. "I'd better get out of here. I told Chuck I'd sort through some research for him. Are you taking Matt to the garden with you this morning?"

"No, Dottie is opening the garden. Matt and I will go over later this afternoon."

Aaron shook his head in playful disbelief, and she cast an amused look back. "I know. Sometimes I can't believe it myself, but Dottie and I have managed to become friends. And…" She paused for a minute, unsure if she should mention what was on her mind. But Aaron kept looking at her, clearly expecting her to finish the sentence.

"…I probably shouldn't talk about this, but I think Dottie's dating again. You know those two women, Mandy and Amy, the ones who write the gossipy Spotlight column for the newspaper? They *called* Rona the other day and came right out and asked her what she knew about Dottie's social life. Oh, to have heard Rona's answer, no doubt evasive. But who knows? Maybe your sister *is* seeing someone."

His eyes widened. "Really? I like that news, gossipy or not. She deserves better than Burt."

"I'm all in favor of it, too."

Aaron kissed her goodbye again. Sonia sat in the window seat and pulled her knees up to her chest. Smiling to herself, she watched Aaron go out to the patio, stopping, she noted, a safe distance from the puddles formed in the dips in the stone. Then he gestured to Matt to come over to him. Whatever he said to their little guy, Matt responded by opening his arms for a hug. Once Aaron let him go, he waved as his daddy disappeared along the side of the house. Sonia tingled with pleasure seeing Aaron and their boy share an affectionate hug.

She stayed put and watched Matt load plastic trucks into his wagon. If she'd been out there with him, she'd have heard him imitating the sound of a train whistle as he stomped through puddles pulling the wagon behind him. He'd always been good at imitating sounds, but she'd never thought it had any significance before.

When he came inside, she'd tell him they were going to the garden to see Aunt Dottie and watch his face light up. Seeing Dottie shower love on Matt made Sonia glad that she and her sister-in-law had managed to do better than simply keep the peace.

As details came out, Sonia learned that Burt had laughed at their rained-out grand opening weekend, satisfied the garden would be a bust and close within a couple of months. Burt didn't know how close to correct his predictions had been. Despite Sonia's PR efforts, they'd attracted only a trickle of local people and tourists their first two years.

Although Sonia kept her chin held high and became quite an expert at forcing an upbeat tone, she learned to live with waves of anxiety when she compared her earlier optimistic projections with the reality unfolding as the weeks ticked by. At one point, she admitted to Rona and Aaron that perhaps her vision had been grandiose after all.

Perhaps because her mother-in-law had been through a transition with the farm before, Rona had refused to succumb to any notion of defeat. Aaron had teased his mother about catching "garden fever," to which Rona had responded, "Damn right."

The sign of a turnaround came when their first annual Halloween extravaganza brought about one hundred and fifty parents and kids to the garden. The newspaper had run a feature story about it, and that PR led her to roll out a couple of holiday and winter festivals. Sometimes Sonia had to wonder at the confident way she'd breathed in that initial whiff of success, excited that she could justify going on another year or two to see if she could turn around the slow startup.

Last year, they'd dedicated a garden of whimsical wooden farm animal sculptures created by a local artist. The exhibit honored both Aaron's dad and his idea, Chapels Farm on the Hill. Sonia had to laugh at the children's book version of farming the pieces created. Between the mother duck and the ducklings lined up behind her and the smiling cows, farming looked idyllic.

Rona made the sculpture garden her own pet project, but what had been a great development for the garden had led to the demise of Dottie's marriage. Burt soon moved across the state and set himself up as a builder. His new life didn't include Dottie.

Sonia came back to the present when Matt stopped suddenly on the patio and waved at her. Then, obviously showing off for Mom, he let out a loud *whoop!* and gave himself a running start before jumping in the middle of the biggest puddle. She held her hands high and clapped, and he returned an exaggerated bow.

* * *

*A*aron tucked the ticket into his pocket and walked away from the counter, looking for the nearest bank of phones. He quickly claimed one of the few not in use and dialed the garden's number. Good, he'd caught Sonia in her office. But her breathless "hello" left him sensing that he'd interrupted something. A familiar feeling over the last few months.

Ever since Matt had started what Sonia called serious cello lessons, her juggling act had taken on a new dimension. Except for their customary late-night phone conversations, he suspected his other calls weren't always welcome.

"There's no way I can pick you up at the airport," she said, after he'd told her that he was flying out of Las Vegas a day early. "Matt has that special lesson, you know, the one I told you about with the teacher in Madison. We won't be back in time to meet you."

"I forgot about that." He tried to hide the disappointment in his voice.

"I'm sorry." She sounded sincere, but distracted. He could almost see the receiver resting between her cheek and shoulder, freeing her hands to leaf through a file or mime an instruction to her new office assistant, Angie.

"No, no, it's okay. Your trip to Madison slipped my mind, that's all."

"How did your work go out there?"

"Not so good. A couple of potential witnesses didn't show up, and one died suddenly. It's a mess. The guy from the local firm says they're regrouping, but I think it's over."

He stopped talking and glanced around him at the flashing lights and crowds of people. He rubbed his forehead with his free hand. "Can you hear all that clinking and ringing in the background? I can't believe the number of slot machines in this airport. The racket alone is enough to make my head pound."

"That sounds awful," she said with genuine sympathy in her voice.

He sighed. "Don't mind me. The way I feel right now, I'd complain about any nitpicky thing to come along."

He quickly explained the way the case had turned into a bust, a huge disappointment for everyone involved, especially Chuck, who'd stayed in the Lady's River office to work on another case. Aaron had tried to warn his boss that it was fifteen years too late to frame a liability case involving faulty building materials produced by companies long out of business. This wasn't a good set of circumstances on which to leverage their reputation as emerging trial strategy consultants.

"Chuck feels even worse than I do, but the truth is, he wouldn't listen to me this time. I'm sorry to say I predicted a bad outcome."

Aaron liked to win out of court and he'd earned a reputation for bringing the opposition to the table, just like Artie Silverman. But on the flip side, he and Chuck never flinched at the sight of a courtroom either. That was the strength of their image and why they were in the running for many good out-of-state cases.

"I can hear your disappointment," she said, her voice softer. "Can Chuck pick you up from the airport?"

"Nah, no sense bothering him. I'll grab a cab." He didn't care about the ride home from the airport. He cared about an evening with Sonia. He'd been in California before his trip to Vegas, so he'd been gone almost two weeks this time.

"I'm sorry," she said again. "We can talk when Matt and I get back."

"I suppose you'll get dinner on the road."

"Uh, I guess we'll have to." She sounded apologetic. "By the time we get back, Matt will probably be asleep in the car and he'll need to go right to bed."

Aaron felt a sigh coming on—a heavy, impatient one. He hadn't approved of taking Matt almost halfway across the state for a special class. But he held back his reaction and cut the call short by saying he'd see her at home. Was his tone clipped, maybe too curt? Probably.

Aaron glanced at his watch. He had over an hour to kill before his flight. Already in a bad mood, he let his mind travel down a selfish path, the one that regretted they'd learned about Matt's talent so early. It had consequences, and not necessarily good ones.

Matt's first teacher over in Sturgeon Bay had worked with him over the summer, but confirmed what Sonia already suspected. Matt showed such unusual promise that he needed a more skilled teacher. It wasn't that Matt didn't need to practice, because, apparently even prodigies, especially little ones, required coaxing to stay focused. But Matt moved on to study with one teacher in Green Bay, a good hour's drive, and now with a cellist in Madison, over two hours away.

Talented or not, Aaron's jaw tightened every time someone referred to Matt as a prodigy. Was that good for a little boy who'd just turned six? What kid wouldn't develop an attitude over that?

Wandering into the bar, he ordered a beer and found a table where he could read a newspaper and try to relax. Grumpy and out of sorts, he was ready to snap at the first person to look at him the wrong way. These big, anonymous airports sometimes affected him this way. He was just another stranger with an attaché rushing down a concourse to catch a flight. Every once in a while, the rushing stopped and travelers like him sat in the lounge or coffee shop to kill some unscheduled minutes or hours.

The time had come to have a serious talk with Sonia about the events propelling Matt's life into this new and strange territory. Aaron understood the idea of mission and a desire to do something gutsy and hard. He and Sonia shared the fuel that led them to follow their passions. Hadn't his own drive been responsible for the role he'd played in establishing a national reputation for a small town law firm? Sonia's vision had turned the farm into a garden that grew more innovative and showy every year and attracted the attention of travel writers all over the country—and even a smattering from Europe and Asia writing about off-the-beaten path destinations.

But when was the last time they'd been out to dinner alone or gone to bed early to make love and talk late into the night. He tossed the newspaper across the table and drained the beer mug. He hadn't expected success to feel so lonely.

* * *

"*M*s. Morton made me drop the bow," Matt said with a giggle in his voice, "and then she caught it. That was so funny."

"Was that to help you loosen your grip?" Sonia asked, glancing down at Matt in the passenger seat. With dusk at their heels, they turned onto the highway and headed home. She'd have expected Matt to look sleepy, but instead, he bounced with energy.

"Uh huh. She said I grip it like I'm holding on to an ice cream cone."

"Really? Well, I guess you caught on. Ms. Morton looked very pleased with you."

From the beginning, posture and hand positions had been the biggest concern about Matt's early habits. His new teacher, Olivia Morton, made a game out of showing him the difference between tension and relaxation in his whole body, including his hands. It's as if she understood that while Matt produced pure, rich tones, he was a little child in every other way.

"Can I go back to see Ms. Morton?"

She smiled at the eagerness in his voice. "Absolutely. When we get home, we'll mark the appointments on next year's calendar. I'll put it up in your room so you can see it." Olivia didn't take children as young as Matt as regular students, but she did see them for special classes. At this stage, Olivia would monitor Matt's progress every couple of months or so. But some years down the road, Matt would likely study with Olivia Morton exclusively. And that, Sonia realized, meant more long commutes to Madison.

"When do we eat?"

Apparently, Matt was done being a prodigy for the day. "When I spot a place that looks good," she said.

Matt craned his neck to look out the window to join in the search.

"Good," Matt said. "I could eat like a pig."

Sonia laughed to hear her own expression come back to her. "Well then, be on the lookout."

A few minutes later, she pulled off the road and into the parking lot of a diner where she let him order his favorites, a grilled cheese sandwich and a chocolate shake. She got a cup of soup for herself, thinking that she'd fix something later after Aaron came home.

They needed to talk. She and Aaron had been out of touch with each other, and not just because of the miles that separated them when he was away. They sometimes spoke during the day, but more and more, those conversations interrupted something else she was doing. Sometimes it felt like the time she needed to help Matt develop his gift threatened to steal not just hours, but the focus and attention she and Aaron once gave each other.

When she'd told Aaron about the class with Olivia, he'd screwed up his face in a disbelieving scowl. The first words out of his mouth gave voice to his disgust. "Are you kidding? Cello lessons over one hundred miles away? This has gone too far."

He'd been right, too, when he accused her of patronizing him with her patient tone, explaining yet again that Matt needed special guidance. But she couldn't help it if he couldn't get it through his head that Matt's talent was no small thing. It—he—was special. Of course his childhood would be different. What did Aaron expect and what words did she have to discover within herself that would make him understand?

"Every time I object to something involving Matt and his music lessons," he'd said through clenched teeth, "it's not because I'm some kind of numbskull who doesn't get it. I'm raising the question because I'm not sure it's good for one interest to dominate Matt's childhood like this."

Without waiting for her to reply, he'd turned on his heel and headed up the stairs. A minute later, she'd heard the door to their home office slam behind him. With Matt already in bed, she'd spent the evening alone in the den. Late that night, Aaron had crawled into bed next to her, but uncharacteristically hadn't whispered goodnight or arranged his body to nestle against hers. She'd finally slept, and the next morning, they'd both acted like nothing had happened.

Earlier in their marriage, when awkwardness defined their relationship, they'd have at least politely agreed to disagree.

She snapped back to the present with the annoying sound of Matt trying to suck up every last molecule of the shake through his straw. "You hit air, buddy," she said, scooting across the leather booth seat. "Let's head out."

Matt slept through the last thirty or so miles of the drive, and she had to jostle him awake to get him into the empty house, and he didn't like it one bit. It was almost nine o'clock and Aaron still wasn't home. Just as well, she thought. Matt whined all the way up the stairs, making *her* question the wisdom of lessons two hours away. And any thoughts of having a heart-to-heart with Aaron when he came home flew out the window. She was bone tired.

11

June 1991

Aaron slipped in next to Sonia at the back of the tent just as Matt played the first bar of the piece, a Chopin minuet. A beaming smile lit her face as she laced her fingers with his before turning her focus back to Matt. But rather than fixing an adoring gaze on their son, she closed her eyes and moved her head ever so slightly to the rhythm. She's playing that piece right along with him, he thought. Aaron envied that ability.

With the wedding chapel still in the planning stage, they'd set up the tent in what the three women in his life had dubbed the wedding field, one of the flat grassy spots at the edge of a wooded hill. Sonia, his mother, and Dottie had put their heads together on the design, creating an entrance with stone stairs and an arbor covered with pink climbing roses. Flowering crabapple dotted the woods surrounding the field.

Not the first wedding in the field that spring, but special because Karen Baldwin, Matt's kindergarten teacher, had asked their seven-year-old to play two pieces during the ceremony. "My first wedding gig," Matt had said, his little chest puffed out.

He'd laughed at Matt using such a grownup word, yet his son's precociousness troubled him, too, especially because of the way Sonia doted on him.

When he challenged her about Matt's insanely busy schedule, she commented that the schedule wouldn't be so crazy if Aaron stopped insisting that Matt's semblance of a normal childhood include playing softball on a team at the park. And don't even get her started on driving their son to Cub Scout meetings, which, she reminded him, meant dents in her schedule, not Aaron's.

"I think I was more nervous than he was," Sonia whispered, when applause for Matt had died down. "He sounded even better than he did at rehearsal yesterday."

Seeing Sonia so delighted, he willed himself to forget their disagreements and instead fall into the spirit of the event. Of course he was proud to see his little boy, poised beyond his years, performing in front of the wedding guests.

When the ceremony was over, Aaron stood back from the crowd, feeling oddly out of place as Sonia, along with his mother and Dottie, mingled with the group of fifty or so. Sonia gave her full attention to each person she greeted, as if delighted to see the very person she'd been waiting for. He smiled to himself, admiring her ability to make everyone feel special.

He didn't recognize the pale yellow dress she wore, or the necklace made of chunky glittery stones. Had she just bought those things? And why did it bother him that he didn't know? As a self-proclaimed clothes horse, she usually enjoyed showing him a unique jacket she'd found or an unusual pair of shoes or a one-of-a-kind piece of jewelry. He appreciated her slightly bohemian, yet elegant look, and she could pull off a bit of flamboyance, too. Seeing her wearing things he didn't recognize saddened him. He wanted their private moments back.

Before long, golf carts arrived to ferry some of the guests up the hill to the terrace, where they could linger and have coffee and iced tea before moving on to the late afternoon reception at a hall in town.

"Ready to go, kiddo?" he asked Matt when he approached him standing with Sonia.

"Good, here you are," Sonia said. "I need to get up to the terrace." She looked down at Matt. "You and Daddy have a good time doing whatever it is he's cooked up."

Matt pulled at the lapels of his jacket. "We're going down to the river, but first I gotta get out of this suit."

Aaron laughed and pulled at his own lapels. "That makes two of us."

Sonia leaned down to plant a kiss on Matt's forehead. "You did a great job today, really fine. Everyone says so."

Telling Aaron she'd see him at the reception later, she kissed his cheek and took off up the hill. Statuesque described her, as she skillfully navigated, in very high heels, the uneven grassy ground and then the stone steps. "Your mother is the prettiest woman here," he said, quickly adding, "and the smartest, too."

Matt didn't respond. He'd taken off his jacket and was spinning it by one sleeve above his head, as if he desperately needed a horse to rope. Aaron laughed, content to leave the prodigy behind and spend time with Matt-the-little-boy.

Later, dressed in jeans and sneakers, Aaron led Matt across the bridge and onto the path that led away from the garden buildings and down to the river. Matt sprinted ahead, stopping periodically to wait for him to catch up. Aaron loped along, relishing the warmth of the sun on his back and shoulders. It had been too long since he and Matt had a few hours to just be together—no schedule to keep, no plans.

Matt got to the river bank first and picked up a stone to skip across the surface of the water. He'd tried to coach Matt's technique, but Aaron had never been very good at the wrist action it took to make stones skip across the water's surface and cover some distance. His dad and Dottie were a different story. On a good day they'd get one pebble after another to the middle of the river, if not almost to the opposite bank.

When he tired of skipping stones, Matt climbed on a boulder and played a sailor steering his ship with an imaginary wheel, swaying from side to side as he navigated through stormy seas. He'd be a pirate next, Aaron mused, and peer through his make-believe spyglass, hoping to spot a sailing ship loaded with gold.

Watching Matt play in his own private world always brought Aaron back to the first time he and Sonia had carried their newborn baby down to the river. Sonia, shamelessly exaggerating for effect, loved to tell Matt about how close he'd come to being born next to the big boulder. She didn't have to stray too far from the truth, though. Matt had greeted the world only a few hours after Aaron had pulled his very round wife to her feet and taken her home. Her water broke almost the minute they'd opened the door to their apartment.

It had meant a lot to Sonia to bring Matt back as soon as possible after he was born, so one Sunday morning in late October, they'd put Matt in his carrier and set out. For reasons he couldn't recall, Aaron insisted that they park at the farm and walk, although

Sonia pointed to the billowing clouds turning the sky gray. But he'd said that darkening autumn skies in Wisconsin were usually all bluff and no bluster. She raised her eyebrows in skepticism, but went along with him.

Naturally, that day the clouds made good on their threat, and once the rain started he'd had to leave her sitting under tree branches cradling Matt inside her jacket while he ran back to the farm to get the car. He expected her to be angry with him, but she thought the whole incident made for a great story to tell Matt one day. And true to her word, she described such a grand adventure that Matt acted like he remembered being a few weeks old when the clouds dumped buckets of rain on them during his first visit to the river.

Worn out from exploring new worlds, Matt dropped his little body next to Aaron and let his hands fall between his bent knees, mimicking him, Aaron noticed. Matt had inherited Aaron's long, slender, almost bony fingers, and his eyes and hair color were nearly identical. He had no idea where his son's musical gift came from. Probably some distant DNA contribution from Sonia's side of the family, he guessed.

"Are you tired from your big day?"

"Nope."

"How did you like playing your cello at the wedding?"

"Good. I like playing for an audience." Matt's tone was grown up and matter of fact. "You know that."

"No, Matt, I didn't know how you felt about performing in public. I'm glad you told me. Since we're talking about what you like, how is softball going?"

"*Baaad.*"

"Huh? Since when?"

"Since I can't hit and I can't throw. Mom said to give it another chance this summer, and then we'd re-eval-u-ate."

Now that sounded like Sonia. She could have been talking about giving an ad campaign one more chance to pay off.

"What about Cub Scouts? Are you enjoying that?"

"Yep, I've got lots of friends in scouts." Matt slapped his feet on the ground, spontaneously creating a rhythm.

What looked like fidgeting in other kids was all part of Matt's abilities. Sometimes he tapped a fork on the edge of his plate, or he'd use his toothbrush as his stick and the bathroom sink as his drum. Lacking an instrument, his feet would do.

"Good. I'm glad you like scouts."

"Mom said you'd be happy."

"She did?"

"Yup. She said you wanted me to do other stuff and not just play the cello all the time."

He wasn't sure if he liked Sonia explaining his opinions to their son. It felt like she was talking about him behind his back, even if supporting his ideas.

"You're very talented, Matt, but I *do* think you need to spend time with friends and try different things."

He giggled. "I know, Dad, you want me to grow up to be a well-rounded person."

Aaron laughed at hearing his words to Sonia circle back to him. He felt a little melancholy, too. Matt would turn eight in the fall, and already it appeared that the days of Mommy and Daddy were gone, and the era of Mom and Dad had begun.

* * *

November 2006

The sounds of conversation and the outbursts of laughter in the house reminded Aaron of a home-for-the-holidays movie, one with a colorful cast of adults and kids gathered in Katherine's family estate in an old-money town north of Chicago. He'd suppressed a laugh when he'd first seen the Tudor mansion her parents had lived in for almost fifty years. About three times the size of the house in Lady's River, Aaron was sure no one had ever dubbed it the Wreck of the Tudor.

In an email to Dottie he'd described Katherine's wealthy relatives as a cross between a competitive, but affable clan like the Kennedys, and more staid British types, who hosted hunting weekends and served tea in the late afternoon. Katherine's family didn't hunt, but neither did a holiday include only a dinner followed by a quick exit. Thanksgiving weekends included killer tennis matches and pickup basketball games if the weather cooperated, and competitive laps in the indoor pool if it didn't.

He and Katherine drove up early that morning, but like the previous year, they wouldn't spend the night. The Nolans, a reserved pair in their seventies, didn't approve of unmarried couples sleeping together, regardless of age. But Katherine claimed her old bedroom as a place to change into suitable clothes for the late afternoon dinner.

The way Katherine's family dressed for the occasion reminded him of what Sonia liked about the holidays, especially Thanksgiving. She may have lacked the stuffy formality of the Nolans, but she'd enjoyed inviting a crowd to gather around their big dining room table, always set with the "good everything," as she'd told Matt every year, and wearing their best clothes, too. "It's a special day," she'd say, "and not just because we get to eat like little pigs. It's a day we get to appreciate everyone and everything we have."

As he followed Katherine up the spiral staircase to the third floor, Aaron recalled the first time Sonia said those words to their son, when they were still living in their apartment and he was about two months old. Cradling Matt in her arms, she'd swayed back and forth, telling him all about the holiday. Aaron couldn't stave off the vision of that single moment in time, even as it seared his heart.

If Aaron had his way, he and Katherine would have gone out for Thanksgiving dinner and maybe taken in a movie downtown. Katherine had scoffed at that idea. Since she made few demands, Aaron acquiesced and later found himself apologizing to Katherine for letting Dennis, her eldest brother, and his wife handily crush them on the tennis court. The loss of the doubles match didn't particularly bother Aaron. He seldom played tennis anymore and had never spent time developing his game. Katherine, on the other hand, hated losing *on* the court as much as she hated losing *in* court. The trouncing created a jittery tension between them.

"The house sure smells good," he said, hoping the meaningless conversation about the aromas of baking apples and pumpkin pie would keep him from sinking deeper into bittersweet nostalgia. If he silently traveled back in time, a part of him would linger in Lady's River and it would be hard to come back. And maybe he wouldn't want to.

Katherine closed the door behind them and then perched her hip on the dresser next to the door. "The other day Dennis asked me what's ahead for the two of us," she said, "and I know my parents wonder, too."

"Your parents?"

"Uh huh. This is your second Thanksgiving with my family, so naturally they're curious about what's going on between us. Frankly, I don't know what to tell them."

"How about 'none of your business?'" He pulled off his damp T-shirt and tossed it on the bed. "I'm fifty years old, for Pete's sake. You're in your forties. We can damn well make our own decisions."

With a jerky motion, she tucked her thick dark hair behind her ears. "My family is close. You're aware of that. Do you really find it odd that they'd ask a few questions about our relationship?"

"I don't know. I'm just surprised." He hated feeling defensive, always conscious of her older brothers watching his every move. "C'mon, Katherine, do you really want to be treated like we're a couple of kids fresh out of college."

She lifted her chin. "My family is traditional about these things."

He felt like tossing off a sarcastic remark about the tradition of minding one's own business, but thought better of it. "But we haven't been together that long, and you told them about Matt and *why* I left Wisconsin," he said, deliberately lowering his voice.

She cocked her head. "Yes, of course. But, Aaron, it has been a while since you and I have had a meaningful discussion about where we're going."

Not knowing how to respond, he sidestepped to the

far side of the bed and pulled out the shirt and tie he'd packed in his overnight bag.

Even as he fumbled around with his clothes, Katherine stayed put, a signal that she expected a discussion. "Look, we're in your parents' home," he finally said, "about to sit down to a dinner with, what, a couple of dozen people? I hardly think this is the time to talk about us." *Damn those blowhard jock brothers of hers, anyway.*

"It hasn't been *the time* since late last summer," she said. "We had begun talking about our future. Maybe moving in together. But then the event in Pearson Pond changed things. You said you didn't want to make plans until you put it behind you, so we put discussions on hold."

Her smile became sweet and gentle and she extended one arm toward him. Three or four steps in her direction and he could take her hand and put his arms around her. But he froze in place.

"And, now, a couple of months after Pearson Pond," she continued, "you're still distant."

He nodded as he spoke. "You're right. I won't deny that. The weekend upset me. It brought up Matt, and all the memories of who my son was and everything he'd done with his life, all seventeen years of it." He swallowed hard. "And I couldn't get my mind off the young man he was on the verge of becoming the day he died. I felt like I lost him all over again."

"I know," Katherine said in the soft voice he'd found attractive when he first met her. "And I think seeing Sonia upset you, too."

"We suffered the same loss. I can't ever forget her." His throat tightened, but he made himself continue. "I told you how we got together in the first place. We were an unlikely pair, she and I."

"The last thing in the world I want to do is bring up painful subjects," Katherine said, "but you also told me that when Matt died you and Sonia lost the reason to be together."

"Yes, that's true." That conclusion had pushed him to leave Lady's River.

"Then why is it so hard for you now?"

He'd asked himself the same question, but nothing he came up with in response helped him dissipate the gloom following him around. Probing too deeply only made it worse.

Unwilling to meet her gaze, he stared out the window at a ravine behind the house. "I feel off balance. When I first came to Chicago, I threw myself into a completely different life, hoping the past would retreat and fade. It seemed to be working for a while, but then the dedication threw me, as if I'd lost ground."

"So this mental space you're in now isn't about seeing Sonia?"

"No," he said, hoping that was true. It was hard, though, to keep his mind from drifting back to other Thanksgivings when he'd had everything he ever wanted.

Smoothing his hand across his forehead and down the side of his face, he tried to explain. "Sometimes I miss Lady's River. Being up here and seeing you with your family remind me of what little family I have. Maybe I—*we*—should visit Dottie and Cal sometime this winter. We could plan a long weekend."

He knew his deliberate change of subject worked because Katherine's features relaxed as she approached him. "I'd like to meet your sister and her family." She kissed him lightly on the mouth and then headed to the bathroom for a shower.

Later, when he took his seat at the long table between Katherine's youngest brother and one of her many cousins, Aaron fell into the good-natured banter around him. Sitting across from him, Katherine's lovely and now untroubled face glowed in the flickering candlelight. She and the others around the table were supposed to be his new family. Plus, Dottie would definitely like Katherine. Yes, a visit home in a few weeks might do him good.

After dinner, the whole family gathered in the living room to watch the kids entertain the adults with songs and skits they'd practiced. Not too bad, at least as far as he could tell. Then Katherine's nephew, Boyd, played a lively piece on the piano, fumbling through a few bars in the middle and flashing silly grins at his cousins. When he'd finished, he hammed it up for the crowd, lifting his hands high off the keys with dramatic flourish.

Katherine leaned in close to Aaron. "I hope that wasn't too hard for you to watch. I know Matt had a special talent, too."

Aaron choked on the cynical chortle he'd tried to hold back and feigned a sputtering cough. He must have done a really poor job of describing Matt and his music. It hadn't been the least bit difficult to observe the boy playing. Even a person as tone-deaf as Aaron could see that the young performer didn't understand or feel the music. Matt's real artistry and his stage presence were the qualities that had convinced Aaron that his son had a gift, an understanding of music extraordinary at any age.

Boyd stood and took a couple of bows. Aaron

watched Katherine's youngest sister raise her arms above her head and clap, the longest and loudest of anyone in the room. If he hadn't already known she was the boy's mother, he'd have picked her out in the crowd immediately. Her expression gave her away. Full of adoration, pride that knew no bounds, and with a little awe thrown in. He knew the look well.

Memories flashed through his brain, threatening to bring on another bout of sadness.

"Sometimes Colleen acts like she's raising a prince," Katherine joked. "You wouldn't believe how she dotes on him."

Oh yes I would. Living with a real prodigy—and that prodigy's mother—had always been interesting.

12

June 1995

$\mathcal{A}$aron stood in the wedding chapel across from Sonia, who looked especially elegant in a sparkly silk suit that matched her blue eyes. Not that he could look into those eyes. As always, when Matt started playing, she tilted her head and closed her eyes and retreated to her private enclave to listen to his music.

Unlike Sonia, Aaron watched his son. Maybe he couldn't hear the same quality of sound others enjoyed when Matt played, but he could see it in his face. And that helped him understand that prodigy wasn't a relative term, as in having an extra dose of talent or promise. When it came to his son, different standards applied.

Prodigy meant having an ear that allowed Matt to produce a pure tone, sophisticated beyond his almost-eleven years. It's what sent him to the piano as a preschooler to sound out melodies and improvise their rhythm. And over the last few years, Aaron, having finally accepted the limitation of his own ear, studied Matt's expression to peer into the sphere his son occupied when he played. A few seconds into a piece of music, Matt closed his eyes and the corners of his mouth turned up ever so slightly, leaving the ordinary world behind him. Matt once said that sometimes he could feel his body move *inside* the notes.

In other ways, though, studying his son's face was like looking in a mirror and seeing himself. Not only the same sandy hair and gray eyes and well-defined features, but a certain intensity in his expressive face.

Aaron watched Matt move his body in quiet ecstasy, seemingly unaware of his surroundings, including the guests at his aunt's wedding and even his parents. Did he inhabit the music, or did the music inhabit him? Maybe that was a chicken and egg question, Aaron mused.

What a great day for the family and the garden. Cal and Dottie's wedding launched the wedding chapel, finished in the nick of time. With every breath, Aaron's nostrils filled with the scent of fresh wood mingling with the fragrance of freshly cut flowers.

Working together as a team, Sonia, his mother, and Dottie had decided to wait to start construction of this building until they knew the garden could afford the glass and stone showpiece. They wanted it set on a hill, with panoramic views of the dense woods on one side, and on the other, the steep grade that led to reclaimed acres of prairie flowers and grasses. Recent rain had turned the woods and fields green and lush.

When Matt finished his piece, Sonia caught Aaron's eye and smiled, almost shyly. But the wedding guests didn't hold back and broke into loud applause, including Dottie, who clapped for Matt as she walked down the short aisle to join Cal and the judge at the front. Aaron and Sonia played their role as witnesses, with Cal's kids and Rona standing close by.

Aaron liked Cal, his sister's second chance. A widower with three kids around Matt's age, give or take a couple of years, Cal showed the good sense to appreciate Dottie. After Cal and Dottie exchanged the vows they'd written, Matt played his aunt's favorite piece, "Simple Gifts," and then they walked back down the hill to the main building and the terrace for the buffet reception.

When Aaron finally crawled into bed around midnight, Sonia started a conversation just as they were drifting off.

"I'm too excited to sleep," she whispered. "Wasn't the wedding grand and gorgeous? And don't Cal and Dottie make a terrific looking couple."

He rolled on his side and rested his hand on her belly. "It was a great day. You make such a beautiful mother-of-the-cellist."

She laughed and chatted about the fun of having Cal's kids in the house with Matt for the weekend while the bride and groom got away alone for a couple of days.

"It's good for Matt to have some cousins around," he said, reiterating what he'd so often told Sonia about the need to make sure Matt had time to hang out with his friends. Despite their good intentions, the push and pull over what was a normal childhood for Matt remained a bone of contention between them.

Bad timing changed things, too. They'd discovered Matt's gift just about the time they spoke of having another child. They'd agreed to wait another year, but that brought trips to Madison and lessons in Green Bay. Those were the years the garden took off and what attention Sonia diverted from Matt was focused on new festivals and marketing campaigns. As for Aaron, out-of-town cases became more frequent. Life was good, and they never questioned the paths they were on. Conversations about having another child gradually became fewer until they dropped the idea altogether.

With Matt a little older now, he spent time preparing for public appearances, one in Green Bay in a month and another coming up in Minneapolis in a few weeks. He'd added extra sessions with Olivia and taken a couple of master classes with visiting cellists in Detroit and Milwaukee. At one point, Sonia and Matt were in one city, while he was consulting on a case in another. Something felt off, but Aaron tried to follow Sonia's lead and simply take it in stride and consider their success a blessing.

"So, what did you think of the wedding chapel?" She turned to face him. "Not bad, huh?"

"It's the best...and I suppose you've already booked some weddings."

She frowned. "Well, not yet, but we've had some bites, and Dottie set up a presentation with some wedding planners—and she cast a wide net. No reason we can't attract weddings from towns all over Northeast Wisconsin."

The previous week, the local TV station had devoted a live segment on the morning news to talk about the new wedding venue in the area. No, that didn't cover it. They called it a spectacular venue because of the natural setting. Reporters wove Dottie and Cal's wedding into the story, so the grand opening drew plenty of coverage. Poor Cal even got dragged into the act, and had joked that now his students would get a glimpse into his private life. "Can't keep a secret around here," he'd said on camera.

Aaron had to laugh at that. Showing off the newest

feature of the garden was all in a day's work to Sonia, and now Dottie, too. Cal had better get used to being associated with a family that regularly found itself in the public eye.

Sonia snuggled closer. "You aren't sleepy, are you?"

He laughed. "Not at the moment." He brushed his hand over her hair. "You glowed and beamed all over the place today—as usual."

"Hmm…thanks…and you, too. I've always said I married a really handsome guy."

He gently pulled her closer. "I'm glad you're not worn out from the day." He cupped her cheek and kissed her gently, immediately responding to her welcoming lips. He slid his hands under her gown and caressed her warm back, as smooth as the petals of the lilies she loved so much. She rose to her knees and pulled her gown over her head, and then he drew her across his chest. Everything else fell away as he buried himself in the scents and tastes and feel of her. Soon his own murmurs and whispers mingled with her urgent moans and soft cries. Tightening his arms around her, he pressed his face into her neck and the slope of her shoulder. She'd given him everything.

When they were ready for sleep, she settled her arm across his chest.

"I still really, really like you," she whispered.

Smiling to himself, he sighed softly into her hair.

* * *

The Chapels on the Hill

The River Gazette
"All in the Family"
By Martha Samuelson

June 25, 1995 - *Chapel's Botanical garden christened its new wedding chapel yesterday, when Dorothy Chapel married Calvin—Cal—Thompson. On Friday, amidst the preparations, Sonia Chapel, the garden's general manager, joked with TV reporters that they hoped the paint would dry before the wedding. "But we're thrilled that the first wedding in the new building is a family event."*

"We wanted a facility that blended into the natural landscape of the garden, and I think we've achieved it," Mrs. Chapel said. "This setting can add beauty to any occasion."

A second marriage for both bride and groom, the groom's three children were present. The Chapels' son, Matthew, already an accomplished cellist, played two pieces.

After the early afternoon wedding, the celebration continued for the day. The reception for the guests was held on the garden terrace. Those who happened to visit the garden on a day trip were invited to stop by and enjoy some champagne or punch in honor of the occasion.

13

October 1996

"You're home," Sonia said. It was almost nine o'clock, but she and Matt were just back from his lesson in Green Bay. "I didn't expect to see you until tomorrow, or did I get the days mixed up?"

"No, no, I finished up in Detroit a day early and changed my flight."

Surprisingly flustered, Sonia set the bag of fast food on the table where Aaron sat reading a magazine. She and Matt had fallen into a routine of their own on these late nights, especially when Aaron was out of town. Not expecting to see him, she struggled for a couple of minutes to adjust to his presence.

"I picked up food on the way into town."

"I can see that," he said, his voice flat. "I raided the fridge and found something."

When Matt pulled out a chair and sat down at the table, Aaron frowned, creating tension in the air, and Sonia could see it centered on Matt. Usually, Aaron's silent disapproval focused on her handling of Matt and his music. Even after all these years, Aaron still found it hard to accept that Matt wasn't a typical kid living a so-called normal childhood.

She went to the cabinet to get plates for herself and Matt.

Aaron joined her at the cabinet and grabbed some napkins. "Hey, Matt," he said, "this is how it's done. You get up out of the chair and help put the food out. I don't want to see you sit idly by while your mother waits on you."

He had a point, but she was beat and not up for a squabble. "It's okay, Aaron."

"No, it's *not* okay."

Matt stretched his long legs out in front of him. "I'm tired."

"Aren't we all?" Aaron thumped the table with his fingertips. "But when your mother is getting food ready, it's your responsibility to pitch in—without being told."

"They're burgers in boxes, Dad. We don't even need plates."

Aaron chuckled and rolled his eyes. "You have me there, Matt."

The sound of Aaron's good-natured laughter lifted the tension right out of the air. But it took a joke at her expense, Sonia realized, and it ruffled her already resentful feelings. Aaron had barged in and taken over, teaming up with Matt to make fun of their fast food dinner. At least that's how she read the banter.

"The point is still the same though," Aaron added.

When he got up to pour them both a cup of coffee, Sonia watched him closely. Barely looking at her, he'd focused his attention on Matt. Aaron was up to something.

When he sat back down, Aaron cleared his throat as if getting their attention. "Say, Matt, did your mother and I ever tell you about the time she called you a lazy butt—before you were even born?"

Matt groaned. "Oh, please, not that story again."

Sonia burst out laughing. "Your dad is never going to let me live that down."

Matt grinned at his dad. "I like the story about getting rained on down by the river better."

"You would," Aaron shot back. "That story makes me look too dumb to come in out of the rain."

She liked this conversation much better than the edgy talk about manners. She listened as Aaron prompted Matt to recite the details of that rainy day. It took no effort at all to put herself back at the river with Matt buttoned up in her jacket, waiting while Aaron ran back to the farm in the rain. How odd that Aaron thought she'd be furious with him. On the contrary, to her the escapade was marvelously funny and had all the ingredients of a good family story. Now, listening to Aaron and Matt embellish the details, she felt downright smug.

The only downside of the dinner conversation was the reminder that they didn't have enough of these good times. After Matt went upstairs to bed, she and Aaron lingered at the table.

"You were surprised to see me earlier, weren't you?" Aaron asked.

"Of course." She laughed and pointed to the calendar on the board next to the phone. "I live by what I write down in those boxes."

"But you looked like I'd thrown you for a loop. It was more than surprise. You seemed preoccupied with other things and had to *adjust* to me showing up."

"Is that resentment I hear in your voice?"

He shrugged. "Probably."

"Maybe you're right. Seeing you here at the table did throw me," she said, her own resentment building that he'd put her on the defensive. "I have a lot on my mind. Matt has been asked to audition for a guest appearance with a youth orchestra in Iowa City, and Dottie and I are planning a new art exhibit at the garden. I felt unprepared or something. I don't know." She folded her arms across her chest. "If I were the one away from home so much, you'd have been thrown, too."

Aaron leaned in closer to her. "I know. It's not rational, but I feel as if so much of our family life goes on without me."

"And your life away from home, working with people I don't know and staying in hotel rooms is a part of your life that seems remote to me."

He again lifted his shoulders in a shrug. "I know. Like I said, this isn't rational."

"You seem satisfied with your work, and I'm happy with mine, but I wish you were home more."

"That's why I got the earlier flight," he said dryly, "to surprise you."

She rose from the table and stood behind his chair so she could drape her arms over his shoulders and rest her chin on the top of his head. "Don't mind my earlier reaction. I'm really glad you're home."

He took hold of her hands and they stayed that way for a few minutes. She needed to talk to him about so many things. The garden, Matt's schedule, and they hadn't had a serious conversation about the way Rona slowed down more and more every day, and her own mother's growing frailty. But she had no inclination to start those conversations when all she really wanted was to curl up with Aaron and go to sleep.

He squeezed her hands. "Every once in a while, it hits me how fast the days and years are ticking by. I don't want to miss our life."

"Me either," she whispered.

"And there are things we need to deal with...I mean..." His voice trailed off as he quickly shook his head.

"Like what?"

"Nothing. Just a lot of things rolling around in my brain. It will all keep."

"Good. Then let's go to bed," Sonia said.

What a relief. She wasn't up for a heart-to-heart conversation about their differing approaches to Matt, and she didn't have to be a mind reader to know that's what his thoughts were about.

* * *

Since Aaron was running late, he'd driven straight from the office to the garden without stopping at home to change into his Abe Lincoln costume. He smiled at the outdoor decorations on the road to the main building and the walkway from the parking lot. Ground lighting and lanterns illuminated gauzy ghosts and witches on broomsticks peeking through the shrubs and trees.

Once inside, he scanned the crowd and spotted Sonia lining up children at the buffet table. She had the style to pull off a fun fortune-teller costume—a red scarf tied around her hair, hoop earrings, and a peasant blouse, along with bracelets ringing both arms halfway up to her elbows. The garish purple eye shadow was a bit much, but she fit right in at their Halloween party. He made his way to her through the maze of tables and tubs set up for apple bobbing, keeping an eye out for Matt along the way.

"I can't find Matt," he said, when he reached Sonia.

"I'm glad you're here." She spoke in a loud voice in order to be heard over the buzz of kids' laughing and shrieking. "It's getting wild in here. We'll be giving out the costume prizes soon."

"Where's Matt? Why isn't he here to help with the games?"

"Oh, he had to practice. He'll be here later."

Once again, Matt used music to wiggle out of an obligation. "Practice for what?" Aaron demanded. "Is something special coming up?"

Sonia frowned. "There's always one performance or another to prepare for. And he has his lesson with Olivia next week."

He puffed his cheeks and blew out air in frustration. "You're telling me he's home practicing now for next Wednesday's lesson?"

Sonia glanced around, her attention clearly on the party. "What's your point?"

Knowing a bad time for a confrontation when he saw one, he overrode his better judgment and plunged in anyway. "My point is that Matt's special treatment is getting out of hand. I try to keep quiet because I've been away so much lately—"

"You can say that again." Her bracelets jangled as she planted her hands on her hips. "It seems we haven't had any time together since Dottie and Cal got married—and that was months ago."

"Oh, Sonia, that's not true." Clever how she'd managed to change the subject.

"As you can see," she said, gesturing at the crowd in the room, "I'm a little busy here making sure the kids enjoy the party."

"That's my point," he said defensively. "This is a

149

family business. Everyone plays a part in the Halloween events, including me. I left the office early to be here. We agreed that Matt should start helping out with the party." He pointed across the room where Dottie, dressed as a scarecrow, handed out balloons, with Cal's three children helping. "See? Cal's kids showed up. I told Matt it's his job to help me supervise the games."

"Right, right." She cast an impatient look. "Why is it so difficult for you to see that he's different? His practice is like his work—a job—and he needs to put in a certain number of hours a day. You still want him to be like every other boy his age. But he isn't. And *he never will be*."

He hated playing the bad guy, but he couldn't sit by and watch Matt turn into a little prince, too good to be one of the group. "Sometimes he acts like he's not part of our family. And you encourage it. Gift or no gift, he's got to learn basic respect for other things—and people."

"Fine, Aaron, if you think it's that important—then go get him." She stalked away.

Angry with Sonia, and unhappy with himself for starting the argument, he hurried to his car and drove to the house. He found Matt in his room with the door open, deep in concentration as he practiced a bowing exercise. Apparently he hadn't heard footsteps on the stairs, so Aaron gave the door a couple of loud raps to get his attention.

Matt's face turned sullen, but he didn't verbally protest when Aaron pointed to the Buffalo Bill costume on the bed and told him to change—on the double. "We all work at the little kids' Halloween party. You know that." He stepped into the room. "Besides, if I can spend the evening as Abe Lincoln, you can manage to become an icon of the Old West for a few hours." He didn't wait for an answer, but he thought he saw Matt smile, just a little.

Once in the car, Aaron, determined to get Matt to talk about something other than his music schedule, asked how his math class was going.

"Fine," Matt said.

"That's it? Fine?" He had trouble hiding the irritation in his voice, and wasn't even sure he wanted to.

"What do you from me, Dad? I'm going to the party in this dumb costume."

"Am I supposed to be impressed? Your cousins are already there doing their part, and I shouldn't have had to come and drag you out of the house and make you show up." Aaron sighed loud and long. "Look, I don't want to fight with you, but I don't like the way you set yourself apart from the rest of the family."

Matt folded his arms across his chest and stared out the window.

"Do you understand what I'm talking about, Matt? Do you?"

"Yeah, sort of."

Sort of. "Let me make it clear," he started, his tone matter-of-fact. "You know your mother has her hands full with the garden and taking you everywhere you need to go. You're old enough now to pitch in when you're asked—but more to the point, even when you're not."

"I know, Dad. I don't need a lecture. I'll help with the little kids. I always do."

Knowing he'd taken this as far as he could, Aaron dropped the subject and a few minutes later, he pulled into the employee parking lot. Matt immediately made a move to get out of the car, but Aaron put his hand on his son's arm to hold him back. "I have one more point to make. I want you to listen carefully. I know you have unusual talent, and yes, maybe your music sets you apart a bit. But your cousins and your friends at school are special in their own ways, too. Just remember that."

Matt didn't respond in words, but he lowered his head in a quick nod.

True to his word, Matt immersed himself in the party for the rest of the evening. Maybe not happily, Aaron thought, but he was nice to the little kids. No backtalk to Sonia either, and Aaron kept his ear tuned in for that.

Sonia pretended like nothing had happened, but Aaron found the whole incident troubling. She'd always been such a great mother to their son, and no one could have been more devoted to nurturing his extraordinary gift. But during the early years, Aaron had been more involved in raising Matt and had even taken pride in their teamwork as parents. Something was missing now, and it was time for him to step up.

Aaron spent the next week in Atlanta and made a point not to bring up Matt and his bad attitude during the nightly calls to Sonia. Soon enough, he would find an opening to start dealing with the issues he saw building in their family of three. In those moments, he regretted that they hadn't figured out a way to have another child or two. But then he admitted Sonia would have been called on to make the lion's share of sacrifice, while his trips out of town continued.

Back home on Friday, he was glad to see Sonia had planned a family dinner. Family was a bit of a stretch though, since he and Sonia carried on most of the conversation. A silent sloucher had replaced the talkative little boy that liked to take his turn telling the best thing about his day. At least he didn't balk about helping Aaron clear the table.

Then, when Sonia asked him to take the trash out to the bin, he responded with a snippy "Later."

Okay, enough was enough. Aaron spun around to face him. "Later? Your mother asked you to do one simple thing."

"I have to practice." Matt walked out of the kitchen, but Aaron took fast long strides to catch up to him, and quicker on his feet, got in front of Matt and blocked the stairway. "Trash first."

Without looking at him, Matt stomped back to the kitchen and with the plastic bag in hand, disappeared out the back door.

"What are you doing?" Sonia demanded in a low voice.

"I've kept my mouth shut long enough. He may be a prodigy, but he's not royalty."

She crossed her arms and stared at her feet. "And you picked this minute to make your point? Your first night home after being away all week—and before you talked to me?"

Aaron looked away, purposely ignoring her rhetorical questions. "Is Jewel coming tomorrow?" Maybe their long-time housecleaner could play a role in his plan to turn things around. Not that he'd thought out the plan in any detail.

"She's coming tomorrow morning. Why do you ask?"

He snickered. "I'm not sure. I'm making this up as I

go along."

She raised her eyebrows in obvious skepticism. "Really? Well, I'm not sure I like it. I have to drive him to a rehearsal in Madison tomorrow and he does need to practice."

"And he needs to be part of this family, too."

She started to respond, but Matt came back in the house and headed for the stairs.

"Not so fast."

"What now?" Matt asked, his upper lip curled in an impudent smirk.

Aaron grasped the counter with one hand and planted the other on his hip. "For starters, you can stand up straight and look me in the eye when I'm talking to you."

"Can I go practice now?" Matt demanded through clenched teeth while looking directly at Sonia.

Aaron glanced at Sonia and read confusion on her face. He kept his mouth shut, not wanting to preempt her, but at the same time fearing she might allow Matt to walk away.

"No, not until your father is finished talking with you." Turning her back to Matt, she picked up a sponge and with great determination swiped it across the edges of the sink.

"You've been avoiding your responsibilities," Aaron said, "and—"

"That's a lie. I get good grades and I practice all the time," Matt's loud voice reverberated through the room.

"That's all well and good, Matt, but you have responsibilities in the family, too. You had a job to do at the garden on Halloween, but I had to come back here and drive you there myself. And at your age, taking out the trash is hardly pulling your weight."

Aaron glanced at Sonia. She was bringing the chrome faucet to a high shine with that sponge.

"Here's the deal. Someone mature enough to perform like a pro in front of hundreds of people is old enough to take care of his own laundry." Aaron pointed toward the stairs. "Go take the sheets off your bed, then gather up your dirty clothes and the towels in your bathroom and bring it all down."

Matt slouched against the wall. "I thought that's why we have *Jewel*? You know, to do all that stuff."

His kid looked stricken! At that moment Aaron knew he should have taken a stand long ago. Giving Sonia a sideways glance, he noted she'd clamped her lips together.

"*We*? As in who? *You* don't contribute to her fee, my friend. And, in case you need it spelled out, Jewel is not a maid. She has her own cleaning business and we're one of her many customers. But from now on, taking care of your room and doing your laundry are two less jobs for her."

Matt huffed sounds of protest and shifted his weight from one foot to the other.

"Are we clear about this, Matt?"

Aaron waited for an answer as Matt nervously began tapping one foot.

"Well? I asked you a question."

"Uh, I don't know how to work the washing machine," Matt said, a look of embarrassment on his face.

Out of the corner of his eye, Aaron saw Sonia struggling to stifle a laugh.

"Well, then, it's time for some father-son talk.

Tonight I'm going to tell you the ancient tale about the journey dirty clothes take from the hamper to the washing machine and back to the closet." Aaron waved toward the hall. "Go on, Matt, let's get this done."

Matt narrowed his eyes, but then he turned on his heel and stomped up the stairs.

Aaron glanced at Sonia. "I know what you're going to say. All that stuff about his gift and being different from other kids. But damn it, he's almost thirteen-years-old and thinks Jewel is his servant. And I'm not going to stand by and listen to him speak to you in that nasty tone."

Without even looking at him, she thrust her palm in his face. "Stop, enough. I don't need a lecture. When you're right, you're right."

Since she never said that unless she meant it, he exhaled loudly and his body relaxed. "Looks like I've got my evening cut out for me."

"Serves you right," she said with laughter in her voice. "But seriously, please don't do any more of these *interventions* without talking to me first. Okay?"

He nodded. "But I couldn't stay silent and let him be so obnoxious."

She tossed the sponge on the counter. "And I'm going to leave you to it." She looked at him with amused eyes. "Besides, if I hang around I'll be tempted to jump in and offer nagging little hints about what to wash in cold or hot water. And you know the ins and outs of laundry anyway—thanks to Rona and your dad, you came to marriage fully loaded." She gave him a devilish grin before slipping into the family room.

And shutting the door behind her, he noticed.

14

December 2006

Sonia opened her eyes to the sound of the rain hitting the window in the den. A disappointing development. She'd hoped the light flurries the previous evening would leave a dusting of snow behind. She needed nature's decoration. Cold rain kept visitors away from the opening night of the Light Up the Holidays festival, and muddy trails discouraged walks to see the light design. But with any luck the rain would stop later.

Resisting the temptation to remain stretched out on the couch, she threw off the blanket and stood. Once in the kitchen, she flipped the switch on the coffee pot, and then turned on the TV to check the weather. She surfed through the channels, ready to stop at the first sign of a weather map. Was there anything that wasn't about the war or a new scandal or lame tips for holiday shopping?

Then, a cheery voice said, "Stay with us. After a short break, we'll be back for a conversation with Aaron Chapel, an attorney representing the Safe Play Council. He'll be reporting some new concerns about toy safety."

Aaron's face flashed on the screen. A split second later a commercial for car insurance wiped away his image.

Sonia dropped the remote on the counter and tried to rub away the tightness in her chest. Why did seeing

Aaron shock her so? She'd seen him on TV before—
many times. Frozen in the chair with her heart beating
fast, she waited impatiently through one ad after another
filled with frenetic images and tinny music. Her stomach
flipped over, alternately tightening and fluttering as
anxiety she couldn't explain continued to build.

Finally, Aaron's image reappeared in a box on the
screen. He smiled politely as the host introduced him as
the spokesperson for the advocacy group dedicated to
investigating reports of unsafe toys.

He sat in front of a glass window showing the
outline of dozens of Chicago's downtown buildings and
a series of bridges spanning the river. It wasn't raining
down there, Sonia noted, about two hundred miles away.
She listened as Aaron explained the Safe Play Council's
stand against manufacturers who had failed to test for
toxins in components that made their way into some of
the most popular toys on the market.

Anxious or not, she took pleasure in watching him
exude both competence and sincerity, and even if she'd
closed her eyes, she'd have heard the passion in his
voice. Shortly before they'd split up, he'd started doing
pro bono work on behalf of the Safe Play Council. So,
he'd kept it up. Good for him.

Before Matt hit the worst years of his adolescence,
Sonia remembered so many times that she'd called
upstairs to let him know his dad would be on TV in a
few minutes. Seconds later, she'd hear Matt's heavy
footsteps racing down the stairs, and together they'd
wait for Aaron to be introduced as a guest expert or a
commentator on many different news shows. Sonia had
always felt her chest fill with pride over his ability to
handle an on-camera debate or field reporters' tough

questions at a press conference. Aaron showed Matt what a person's passion looked like in the world. He'd been mentored by Artie Silverman, and now he was a Silverman himself.

And that's why Matt had gone away, to follow his passion. Sonia sighed and massaged her temples as if trying to rub away these thoughts—they always came back to still missing him so much.

Watching Aaron talk, she noted how worn out he looked, even more than when she'd seen him in Pearson Pond. Did the new woman in his life, whoever she was, see the deep lines around his eyes, which even TV makeup couldn't hide? Did she ever urge him to turn off the computer and sleep?

Ha! For all the good it probably did her. Once immersed in something, Aaron wasn't easily pulled away.

Aaron's hair, thinning slightly now, had transformed into a white-gray shade that made him even better looking, and magically, didn't add years. Aaron was lucky that way. She remembered a time when she caught him studying his reflection in the mirror in their hotel suite in Chicago. He'd turned to her and frowned as he pointed to the few strands of gray. She'd mocked him by grabbing her glasses and pretending she had to search to find even one gray hair. He'd grinned, but turned back to the mirror and frowned once more.

Now why would she start thinking about that Chicago trip? If she got lost in the maze of memories, she might never find her way out.

The TV host finished the interview, all of three or four minutes of it, and thanked Aaron for coming into the studio. He nodded graciously. Good TV manners, as always, Sonia thought. If Artie Silverman were still alive, he'd give his protégé a hearty slap on the back.

She turned off the TV and rested her forehead on her folded hands. Her heart filled with pride over Aaron's passions—and all he'd accomplished—but at the same time, a wave of sadness hit so hard her chest hurt.

Restless, Sonia slipped off the kitchen stool and went to the back patio door and stared into the yard. Aaron and Matt's bird feeders clustered near the ancient concrete bird bath Aaron had spotted at a flea market. She smiled remembering the father-son comedy routine when they rolled the bird bath across the yard, a feat in itself, searching for a spot flat enough for it to sit reasonably straight, but still visible from the kitchen. Standing at the patio doors, she'd watched the silly antics of their trial and error caper until they found the right spot and pushed the bird bath up into position. Still laughing, they'd flashed her a triumphant thumbs up sign.

Now, although she managed to keep the feeders filled, she paid little attention to the birds. Some days she didn't bother opening the blinds, maybe because, like now, so many memories came in along with the sunlight. Sonia turned away and drew in a deep breath. Hadn't she made progress building a new life, dating Ben, staying in touch with new friends from the Unity Flight Family Group? The dedication in Pearson Pond had changed her, and not for the better.

Sonia closed the blinds, blocking the sight of the bird bath and the feeders. She headed for the stairs, determined to start her day. *I will stop these trips into the past—I have to.*

* * *

Aaron shook hands with Keisha, a producer he'd worked with a few times, and then slipped out of the studio. He bought a coffee from a vender in a kiosk in the lobby and decided he wasn't ready to head to the office and face emails and phone calls. The December wind blew cold off the lake, but he headed to the bridge, stopping in the middle to gaze at the view to the west. The mixture of old and newer buildings framed each side of the river, always reminding Aaron of soldiers standing at attention.

He continued down Michigan Avenue, switching the cardboard container of coffee from one hand to the other, letting it warm his gloveless hands. He'd had a dream about Matt, but couldn't remember the details, though he'd stayed in bed long enough to try to lure back the gauzy images. But when he could call up nothing other than a vague memory of a lion and Matt's face moving in and out of the dream pictures, he forced himself to put the night and hopes of sleep behind him. Besides, he'd been due at the TV studio, luckily only a few blocks from his apartment.

Glancing at the familiar surroundings as he walked, Aaron was struck by how little he knew of Chicago other than these downtown streets and the Gold Coast and Lincoln Park. With his office just off Wacker Drive, he seldom had reason to venture into the neighborhoods, the real city. He'd made a pilgrimage to Wrigley Field a couple of times, and he and Katherine had a favorite Hyde Park restaurant, but he'd done most of his exploring early on, back when he'd kidded himself into believing he could start over.

He picked up his pace as he crossed Madison and

then Monroe. Once he reached Adams, and the lions guarding the Art Institute came into view, he realized they were the lion sculptures that had come to life in his dream about Matt. It wouldn't be the first time shadowy outlines of that landmark—and of Orchestra Hall across the street—floated in and out of his dreams. Paradoxically, waking from the dreams sharpened the pain of his losses, but also filled him with longing to hang on to the much too fleeting images as long as possible.

The Art Institute wouldn't open for hours, but that was okay. He didn't plan to go inside anyway. He sat on the cold steps and took the cover off the cup, letting the hot steam escape. Passersby looked at him curiously, but he didn't care. He glanced up at the landmark lions and smiled. It was as if Matt, the young Matt who posed for pictures with the lions and performed at Orchestra Hall, had joined him on the stairs to watch the passersby on what had been their favorite stretch of Michigan Avenue.

* * *

December 1999

"*This* is great—an entire afternoon to ourselves." Aaron stood with Sonia in front of Orchestra Hall, relieved that he'd managed to coax her out of the building and leave Matt to rehearse with the orchestra and the other guest musicians. "So, what will it be? Marshall Field's? The Art Institute? Browsing the bookstores?"

She grinned. "I know you're trying to distract me, but I can't get my mind off our boy in that huge hall with all those musicians around him. Wow, such pressure."

He cupped her face in his hands and planted a kiss on both cheeks. "But he's fifteen now. Let him be. He's supposed to handle these performances on his own. Besides, *Olivia* holds the reins on this event, not you."

Despite what he'd said to Sonia, Aaron wanted to jump out of his skin from a bad case of the jitters. Being invited to perform as a guest soloist with the Chicago Symphony Orchestra had sent them all soaring. Without question, this represented the most important appearance in Matt's still budding career. He'd been one of only three young musicians in the Midwest chosen for this honor. Matt showed more anxiety over these two performances than he had over any others, which was undoubtedly why Olivia and the other musicians' teachers had more or less ordered all the parents to leave the rehearsal. She wouldn't allow their apprehension to compound the problem.

Sonia slipped her arm through Aaron's and snuggled closer, hunching her shoulders in joyful contentment.

"It's all so thrilling," she said, her smile bright and dazzling, "but Olivia knows what she's doing. I'm so jumpy I'd probably make him frantic if I hung around." She pointed across the street. "How about the Art Institute first and then let's explore some bookstores?"

A few hours later, they each carried loaded shopping bags back to the hotel and up to their suite. Sonia kicked off her shoes and collapsed on the couch, exaggerating her fatigue for show.

"We more or less finished our Christmas shopping," she said to Matt, who came out of his room, dressed for the pre-concert dinner with Olivia and the two other guest soloists and their teachers.

"How are you doing?" Aaron asked Matt. "You look ready for your big evening."

Matt grinned and pulled at the lapels of his black suit jacket. "I'm okay. I'm getting used to dressing up like this."

"You look heartbreakingly handsome," Sonia remarked. "I—we—are about to burst with pride."

Matt rolled his eyes. "That's what Ms. Morton told me you'd say."

Aaron laughed. "Well, it's true. And you look all grown up." He lowered his head and looked away, wincing. He looked up to return Matt's quick wave, and then his gangly son was out the door.

"You were thinking about Rona just then, weren't you?" Sonia asked.

He nodded. Of course, Sonia noticed. "It's like a wave that crashes suddenly and without warning."

She touched his arm. "It happens to me that way, too. Rona wasn't my mother, but she became my good friend—she was the best. And it's never easy when someone dies without warning."

But in her sleep. Over the previous couple of months, Aaron hung on to that simple fact. It comforted him to know that she'd been spared a long illness or a frustrating, slow decline into old age. But she'd been excited about coming along on this Chicago trip, such a milestone for her grandson.

"Looking at Matt just now," he said, "I couldn't help but think how proud she'd be of him. She wanted to see him play in Orchestra Hall."

"I know. Rona believed in our son."

He could see Sonia blinking back tears. He put his arms around her and held her tight. "My mother believed in *you*, too, and admired your passion for the garden, and especially what you've done for Matt."

He broke the embrace and in silence, they finished getting ready. After a quick dinner in the hotel restaurant, they walked down Michigan Avenue to Orchestra Hall. Aaron kidded Sonia about the electric energy she exuded. Strong enough to power the streetlights, he quipped. Then they spent a few minutes with Matt backstage before taking their seats alongside the parents of the guest violinist and pianist, both girls about Matt's age.

"He towers over those two," he whispered to Sonia. "He looks like a young man now, all long arms and legs."

"He looks like you," Sonia whispered back.

Aaron reached for her hand when Matt walked to the center of the stage, then took his seat and placed the cello between his knees. As the lights dimmed in Orchestra Hall, Aaron glanced at Sonia just to enjoy the happy glow on her face.

As usual, Sonia closed her eyes, but Aaron kept his gaze riveted on their son as he played a lively Dvorak concerto, a piece Aaron had heard many times over the past few months, especially the troublesome sections that Matt practiced in his room with the door closed. Self-consciously, Aaron watched his son's face, undeniably a younger version of himself. Yet, when Matt closed his eyes and the corners of his mouth subtly turned up, Aaron saw glimpses of Sonia.

Near the end of the piece, Aaron again looked at Sonia, knowing what he'd see. Tears spilled from her still closed eyes and dampened her cheeks, and the ecstasy in her smile sent a warm shiver through him.

Then the piece was over, and he and Sonia stood with everyone else in Orchestra Hall to give their son a standing ovation. Aaron's breath caught in his chest as he watched their son rise from the chair and shake hands with the conductor. Matt then faced the orchestra and bowed in acknowledgment. No longer a child, but a young man who now occupied a world with its own rites of passage and rituals Aaron himself would never completely understand. The whole range of emotions, including the pride Aaron had no words for, repeated when later, Matt played his second piece with the other two musicians.

After the concert, he and Sonia joined Olivia and the other guest performers and their families and teachers for a drink in the hotel bar.

When they'd settled at a table, Sonia had pressed her graceful hands together and said, "How wonderful to be with people who feel no need to be modest about their children."

Everyone had laughed at Sonia's declaration, including Matt. Watching Sonia chat with the other parents, Aaron quietly observed her exhilaration, and a touch of relief, too, in how remarkably well Matt had played. She lit up the table in her red silk dress, new for this occasion, and the bold necklace of gold and black beads he'd bought for her in Miami, not for any particular occasion, but because it reminded him of her style.

With her short blonde hair softly framing her animated face, Aaron had never seen her more beautiful—or happier—than in that moment. *Gratitude.* The sweetness of it traveled through his body, filling him up, tightening his throat and leaving him unable to speak.

A couple of hours later, up in their room in the suite, but too keyed up to sleep, he and Sonia talked in low voices, going over every minute of the evening and reveling in how grown up Matt had looked—and acted. Sonia spoke of Olivia's pleasure in the evening, but Aaron focused on his son's professional poise. No, he hadn't heard the genius in the performance, but he'd forever hang on to the manner in which his young son had turned to the conductor and the orchestra and nodded in respect. Punctuating their talk of Matt with kisses that grew hungrier, he and Sonia made love with intensity, releasing pent-up energy and pride in their son they didn't have words to express.

Dim morning light slanted through the gap in the hotel room drapes when he and Matt, dressed in jeans and heavy sweatshirts, left the suite to make the trek to Soldier Field because Matt wanted to see the legendary landmark in person. Aaron had left Sonia dozing, but alert enough to declare them both crazy to leave warm beds just to see their arch rival's football stadium.

"The only bad thing about the second concert is that I'll miss watching the Packers' game this afternoon," Matt said, when they'd walked about three blocks straight into the wind.

Aaron yanked his knit hat down over his ears and then rubbed his hands together. Even wearing gloves, the blustery morning left him feeling cold all over. "I'd keep that thought between us," he said dryly. "Olivia might never recover, and your mother's frown would not be a pretty sight."

Matt laughed. "I've got my priorities straight. Cello first, following the Packers a very close second."

When they reached the stadium, Matt took his camera out of his pocket and snapped several photos of the main gate. Then they took pictures of each other standing in front of it. Later, Aaron called Sonia on his cell phone and she met them in front of The Art Institute to take another round of photos. They stood on the stairs next to the lions with their arms thrown around each other's shoulders, with big grins for Sonia and her camera. Then the three of them hunted up breakfast before Matt's early rehearsal for the matinee concert.

Back at the hotel, he and Matt showered and dressed in their suits.

"We need more pictures," Sonia announced with determination. "Let's go back to those lions. I want pictures of you dressed up in your handsome topcoats."

Matt groaned.

"Might as well stop the protests," Aaron teased. "This is one photo op you're not wiggling out of. Besides, get used to it. From here on out, you'll be posing for a lot of pictures."

"I still get tired of her and her camera," Matt said, once he was out of his mother's earshot.

They hurried across the street and down the block to the museum. Bright sun warmed the day. When they reached the spot next to the lion, Sonia looked into the viewfinder. "Ah, now this is more like it." She grinned. "Am I a lucky woman or what?"

Aaron glanced at Matt, who rolled his eyes in the way only a boy indulging his doting mom could do. The kid had no idea how lucky he was. Maybe one day Matt would understand what his mother had done for him.

Part III

15

April 2000

"Come quick, Matt. Your dad's on TV," Sonia said. Aaron stood at the microphone with a crowd gathered behind him outside the capitol building in Madison. Wow, he looked grim. Sonia stopped chopping green peppers on her cutting board and turned to Matt, who had just come through the door. "Remember? Your dad was scheduled to testify today about a landfill proposal. From the way he looks, the hearing must have gone badly."

Matt kicked off his shoes on the mat inside the back door and brushed past her and headed upstairs without a word. She braced her hands on the edge of the counter. She'd never been one to count to ten to ward off an explosion, but now would be a good time to pick up the habit. She settled for an exaggerated sigh.

If Aaron had seen Matt walk away, he'd have followed him to the stairs and called him on his rude behavior. But she just didn't have it in her to chase after him and launch into a lecture about manners. Besides, no matter where they started a conversation, they always ended up in an argument about why—with no explanation—Matt cancelled his classes with Olivia. Only once had he come right out and said that he wasn't *into* the cello anymore. *Wasn't into?* What did that mean? He couldn't will his talent away.

That evening, after Aaron came home, the two of them ate shrimp stir fry alone in the kitchen, while Matt went to a friend's house for dinner, supposedly to study.

"Spending this much time with friends is new for Matt," Aaron said, his tone matter-of-fact. "I know it's hard for you to accept, but maybe he just wants to have a life that's more like a normal teenager."

She bit her tongue. Most every argument they'd had somehow involved Matt. Too much of his time devoted to music, not enough time with school friends. Those arguments were moot now, ever since Matt abruptly walked away from the cello. He did his chores in a sullen robotic way, but had little to say otherwise.

Sonia still harbored resentment over what at times seemed like Aaron's less than wholehearted support for their talented son. Always excited and up for the big events, Aaron hadn't shown as much interest in the day-to-day routines that made the extraordinary occasions like concerts in Orchestra Hall possible.

"But it's almost May," she pointed out. "He played at a Christmas Eve wedding, and I don't think he's touched his cello since. It's been months since his music filled the house." She got up from the table to avoid his eyes. "I can't help it, it breaks my heart."

"Didn't Olivia tell you that she's seen this before? You know, that sometimes resistance sets in, that teenagers confront the reality of what a life in music means. Sometimes, they take a break to figure out what they really want."

He followed her to the counter and stood next to hear. "Don't you see? The Chicago concert may have triggered it. As wonderful as it was, it may have hit him that he'll eventually need to leave behind all the familiar things, including us. Perhaps a part of him is reluctant to say yes to that kind of commitment. It's a big decision, Sonia."

She snickered and looked into his face. "Will ya' quit confusing me with the facts?"

He patted her back. "I'm only repeating what you told me."

"But you sound so reasonable." She tapped her fingers on her lips, but then stopped abruptly. She'd resolved to stop that nervous habit. "I wish I had the patience to wait this out. But after—"

They both turned to the sound of the phone ringing. Her first thought was to ignore it, but Aaron reached to the end of the counter and picked it up. He gave her a quick sideways glance and then his face wrinkled up in a deep frown.

"Okay, we'll be right there."

Suddenly unsteady, she leaned against the counter for support. "What?"

"It's your mother," he said, coming closer and enveloping her in his arms. "She's had a stroke."

* * *

The house was dark and silent, but when he flipped on the kitchen light, he saw the note on the table.

> Aaron,
> I'm at Open Meadows visiting my mother. Matt's at school for a Spanish club meeting. He'll get a ride home with Tom's older brother. I'll be late. I

have an evening meeting at the garden. Why don't you and Matt make omelets or order pizza or something? I'll eat later.
  S

She always signed her notes with that simple "S." He could almost hear the gears working in her brain as she quickly relayed all the necessary information—the who, the what, the where—and then she couldn't resist adding a suggestion about what he and Matt should have for dinner. He'd go along with whatever Matt wanted, to the extent the kid deigned to express his thoughts about anything.

Aaron had clung to the conviction that the cause of their son's sullen attitude, even his chronic slouch, was nothing more than adolescent angst that he'd soon outgrow. Aaron could accept that Matt's focus might change. Prodigy or not, something else captured his imagination. But he hated seeing Sonia so sad.

Even worse was the burden Sonia carried over her mother, especially after a second stroke quickly followed the first. He'd held Sonia's hand while they listened for a hint of good news in the doctor's words, but even Sonia, usually so optimistic, accepted that reasons for hope were scarce.

In his own heart, Aaron was saddened by this turn of events because Vivian had been a terrific mother-in-law, once she'd seen that he and Sonia had fallen in love. Aaron still wished that Sonia's stubborn dad had lived long enough to witness how it all turned out—Matt, the garden, but most of all, the life Aaron and Sonia had created. Sonia wasn't one to dwell on old hurts, but her dad's death had left a wound in her heart that never quite healed.

They'd marked another wedding anniversary just last week, passing the evening at Vivian's bedside at the acute care center at Open Meadows. Back home, after they'd climbed into bed, he'd put his arm around her and listened as her breathing became shallow and even. He'd smiled to himself, thinking of their wedding night when he'd come to bed after his shower, only to find that she'd already fallen asleep, or to use one of Sonia's favorite phrases, conked out.

Standing in the kitchen, Aaron scanned the calendar. Until recently, the box for each day had been filled with Sonia's color-coded writing. So many empty spaces now. Aaron couldn't remember the last time he'd seen the red lettering marking a performance date for Matt, or the black O, meaning a lesson with Olivia.

He studied the rest of the month and noted a small blue X in the corner of five boxes in a row starting the end of next week, designating the days he'd be out of town. Still looking at next week, Aaron frowned at the notation about the appointment with Dr. Waters, their family doctor. When Sonia had told Aaron she'd set up the visit, he'd asked if Matt was due for a checkup.

She'd shaken her head. "But no kid walks away from the kind of gift he has. There's something wrong."

He hadn't argued with her, but he had his doubts that a checkup would reveal anything.

Aaron opened the refrigerator and grabbed a cold beer and sat at the table. The house felt empty. Granted, it was unfair, but he resented that here he was, in town for the week, yet he again came home to an empty house. On the other hand, at least he didn't have to witness Sonia's puzzled eyes following Matt's movements around the house.

Aaron conceded Matt no longer seemed like himself. Uncommunicative in the extreme, their son avoided looking either of his parents straight in the eye. But Matt still brought home good grades, even an A+ on a complex history paper. The boy showed genuine interest in the U.S. Constitution. *Like him.* Aaron smiled to himself. At the last parent conference, every one of Matt's teachers reported that he was more involved with his classes and other school activities than he'd ever been. So, the kid stayed busy. Hell, Aaron had lobbied for a so-called normal life, and now it appeared his wish for Matt had come true.

Restless, he sorted through the mail on the counter, leafed through catalogs and magazines and gathered up his clothes and shirts to take to the cleaners the next day. Mostly, he felt out of sorts. When Matt came home, they ordered pizza and ate off paper plates. Aaron welcomed the distraction of watching a basketball game on TV while they ate. No need to communicate with a teenager who preferred silence.

Sonia came in as they were finishing up. She acted friendly and like her usual self, or she tried to, as she reported no change in her mother's condition. Translated, that meant her mother lingered, unconscious and helpless.

During the night, something stirred him from a deep sleep. He opened his eyes and in the dim light coming through the window, he saw Sonia slipping into her robe. Then she quietly left the room. From the slow, careful way she closed the door behind her, he could tell she'd tried to be as quiet as possible. He stayed in bed and waited for her to come back. It wasn't like her to get up in the middle of the night.

The minutes ticked by. Sensing something was wrong he went downstairs, finding her curled up on the couch in the den.

When she looked up, her red eyes gave her away.

"What is it?" he asked as he sat next to her.

"A little bit of everything," she said. She patted her wet eyes with a tissue and then wadded it up and held it in her closed, tight fist.

"Tell me," he said, stroking her hair.

"I'm taking Matt to see my mother tomorrow after school. I'm insisting on it. I don't give a damn about his sarcastic, rude smirks. He's going. If you want to sit with her, maybe talk to her, whether she can hear you or not, you should go over there soon. She's dying, Aaron. It's only a matter of time."

Why was he hearing about his now, in the middle of the night? "Why didn't you say something earlier? The doctor predicted she'd regain consciousness, at least."

She shrugged. "I didn't feel like talking. Matt barely had a pleasant word to say, and when I looked at him clearing the table and cleaning up, all I could think about was the untouched cello up in his room."

He leaned in closer. "Why don't you try to forget about Matt and his music for now? Focus on your mother. There's nothing you can do about our son. He's either going to pick up the cello again, or not. It won't be up to us. But right now, your mother needs you—she needs us—and she might wake up before she…you know, before she dies."

"I suppose."

Taking both her hands in his, he gently pulled her to her feet. "Do you want me to fix some tea?"

She shook her head.

"Then let's go back to bed. You need the rest. I'll visit Vivian first thing in the morning." He pressed his lips to her forehead.

When they crawled back into bed, she snuggled her back against him and he held her until she fell asleep.

The phone startled him and he fished around in the dark to pick it up. Just as Sonia turned on the light, he heard the voice announce herself as Billie Burke from Open Meadows. He took the message and hung up the phone. From the look on Sonia's face, he could tell she already knew.

Aaron felt awful for Sonia, but also for Matt. He'd never known his two grandfathers, and now both grandmothers were gone, too.

He cradled Sonia, holding her as she cried out her grief.

* * *

Matt slammed the car door. "What a waste of time."

"You can say that again," Sonia said, jamming the key in the ignition.

"I told you there's nothing wrong with me." He brushed his long hair off his face. "I'm not sick…you know…*depressed.*"

Sonia could accept the long bangs swinging down to say hello to his eyelashes, a familiar sight these days, but the cold resentment in his voice transformed Matt into someone she didn't even know.

As if Matt could evaluate his own psychological state, she thought. Bruce Waters might have been good with earaches and sore throats, but as far as she was concerned, Matt had seen their family doctor for the last time.

"We wouldn't have wasted the time if you had communicated with me," she said.

"You never listen anyway."

"Right. I've only devoted the better part of a decade either listening to you or driving you from one place to another so that other people can give you their full attention."

If Aaron had overheard that remark, he'd have rolled his eyes. Okay, she sounded like a damn martyr. What of it?

Matt stared out the window and kept his mouth clamped shut for the rest of the ride home. Sonia was too riled up to risk breaking the silence herself.

If her mother had been alive—and still well—she'd have gone to see her and poured her heart out about the way her son took his talent for granted, something he could toss aside. As if life handed out such gifts every day.

As Sonia grew older, she'd needed her mother's approval less and her friendship as an equal more. Foolishly, Sonia had counted on more years to have lunch dates and heart-to-heart talks. After losing Rona so suddenly, why hadn't she learned the lesson that no one was guaranteed more time? Every day she awakened conscious of the dull ache left behind by the loss of both Rona and her mother.

Matt barely waited for her to come to a complete stop in the garage before he got out of the car and disappeared inside the house.

"*Ha!* And you say he's acting like a normal kid," she said aloud, mentally challenging both Aaron and Dr. Waters. Just as well that Aaron was still working on a case in Florida or she'd likely take her frustrations out on him the minute he walked through the door.

Climbing out of the car, she gave the hood an angry whack before going inside. Up in her room, she shed her pantsuit and pulled on jeans and a shirt and stuck her feet into sneakers. She hurried down the stairs and opened the front door, but stopped suddenly. Just because Matt had turned moody and fallen into bad habits that didn't entitle her to act like a rude adolescent.

She went into the kitchen and scribbled a note to let Matt know that she'd gone out, adding a line about the leftover stew in the fridge and the frozen dinners he could throw in the microwave. *Oh brother, maybe Aaron was right.* Reading back her words, she saw the evidence in black and white. Sometimes she *did* act like Matt needed her to tell him what and when to eat. She grabbed her cell phone out of her handbag and stuck it in her pocket before heading out the side door.

The bright afternoon light didn't match her mood, but she headed over the footbridge. Instead of walking toward the garden buildings she hurried down the path that led through the fields and to the river.

A few minutes later, she sat on the ground with her back against the boulder. She closed her eyes and listened to the water flowing past in the lazy warm breeze. She drew air deep into her lungs and then emptied them slowly, the way Leslie, who practiced yoga religiously, had taught her years before.

She felt herself finally start to relax, but then jumped when the phone rang. She quickly dug into her pocket to get it.

She chuckled softly in response to Aaron's voice. "You won't believe where I am."

"Try me." His voice sounded pleasantly teasing.

"I'm watching our favorite willow trees caress the river."

"My poet is back," he said softly. "Must be a nice afternoon, huh?"

"It smells alive and green—like summer."

Knowing she was prying the top right off a can of worms, she showed no mercy for Dr. Waters in explaining what had happened at the appointment. "He actually declared Matt as normal as any fifteen year old on the planet, which even he agreed was damning with faint praise. But he completely dismissed my concerns about behavior changes and depression—all of it." She paused for a second. "And I suppose you agree."

"That's not important, Sonia."

"Yes it is," she said, detesting her plaintive tone. "According to him, you're more or less right. He said it wasn't unusual for a teenager to drop one interest and pick up something else."

"I suppose that's about what I said."

She felt like screaming in frustration. "You think Matt's talent is a mere interest?"

"At one time, yes, but I know better now."

Ah, at last, a concession.

"I've been more concerned with your unhappiness with this situation," Aaron said. "Do I like Matt's choices? Do I like the way he's been behaving? No, I don't."

His heavy sigh sounded like a gust of wind coming through the phone. "But I think his refusal to talk about his music," Aaron said with conviction, "especially with you, is part of his need to pull away and make some choices on his own."

"You may be right. But Bruce Waters dismissed me

as some kind of nutty stage mother."

"He said that?"

"No, he didn't use those words…he didn't have to. He looked at me over his reading glasses with a mixture of pity and disapproval. Completely patronizing."

"Apparently, your walk down to the river hasn't quite done the job yet," Aaron said with a soft laugh. "You sound pretty tense. But I'll be home late tonight. And then tomorrow, let's get away from our offices and meet for lunch."

"Another one of your soothing lunches, huh?"

"I'm not just trying to soothe you. I *miss* you."

When they ended their call, she was uncomfortably aware of the irony that she felt like a piece of her had gone missing. Without managing Matt, keeping his color-coded schedule of lessons, rehearsals, and appearances, she'd lost track of a distinct part of her identity. But as if compensating for one loss, she'd opened up more room for Aaron.

16

November 2000

Sonia was standing at the bottom of the stairs when she heard Aaron call her name from the backdoor. She put her index finger to her lips to shush him. And his eyebrows shot up in surprise.

"I've been listening for the better part of an hour," she whispered, slipping her arm around Aaron and leaning against his chest. Matt had started with scales and bowing exercises before he played a full piece through. Then he went back to practice the trouble spots again...and again. A good sign, she told Aaron.

"Does he sound rusty to you?" Aaron whispered.

She bobbed her head back and forth. "Hmm, sort of. But Olivia told me this could happen. She said that the love of playing itself could bring him back, but he'd have to accept working hard to catch up." She glanced up the stairs. "I'm certain he'd never play in public without practicing."

They stood together listening. When the music stopped, she gave Aaron a happy kiss. Then they headed to the kitchen.

"Something's making the whole house smell good," he said, sniffing the air.

"I made one of my mother's old recipes. I unearthed it when I went through her things. It was scribbled on the back of an envelope and stuck inside an old paperback book." She picked up the lid on the sauté pan and inhaled the garlicky chicken. "I'd forgotten all about it."

"Well, lucky for us, you found it." Aaron took plates out of the cabinet and set them on the table. "Do you know what prompted Matt to play?" he asked, keeping his voice low. "It's been a long time since I've heard music coming from his room."

"I have no idea. The whole episode is a big mystery." She'd come home from the garden and heard the music. "What do you think? Should we ask him?"

Aaron narrowed his eyes in thought. "Not yet. Why don't we let him tell us when he's ready?"

At one time, she'd have been inclined to argue with Aaron, but not anymore. Throughout the desolate past year, she'd leaned on him and allowed the comfort he offered to wash over her. Between Matt rejecting music—and her—and her mother's death, she'd clung to Aaron.

Matt kept quiet during dinner, but that was nothing new. She and Aaron made light conversation about upcoming holiday events at the garden.

"So, how was your day, Matt?" Aaron asked in the friendly tone he always maintained, despite Matt's sulky face.

Sonia tried not to fix her gaze on Matt, but out of the corner of her eye, she watched him gulp down half a glass of water. Then he glanced at her. "While you were at work, Leslie asked me to play a couple of pieces at her wedding."

A pleasant buzz traveled through her body. Bless her best friend's generous heart. How smart of her to ask

Matt directly. Like Aaron, Leslie had advised Sonia to quit arguing with Matt. With any luck, this wedding would give him a doorway back into music and he could again embrace what he loved. Aware that she was getting way ahead of herself, she decided she wouldn't think too far ahead.

"I thought I heard you playing when I came in the house," Aaron said casually. "So, what did you tell her?"

"I told her I'd think about it."

Aaron jerked his head back. Forcing herself not to respond the same way, Sonia stabbed her fork into the last mushroom on her plate. Good thing Leslie had teenagers, or Sonia would have been mortified by what sounded like a flippant, rude response. She mentally lectured Matt about the hospitality Leslie offered them on their many trips to Minneapolis. She'd given them a welcoming place to stay when Matt performed in that city, even twice when he was on public television. Leslie's twin girls, only two years younger than Matt, were like cousins to him.

On her own for many years, Leslie had chosen the garden as the site for her second wedding. Sonia's happiness for Leslie made Matt's snippy insensitivity all the worse.

She put down her fork, mushroom and all.

Aaron pushed his plate back and got to his feet. He gave Matt a light thump on his shoulder as a reminder to start clearing the table. Glad for a few minutes alone at the table, Sonia sipped her white wine while Matt and Aaron loaded the dishwasher.

The tone of their conversation changed as the topic shifted to the football game coming on TV later. The three of them had the chance for a pleasant evening, and she intended to push Leslie's wedding out of her mind and at least pretend interest in the game.

That night in bed, as they were drifting off to sleep, Aaron suggested another one of their lunches at the River's Bend Café.

"We're becoming regulars there," she said.

"And I like it," he whispered.

The next day, she smiled to herself as she claimed an empty table in a back corner of River's Bend, remembering again the polite, but awkward New Year's Day brunch they'd shared after their embarrassing New Year's Eve night. The café had been a tiny place almost seventeen years before, but new owners had expanded into the storefront next door, more than doubling its space. Putting aside the old memories, the noisy café, with its walls covered with photographs showing over a century of Lady's River history, had recently become one of their favorite places to meet.

Sonia glanced at her watch and then toward the door just as Aaron came in and scanned the restaurant. He grinned when he spotted her and hurried to their table.

After they gave their order to the waitress, Aaron leaned in toward her. "Okay, here's what I think about Leslie's invitation. I think we should stay out of it. When it comes to Matt and his music, we've backed off and we should stay that way."

She let out a hoot. "You didn't waste a minute, did you? Besides, you really mean that I should stay out of it."

"Not really." He reached out to squeeze her hand. "It's not that simple anymore. But his music isn't as personal for me as it is for you. But I think this should be between Matt and Leslie."

"I agree…reluctantly," she said with a laugh. "As hard as it is, I know backing off is the wisest thing to do. He practiced yesterday, and maybe he'll pick up the cello again today." How she longed to hear him play again.

"So, we're agreed then, we'll wait for him to come to us."

"If he accepts Leslie's invitation, shouldn't we let him know that we'll help him start his lessons again? You know, offer him the support he needs."

With his hand still over hers, he shook his head. "He knows he can count on us. Besides, he's sixteen now, so he can drive himself back and forth to lessons with Olivia. Despite how he's behaved recently, he's mature for his age. And like you used to tell me, his life isn't going to follow the usual path—"

"You still think his rebellion was my fault, don't you?" she interrupted, pulling her hand away. "That he walked away from music because I turned into a stage mother, always pushing and managing."

He flopped back in the chair, as if defeated, but then quickly propelled his body forward again. "Listen to me. I've tried to explain so many times how I felt about his childhood being dominated by music. And I admit I used the term 'stage mother' once or twice. But none of this is your fault."

She sighed. "But I have to back off now. I know that—as much as I want to be there for him."

"He has to set his own course. Let's give him the space to work this out within himself."

"*Oh, okay,*" she said, exaggerating her surrender

and making him smile. To keep the light mood going, she pursed her lips in mock disgust. "Has he told you about the rats?"

"Rats? Where?"

"Not in the house, you'll be happy to know." She pretended to swipe sweat off her forehead. "He's working on a science project with some other kids. It involves putting rats on different types of weight loss plans."

He grinned. "I'm glad you mentioned it. Maybe if I ask *very* nicely, he'll tell me about it at dinner tonight."

"I suppose," she said. "At least this strange creature we live with is interested in something."

Later that afternoon, Sonia heard Matt practicing, and again, she stood at the bottom of the stairs with her eyes closed, taking in the sounds she loved so much. Even playing rusty, he managed to coax the pure, beautiful tones she loved so much.

The next day Leslie called. Matt had sent her an email thanking her for the chance to perform at her wedding and asking what pieces she'd like him to play.

"Thank you," Sonia murmured into the phone.

"I have a strong feeling that something is shifting in Matt," Leslie said. "He sounded serious in his email— very professional—although he refused my offer to pay his going wedding rate."

"I should hope so," Sonia said, "and I hope you're right, you know, about this shift or whatever." She got up from her chair and walked to the window. "But this wedding is about you, not solving our problems with Matt." She chuckled. "So, let's talk about caterers."

Being part of planning Leslie's wedding made her feel girlishly giddy. But the prospect of Matt playing again touched another place inside her where her deepest hopes lived.

* * *

The River Gazette
January 14, 2001

Spotlight on Lady's River People

Is Chapel's Botanical Garden becoming the venue in town for second marriages? Yesterday, former Lady's River resident, Leslie Manley, married Tom Shoemacher of Minneapolis, now home to Leslie and her children. The couple held their winter wedding at the chapel in the garden, and Sonia Chapel was matron-of-honor. Matthew Chapel performed two pieces on his cello. We'd heard that he'd lost interest in music, but apparently, the prodigy is back.

Mandy & Amy

17

October 2001

As they waited for Matt's first flight of the day, Sonia did her best to suppress her mixed emotions. Watching Aaron stay out of the way while Matt checked in at the airline desk touched her in a way she hadn't expected. Not only had Matt come into his own as a musician, but he'd turned into a young man who no longer relied on her or Aaron to steer his course.

When they'd talked after Leslie's wedding, Matt had made it clear that he had to take charge of the decisions that would shape his future. Without saying it in so many words, Sonia understood the time had come for her to step back and make way for Olivia to move to the head of the line of advisors, at least when it came to his career. Sure, she'd always be his mother, but he needed professional guidance now more than ever.

"It's the combination of everything that has me a little…well, not so much sad, but kind of nostalgic," she'd told Aaron last night. In bed, they'd snuggled in each other's arms, finding it difficult to sleep knowing their teenager would fly away without them in the morning.

"I understand," Aaron had said. "I still remember him playing at Karen Baldwin's wedding, when he called it his first 'wedding gig'."

"And we can't forget Chicago," Sonia had added, knowing that event, more than any other, had made an impression on Aaron. He'd finally allowed it to sink in that Matt's life would never mirror theirs, that his path was unique, its twists and turns shaped by his gift.

Now, looking at Aaron and Matt going through the check-in routine, her heart filled with joy over how well they'd come through the hard days when Matt barely spoke to her, and even less to Aaron. When she caught Aaron watching her, she grinned self-consciously, knowing she wore her pride on her face.

Finished at the counter, they rejoined her. Matt carried his cello, drawing attention from others in the crowd. With his cello case looking like an extension of himself, he'd always stand out in a crowd, Sonia thought.

Matt glanced at his watch and shook his head. "I told you we'd have time to kill."

"You might say we're a bit early," Aaron said, adding, "but you can never be too early for a flight."

It went unsaid that they'd deliberately allowed extra time for all the added security. Yes, it was a difficult time to travel, and the garden attendance had dropped off dramatically in the last few weeks. Thankfully, Aaron agreed that they'd not allow the specter of 9-11 to immobilize them or keep them frightened all the time. And Matt himself had brought it up, giving voice to what was on all their minds. But, he'd shrugged off the idea of making other arrangements, even remarking that statistically, driving to Springfield posed more danger than flying.

"So what are you two going to do the rest of the day?" Matt asked.

"We're celebrating our kid's big day," Aaron said. "We're going out for an early lunch and gloat. By the time we're done, even we won't be able to stand ourselves."

"Stop, stop," Sonia said through her laughter. "Do you hear what he said, Matt? This is the effect you have on us."

Aaron slipped his arm across her shoulders. "Somehow, though, we'll get by without you. This is only a preview of next year when you're off to Julliard, or some other equally impressive place."

"You two are so busy, you'll hardly notice I'm gone," Matt said. He glanced at the security line and fidgeted with the handle on his cello case. "I suppose I should get over there."

Maybe he's a bit nervous after all.

"We'll say goodbye here, Matt," Aaron said, opening his arms for the first hug.

"I'm so proud of you," Sonia whispered when she wrapped both arms around him and put her mouth close to Matt's ear. "I know this is going to be a wonderful experience. And you've earned it."

When she let him go, Matt nodded and then started toward the line. About halfway there, he turned his upper body around and waved, but kept walking.

Sonia kept her eyes on her son, hoping he'd turn around one more time. Aaron made that happen when he called out a reminder to Matt to let them know when he'd settled in. Matt said something back, but Sonia couldn't quite catch it.

"What did he say?" Sonia asked.

Aaron touched her cheek with his fingertips. "He thanked you, Sonia, for everything."

She quickly skimmed away the sudden tears pooling in her eyes. She opened her mouth, hoping words would form, but they didn't.

"Let's watch by the glass," Aaron said. "I know it's still a long wait, but…"

Sun streamed into the observation area, offering a panoramic view of the runways and the woods and fields beyond them. "Just look at that blue sky," she said. "What a perfect day."

* * *

December 2006

Aaron poked his head through Katherine's open office door, and although she was busy at her computer, he welcomed her expectant look. He leaned against the doorjamb trying to appear casual and keep things light. "Why don't we act like normal people and leave the office at a reasonable time, say five o'clock? Let's have a drink and then get some dinner."

Her quick "okay" lacked enthusiasm. It didn't take a genius to figure out why her tone cooled the atmosphere. She'd likely had it with his edgy moods and worse, his retreat into his shell. Over the past weeks he'd shut out the rest of the world and spent his evenings cooped up in his apartment. But that morning, as he stood in the shower under a stream of hot water, he resolved—again—to live for the future.

During his first months in Chicago he'd built an optimistic façade and convinced himself that it was possible to leave the past behind, even telling Sonia in a letter that he'd likely never return to Lady's River. That's the mindset he'd hung onto when he'd first met Katherine, the lead attorney on his first case at

Weintraub, Smith & Lincoln.

No man could have missed the beauty of her soft brown eyes and her womanly small frame. But her sharp mind had held his attention. He soon discovered that they filled in the blanks of each other's ideas, and that's what led to late dinners and weekends at the office. His life in Lady's River soon blurred into a collage of images and feelings he forced into a container that he tucked into the back of his mind. He'd entertained the notion that he could start another family. He'd never forget Matt, but maybe, just maybe, he could start over for real.

Back then, he'd still felt raw bitterness over the way Sonia so easily let him go. Still, when he'd told Katherine why he'd left Lady's River, he'd taken care not to pile on more than half the blame on Sonia. Katherine herself had been through a divorce four years earlier, so she understood the pain of a breakup. No wonder their professional friendship had taken a romantic turn, although she'd made it clear having a child at age 40 was not, as she put it, on her radar screen. He accepted that with his eyes wide open. Lately, though, his end of their romantic bargain needed repairs. For over a month, he'd avoided Katherine, and that had to stop. He couldn't expect her to put up with his moods indefinitely.

That afternoon when they left the office, he suggested they go to Katherine's favorite sushi bar. He'd hailed a cab and twenty minutes later, they were settled in a corner booth and had given their order to the waiter. Aaron liked that about the quick pace of his downtown life.

"So, you seem to be in a good mood," Katherine

commented.

"Better than my evil twin, the withdrawn, silent guy?" he joked.

She reached across the table and patted his hand. "I know you've been having a hard time. But for tonight, let's talk about other things."

Good idea. He started by asking about the aftermath of the cancer fundraising event. As an escort, Aaron thought he'd done okay, and only he knew how much effort it had taken to be attentive and friendly to the dozens of people Katherine introduced him to. His grief over losing Artie Silverman had darkened everything. He'd downplayed his connection to the celebrity lawyer because it helped him keep his sadness to himself.

"Are you going to chair the committee again?" he asked.

She looked past him and out into the restaurant. "I'm not sure. It depends."

On me. No need to ask. They'd agreed to talk about moving in together after the first of the year.

The waiter brought their platters, saving him the need to respond. Then Katherine changed the subject to movies she wanted to see and filled him in on some office gossip. Over coffee, she asked him if he'd like to go back to her apartment. Without over thinking it, he agreed.

When they walked outside, the light snow blew in frenzied circles in the blustery wind. By the time their taxi pulled up to her building on south Michigan Avenue, white patches were sticking to the sidewalk.

"This weather makes me glad I live close to the office," Katherine said with a mock shiver as she unlocked the door to her loft.

"Snow gives the city a peaceful feeling, though," he said, aware that he sounded wistful.

"I'm glad somebody likes it," Katherine remarked.

They tossed their coats on a chair and Katherine went straight to the kitchen area in the open loft space and took two wine glasses out of a cabinet. She handed him a bottle of Chardonnay and a corkscrew, and while he opened it, she lit tea candles in matching silver holders on the two end tables.

"You weren't yourself at Thanksgiving, but you're less edgy now," she said from the living room.

He nodded, but didn't look up while he filled their glasses. He avoided looking her in the eye when he carried them to the couch.

She smiled brightly. "And now we're just a few weeks from Christmas."

"So we are." Why did she have to bring up the holiday? Even the candles she'd lit smelled like pine trees…sort of. No artificial scent ever came close to the real thing.

He sat down and gulped a mouthful of wine.

"Now that you're back to your old self, I'd like to talk about making plans for Christmas week."

His jaw immediately tightened. He'd hoped to have an evening where they avoided conversations about tomorrow or next week or next year. *Stay open, hear her out.*

"The other day I went over to GetAways and asked Judy to put together some ideas for holiday trips." She reached to the shelf under the end table and pulled out a fat manila envelope.

Talking to Judy made sense, since the firm worked with GetAways for business travel. Irrationally, it felt as if Katherine had gone behind his back, tricked him in some way to do something he wasn't ready for. His heart pounded hard and he took a deep breath in hopes of stopping the rising panic. Besides, theoretically, escaping the cold of the Midwest during the holidays should appeal to him. He needed a second or two to adjust, that's all.

Her face brightened as she fanned the brochures across the coffee table. "See? We could get a villa in the Virgin Islands or Jamaica—or, look—visit one of the less crowded islands in the Bahamas. We can have Christmas dinner with my family and then leave that night, or the next day. We could stay through New Year's."

His head buzzed as she pointed to white beaches and the aqua and turquoise sea. Shapely women in bikinis and straw hats and muscled, tan men lounged around private pools. Message received, he thought. Luxurious surroundings and lazy days and rum drinks, all for the asking. The literal price tag didn't matter, not to him, not to Katherine.

He nodded vigorously and mumbled some words about how great it looked. Why was it so hard to breathe?

"So, what do you think? We still have time to book a place."

The room moved in a circle, not so fast to make him dizzy, but enough to bring on a bout of nausea. He managed to croak out the words, "I can't do this," before his throat closed.

His mind raced back to the night Sonia had told him she was pregnant and he'd fled to the men's room. He'd felt queasy and gripped the counter to regain his balance. But within minutes, he was back at the table shocking Sonia by bringing up marriage. Over two decades ago, he'd married a woman he'd liked and admired, but then fortune shined on him and they fell in love. Sonia had been his second chance. Deep down, Aaron knew that kind of magical good luck wouldn't—couldn't—happen again.

Turning to face Katherine, he hoped he could find the right words to make her understand.

Too late.

Using both hands, she pushed the brochures into a single pile and stuffed them back into the envelope. "I think you should go now, Aaron." She rose and walked across the room.

"Katherine, please, I need to explain…" He didn't know where to pick up again, except to say he was sorry. He bumped his knee hard on the edge of the coffee table on the way to his feet. He winced and rubbed the wounded spot, but then took a few steps toward her. She held up her hand to keep him back.

"I decided to give this one more chance," she said. "During the first couple of weeks after the trip to Pearson Pond I ignored the way you distanced yourself. You needed space, and that seemed reasonable. Seeing Sonia one last time had to be difficult—even traumatic. I tried to respect your need to sort things out," she scoffed cynically. "For all the good it did me."

"I thought that's what I needed, too," Aaron said, "and that it was only a matter of time before I could find my center again…or some such thing." He nervously ran his hand through his hair. "I know that sounds like a cliché."

She shook her head. "The way you acted at

Thanksgiving gave me a huge clue," she said through clenched teeth. "All your bluster about my brother needing to mind his own business, but a man who's in love with you doesn't resent questions about the future."

He opened his mouth to argue, but he could think of no words to contradict her. "I haven't been very good at masking what was going on with me. You deserve a lot better than what I can give you."

"You bet I do. When you first came to the firm, you were quiet, even withdrawn, but when we started going out I saw your lively, funny side. I thought you were making a life here, a life with me." She turned away. "And I was dumb enough to think we wanted the same things."

She brushed past him to pick up their still half-full glasses off the coffee table. She carried them to the sink, and with her back to him, she dumped out the wine in his glass and turned on the faucet.

"This was my mistake, not yours," he said, extending his arms as if pleading with her to understand. "I led you to believe that I could move forward, despite the hole in my heart over losing my son. And I fooled *myself* into thinking I was over my past…my life before Matt died."

With the water still running, she spun around to face him. "Go ahead and tell me the truth. You're still in love with your *ex*-wife."

He flinched at her uncharacteristic harsh tone. "She's not just any woman. I was married to her for twenty years."

"But you divorced her, and then you acted like a man who was free to love someone else. *That* was your lie." She turned away again, rinsed the empty glass and grabbed a towel.

He waited to speak until she faced him again. "I never intended to hurt you, Katherine."

She swatted the towel in his direction. "Damn you, that's hardly the point."

He lifted his coat off the chair. "I screwed up. All I can do is apologize and hope you'll eventually be able to forgive me."

"Let me tell you something," she said, walking toward him, "you should either try to get Sonia back or take time to really get over her. Stop pretending you're available when you're not. It's a lousy thing to do to someone—not just to me, but to the next woman you meet and the one after that."

On the defensive, he tried to think of more words that would explain his actions, but he didn't fully understand them himself. "What about work? I mean—"

"You mean post-breakup office behavior?"

"I suppose that's what I mean."

"Don't worry about it. I'm a big girl. I can handle it."

She'd spit out the words. He'd never known her to be so cold.

"From here on out, Aaron, we're professional friends." She took the few steps back to the kitchen and the next sound he heard was the clang of the corkscrew landing on top of other utensils in the drawer.

He wanted to wish her well, but anything he said would only sound empty and lame. Besides, she wasn't listening. He let himself out. Anxious to the get into the open air, he bypassed the elevator and hurried down the four flights of stairs to the lobby and through the heavy brass and wooden door to the street.

The muscles in his throat relaxed, despite the cold night air. He leaned against the side of the building and lifted his face to let the cold flakes land on his skin. In the force of the wind the snow skimmed the surface of the street in swirling clouds of white. *Was it snowing in Lady's River? Would the path from the house to the garden be covered by morning?*

He walked north, checking behind him every few seconds for empty cabs. Finally abandoning that idea, he thrust his bare hands in his pockets and decided to walk the couple of miles instead. If it had been summer, he would have headed to the rose garden in Grant Park. Sometimes he drifted that way, as if following an instinct to find one of the many garden oases in the city.

When he crossed the bridge over the river, the white lights circling the branches of the trees along Michigan Avenue sparkled in the falling snow. No wonder they called this The Magnificent Mile. Last December, he and Katherine had gone up one side of the street and down the other, enjoying the sight of bundled-up people weighed down with shopping bags. Now he felt lonely—and guilty. With his shoulders drooping, he must look like an old man. Self-pity was such an ugly creature. He abruptly stopped walking to straighten up.

Back at the dedication at Pearson Pond, Sonia had reminded him about second chances. Beautiful and smart, Katherine deserved her second chance. He'd had his in Sonia, and he'd used it up. Maybe, in the end, he'd thrown it away. But he needed to figure this out once and for all.

Part IV

18

October 2001

She wanted—demanded—that some part of her, a hand, a shoulder, a leg, touched him at all times. That need started the moment the phone began ringing and they turned on the TV to hear the news.

At first, Aaron held her close and offered to go to Pearson Pond alone. Cal would take him, he said, and help do whatever needed to be done about Matt. He'd kept his voice low, barely above a whisper. Sonia could stay at home with Dottie, he suggested, so she wouldn't be alone. And besides, was there any point to them both going?

No, no, no, she'd said, shaking her head with all the strength she had. Absolutely not. She had to go to Pearson Pond with Aaron. *But why?* Certainly not to make what happened more real to her. Sonia didn't feel a sense of disbelief. She hung on to what the TV reporters and the airline representative said, and she knew it was true. Aaron tried to coax her into turning the television off, but she'd insisted on watching. And if Aaron left for Pearson Pond without her, she wouldn't be able to touch him.

Pulling back from his embrace, she'd stroked his cheek. "No, I have to go. I don't want to be without you, not even for a second. We shouldn't be apart."

"I understand," he said, his gray eyes glistening with tears. "I don't want to be without you, either."

Hand in hand, they'd climbed the stairs to gather a few things. Toothbrushes, a change of clothes, extra shoes. Sonia had seen Aaron grab a 3 x 5 picture of Matt off the dresser and slip it into his pocket. At the last minute, he'd gone back for their rain jackets.

"It's true what people say about shock," she told Dottie after she'd climbed into the backseat of Cal's van. "It protects you. I'm numb right now, but some part of me knows that if my feelings were turned loose, I'd go mad. It's as if I can hear a little voice telling me not to think too far ahead."

"I know," Dottie said, twisting around in the front seat so she could look at her.

Sonia nodded toward Cal and Aaron, who stood close together outside the van. "What are they talking about?"

"They're figuring out the best route to take," Dottie said, clearing her throat. "They want to avoid Milwaukee traffic."

"Oh."

"It's going to be rush hour soon," Dottie added.

"Aaron said the airline representative told him where we can stay when we get to Pearson Pond." For a second, Sonia was confused. Why would they stay in some strange town?

"Yes," Dottie said quietly. "Sonia…I don't know what to say. I'm so sorry…my heart…"

Sonia nodded at Dottie, and then stared at Aaron

and Cal, still outside the van. "I wish they'd hurry. We need to get this first part over with." She glanced at Dottie, whose eyes brimmed with tears. "I want it done with so that I can come back home and think. Those people from the airline...they don't know Matt. They don't know who he is."

Dottie turned away, but not before Sonia saw her wiping away tears with the back of her hand.

After the two men climbed into the van, Cal backed down the driveway and Aaron gripped her hand and lifted it to his lips before letting their clasped hands rest on his thigh. As they turned to head down the street, Sonia pointed out the window to a woman standing alone across from the house. "There's Martha Samuelson, the reporter," she said. "We should probably stop and talk to her."

"I suppose," Aaron said flatly, "but I can't right now."

Sonia grabbed the door handle, but then let it go.

"I'll go," Dottie said, already halfway out of the van.

Sonia stared at Dottie and Martha, who skimmed tears off her cheeks as Dottie's mouth moved and her hands gestured. Feeling dizzy in the hot, stuffy car, Sonia wiped sweat off her upper lip. Hadn't the breeze been cool that morning? Hadn't they commented on that in the airport? A typically crisp October day, with a clear blue sky.

Martha caught her eye through the window and lifted her hand in a weak wave. Sonia returned the gesture.

"What did you say?" she asked when Dottie got back into the van.

"Not much. I told her how he happened to be on that plane…you know…where he was going. I hope that was okay."

She and Aaron both nodded.

No one spoke again as they headed out of town. Knowing she drifted into dangerous waters, Sonia did a rerun of what they'd done that day, from the moment she'd thrown the sheet back and jumped out of bed. She'd stretched her arms over her head and grinned at Aaron. Such a big day. And she'd swelled with pride when she'd stared at the look-alike father and son at the check-in counter at the airport.

Self-assured and confident, Matt had given her a final indulgent grin before he disappeared. And he thanked her, too, another sign that he'd grown up. Then, after going out for a long, festive lunch, they'd gone home, intending to enjoy a day off, and maybe even walk down to their spot by the river.

Aaron got the call on his cell phone from Cal, who told him to turn on the TV. That moment everything changed. Aaron called the airline, and confirmed the truth. Then, while Sonia sat staring at the TV screen, he talked to Dottie and now they were in the van driving to a town she'd never heard of.

"He didn't suffer," she said to no one in particular, looking out the window as they passed through farm country with silver and blue silos rising on the horizon. Fall reds and golds still brightened a few spots, but a stiff wind a couple of days before had left many trees nearly bare.

"No, it happened fast," Aaron whispered. "We don't *ever* have to worry that he suffered."

In the front seat, Dottie and Cal exchanged a quick

glance, but stayed silent.

That's when it struck her that she and Aaron had instantly turned into people no one knew how to talk to. "For a while, people will be a little afraid of us," she said, immediately regretting that she gave voice to her passing thought.

"What do you mean?" Aaron asked.

"People won't know what to say, so they'll be afraid to say anything. Like they're nervous around us, or something."

"I've felt that way around clients," Aaron said sadly, "but I never imagined it happening to me...to us."

Cal looked at them through the rearview mirror and nodded.

He's counting his own live children, taking an inventory, Sonia thought, and feeling grateful that his kids are alive.

She rested her head on the back of the seat and closed her eyes. When Aaron let go of her hand and put his arm around her, she let her head fall onto his shoulder. He brushed his cheek over her hair.

Later, when Cal drove off an exit ramp and pulled into a gas station, she robotically followed Dottie into the restroom.

"I can't believe I'm doing this," she said, pulling out her makeup bag. "I'm putting on lipstick. My lips are so dry."

"Mine, too," Dottie said. "Stress does that."

"Where's Matt now?" she asked suddenly, as if she could go to him once she knew where to look.

She glanced down at Dottie's fingers as they circled her wrist.

"We're going there now, Sonia. He's in Pearson

Pond."

She let out a sharp, too loud laugh. "No, I don't
mean that Matt. I mean the real Matt, the one who plays
the cello and isn't going to grow old. Or even grow up."

Again, she felt the pressure of Dottie's hand.

"I don't know. I wish I did."

"Maybe he's with his grandparents," Sonia said,
feeling a lift of hope. "All four of them."

"Maybe." Dottie glanced away. "We better go."

Sonia turned, but lost her balance and grabbed the
edge of the towel dispenser.

"You need to eat something, Sonia." Dottie nodded
toward the door. "I'll pick up some meal bars."

"Okay." She had to be strong for Aaron, and that
meant staying on her feet, not falling over in a gas
station restroom. "Aaron should eat, too."

Dottie opened the door, and then cupped her elbow
to guide her out.

Aaron stood waiting by the entrance. Sonia saw his
pinched features relax into relief. "I was getting
concerned about you."

"I was putting on lipstick," she said.

His face was blank, as if he hadn't understood her.

"We need to eat, so Dottie is buying something. I
forget what."

"That's fine, sweetheart. Let's go back to the van."

"How much farther is it?"

Aaron frowned. "I'm not sure. Cal told me, but it
slipped my mind. Maybe another two or three hours."

Back in the van, Sonia drank water from the plastic
bottle Dottie handed her to wash down a bar that tasted
vaguely like oatmeal and nuts.

"You don't have to leave town soon, do you?" she

asked Aaron.

"Of course not." Aaron spoke in the same low voice he'd been using for hours. He laced his fingers with hers. "We'll get through this together."

"We can bury him in the garden," she said, suddenly envisioning the tall obelisk that would mark his grave. All their visitors would see it.

Aaron's body stiffened. "Let's talk about that later."

She brushed away the tears threatening to spill down her cheeks. No tears, not yet. Better to keep her mind busy designing the stone monument to Matt. They'd create something beautiful and everyone would learn about their gifted, incredible son.

Seeing the sign broke into her thoughts. *Welcome to Pearson Pond.* "No, no," she said, her voice cracking. Choking on a sob she struggled to stifle, she covered her eyes with her hands and bent forward. The damned seatbelt held her back. She reached to her side, fumbling to release it, desperate to free herself.

Aaron touched her back and then she felt his arms drawing her to him and gently rocking her as she buried her face in his shoulder. And the tears finally flowed.

* * *

January 2002

Aaron found her in Matt's room, sitting in a chair in front of the row of casement windows. But she wasn't looking out at the snow-covered branches of the trees in the backyard. From what he could tell, all her attention was focused on the stacks of music at her feet. When she didn't raise her head to acknowledge him at the door, he realized she was far off in another world and hadn't heard him come up the stairs.

"Sonia?" He kept his voice soft so as not to startle her.

She looked up and smiled faintly. "Hi. I didn't hear you come in."

"I could tell. Uh, what are you doing?" Maybe she was finally going through Matt's things. So far she'd refused his offer to help, making it clear that she'd control what happened to Matt's room.

Sonia worried him for many reasons, including her shrinking interest in the garden, always a source of joy and satisfaction with her life. Now, with the holiday garden events behind her, she spent more time at home. But doing what? He didn't know.

A thoughtful expression crossed her face. "You remember Kenny, don't you? I guess I should call him Ken, now that he's practically an adult."

"Sure, I remember him," Aaron said, recalling Matt's old Cub Scout pal, a skinny kid perpetually stuck in an awkward stage.

"He called earlier and asked if he could stop by with a couple of friends—Matt's friends." She clutched a sheaf of sheet music to her chest and hunched her shoulders, as if drawing herself in. "Ken said they wanted to see how we were doing, but I think they wanted to stop by—to be here, where Matt lived."

She quickly scanned the room. "I brought them up to see if there was something of Matt's they'd like to have. You know, a photograph or a book or CD. I gave one of the kids Matt's school jacket—it fit him perfectly."

"Good," he said. So far, going through the room had yielded a couple of bags of clothing Aaron had dropped off at the homeless shelter just before Christmas, but after that, the room remained untouched.

"His friends are so young," he said with a sigh. "This is a terrible thing to go through when you're a teenager and still believe you're invincible."

She nodded sadly. "By the way, did he ever mention a girl named Tessa to you? She came along with the three boys."

Aaron shuffled through memories of Matt's classmates and tried to sort them out. "The name sounds familiar. Maybe I met her at the memorial. What about her?"

"I think Matt had special feelings for her. It was the way Kenny introduced her, not saying as much in so many words, but she studied everything in the room—in a sad kind of way."

Aaron exhaled, hoping to breathe away the pressure in his chest before it built into a crushing weight over his heart. But the things Matt would miss…a special girl, getting married, having kids of his own some day. Aaron hadn't even known about her. "He never said anything to you about a girl?"

Sonia shook her head. "He was even more private about his friends when he went back to his music and took charge of his own direction."

When she rose from the chair he opened his arms and she stepped into them. "He went out with groups of kids," Aaron said, "but at his age, of course there'd be someone special."

"She's pretty in a fresh, young way, and has lovely long black hair," Sonia said. "It hurt me to see her glance around, as if taking it all in quickly. She mentioned hearing him play at the grand opening of the new library. Do you remember that?"

Aaron remembered the afternoon well. Matt played with two other musicians from the school orchestra. Aaron still remembered Matt's big smile when the trio broke into a few minutes of improvisation, literally jazzing up Mozart.

Playing as one musician in a trio had been relatively new for Matt, because he hadn't participated in the school's music programs. The orchestra teacher, a guy with a permanently sour expression, considered Matt so advanced that he bluntly said he didn't want to deal with him. But Olivia had taught him collaboration, which helped allay Aaron's fear that the little prodigy might develop too much swagger. Oh, the dumb things he'd wasted time fretting over.

He couldn't stop thinking about the girl, but didn't want to say as much for fear of upsetting Sonia even more. Sometimes she appeared sturdy and resilient, but on other days, slow, tentative steps and hunched shoulders replaced her familiar long, sure strides. He wouldn't have called her fragile so much as unpredictable. In the middle of a conversation, she might lose track of her words, as if the qualities of focus and concentration he'd admired for years had taken to periodically hiding. But who was he to talk? He never knew how he'd feel from one second to the next.

"Did you give Tessa something of Matt's?" Aaron asked.

"I gave her one of the CDs he made at the end of the summer. And then she picked out some sheet music."

"That sounds about right. Those are characteristic things. They're all about Matt."

She stepped back and caressed his cheek.

"Let's go out to dinner," he suggested. "It's time we got out."

She looked back over her shoulder at the pile of music and didn't immediately answer, but finally, she looked into his eyes and nodded. She stepped away from him and glanced down at her gray sweater and slacks. "I'll go change into something more...I don't know...colorful."

He went downstairs to wait for her in the kitchen. When she joined him, she'd changed into a beige skirt and boots, and a bright red sweater he and Matt had given her for her birthday a couple of years before. She'd have looked like her old self, but for the strain in her face.

"Is the River's Bend Café okay?" he asked on the way to the car.

"Sure," she said, but looked away.

"We could go somewhere else if..." If what? He didn't know.

"No, it's fine. There's always a first time. I mean, we haven't been out for all these weeks."

True. In the days immediately following the memorial Sonia had thrown herself into overseeing the preparations for the Light Up the Holidays festival. Last January, she and Dottie had put into motion their plan to make the 2001 event the most spectacular light show in the garden's history. Somehow, they'd pulled it off. When she had talked to him about it, his mind drifted and her words were collections of sounds without meaning. Sometimes he'd have to shake himself alert, as if he'd been caught sleepwalking and didn't know where he was.

Many pairs of eyes watched as they followed the

hostess to an empty table in the café. Because of the garden and Matt's music and then the tragedy of his death, Aaron and Sonia were recognizable in town. For all he knew, some of the diners in the café that night were among those in Lady's River who had sent condolence cards. He and Sonia had written thank you notes to every person. At first Aaron felt odd writing to people whose names sounded familiar but whose faces he couldn't call up in his memory. Yet, when the last card was mailed, he'd felt anxious, even empty. What would fill the void?

"Everyone stared at us all the way to the table," Sonia whispered when they sat down, "and with eyes filled with pity."

"I noticed people watching us, but they know who we are, Sonia. Of course they'd sympathize."

"It's not easy to ignore those sad expressions on their faces," she said, looking down into her lap.

"It won't be long before everyone will get used to seeing us around town again," he said, "and what happened will recede into the background…for them."

"You sound so sure."

What had he said to bring on such a cold tone? "What is it?"

Still not looking at him, she opened the menu and kept her eyes on it. "Nothing, it's not you, it's me. I pity myself and I pity you. But still, I hate knowing all these people see us as the poor couple who lost their only child."

He reached out to take her hand. "Look at me, Sonia. You haven't looked at me since we sat down."

"I'm sorry. Maybe this was a bad idea." When she shifted her gaze from the menu to him, he saw her struggle to hold back tears.

"Do you want to leave? We can get up and walk out of here right now."

"No, this café is our regular place and I want to be here. Besides, you're right. It's my problem. People tell me this sort of thing gets easier with time."

He searched for the right words. "But, no matter how bad we feel, we keep making it through another twenty-four hours. Let's just try to enjoy this one normal thing. Going out for dinner—being together."

"Okay, then," she said with conviction, "let's order some wine."

He squeezed her hand and held her gaze, enjoying the familiar affection in her eyes. He picked up the wine list and they settled on a Lady's River merlot.

After ordering their dinners, Sonia asked him about the firm and his new cases. Consciously avoiding any mention of what occupied most of his free time, Aaron gave Sonia short answers and then shifted the subject to the spring programs in the garden.

No matter what anyone else said in the early investigations, Aaron hadn't ruled out the possibility that someone had sabotaged the plane, intentionally making it fall out of the sky and crash on a soybean field in Illinois. He'd mentioned his suspicions to Sonia a few times, but her alarmed expression put him off and he feared upsetting her when he couldn't prove his theory.

The last time he'd tried to broach the subject of sabotage, she'd interrupted him mid-sentence to point out that the lawyer hired by the newly formed Unity Flight Family Group, made up of relatives and friends of those lost, believed the evidence pointed away from terrorism or any form of sabotage. With that, Aaron decided that until he had a specific list of points to argue, he'd keep his research to himself.

"By the way," she said, "I've been in touch with Madge Watanabe at Fitzgerald College. Remember? She oversees endowments. I told her we were going ahead with the scholarship in Matt's name."

"Good. I'm glad we're doing that," he said, surprised by the lift that gave him. "Matt would want that—and so would our parents."

"She'll make the announcement at their graduation ceremony in May." She paused and took a breath. "Madge said she hoped we would come."

He nodded. Yes, of course they would be there.

Sonia stared out into the restaurant, as if her mind had moved on to other things. When she spoke, it was about the meditation garden she planned in memory of Matt.

He listened, but then his mind dipped back into his own thoughts and got stuck on one word, *blame.* The scholarship, the meditation garden, all well and good, but what—or who—had killed their son?

"Aaron?"

He snapped back into the present.

"You seemed to wander away, as if you stopped listening to me."

The disappointment in her voice hurt him. "I'm sorry. I do that a lot lately."

She smacked her lips. "Me, too. What were you thinking about?"

He waited to speak until the approaching waiter set a basket of hot bread and plates in front of them and left.

He picked up his knife, but then put it back down. "I don't care what the lawyers and the government agencies, even the FBI says, I'm not ruling out sabotage—terrorism. That's what I was thinking about."

When she glanced down and smoothed her long fingers over the napkin across her lap, she transmitted silent disapproval. Not looking at him bought her time to think about a response.

"If that theory is still on your mind, Aaron, then help me to understand why."

Did she hear herself? Her patronizing tone came through loud and clear. "You sound like you're trying to placate an incoherent child," he snapped.

She settled back in the chair and dropped her arms to her sides. "What am I to do? Just shut up and go along without asking questions? You know me better than that. If you believe this…other situation…is a possibility, I would *never* try to stop you from investigating. But I'm struggling to understand."

She couldn't even say the words—terrorism, sabotage. "You don't approve. I'm a lone voice in the wilderness and you've closed your mind." He hesitated, but then sputtered out words he hated to say. "You don't trust my instincts."

"It's not a matter of trust." She nervously rolled the edge of the napkin in her lap.

"Really? Then what is it about?"

"Facts," she blurted.

He threw back his head and laughed. "Ah, I see. You're convinced it was a mechanical failure, a maintenance issue, because that's what everyone else involved says. You accept the conclusion—an early conclusion, mind you—that our son died because someone carelessly failed to note a flaw in a wing fastening. Are those the so-called facts you're talking about?"

She glanced away for just a second. He knew why, and it had nothing to do with the facts. No, the word he used had upset her. *Careless*. She'd never stopped her offhand remarks about the way they'd brought Matt into the world. Now she couldn't quite grasp that a careless mistake could have taken him away. He struggled with the irony of it himself.

She rested one elbow on the table and cupped her chin in her palm. "I'll hear you out."

An argument in a restaurant was the last thing he wanted. Sonia's generous spirit, her willingness to listen to his ideas had been a constant in his life. But if his suspicions meant being out of step with the person he loved most in the world, he'd learn to live with that. He'd have to.

"I'm going to Washington in a few weeks and while I'm there, I'm seeing Senator Robbins. She's chairing the subcommittee that's holding hearings on a series of recent industrial accidents whose causes aren't easily identified. Her committee is bringing in expert witnesses to examine the data. Sabotage can be subtle and often overlooked—and originate deep within an organization."

Sonia nodded, but her interested expression looked forced, and worse, it masked the concern written all over her face.

"I didn't know you were going to Washington."

"I'm going to attend a board meeting of the Safe Play Council. I arranged a meeting with Senator Robbins because I'll be in town anyway."

She cleared her throat. "You have a trip planned that I don't even know about. Or, did you tell me and I forgot? Either way, that bothers me more than I can say. And I've got things on my mind, too, but I don't want to bring them up now, not when we're finally out by ourselves trying to live like a normal couple." She took a sip of her wine, and then another. "As if we'll ever be that again."

How could he argue? Eventually, they'd create a *new* normal. Small consolation.

"I was going to tell you about the trip. It's not a secret, but it slipped my mind until now."

"It seems that we're both so tired we hardly talk at all." She pursed her lips. "But, I don't want to lose you."

"*What?*"

She responded with a helpless shrug. "I've read about parents breaking up when they lose a child. They go off in different directions. Sometimes they blame each other for what happened."

"But we don't blame each other."

"Not directly."

That felt like a warning punch in his gut. "What does *that* mean?"

"Nothing. Forget I said anything." She stared thoughtfully into space. "Maybe it's that I really blame myself. Some days I'm consumed by speculation. What would have happened if I hadn't encouraged Matt to take his music seriously? He probably wouldn't have been on the plane."

The pain in her voice cut deep into his heart. "But Sonia, of course, it's natural that we'd question every decision we made. I wish I'd said no to the out-of-state trip. I wished I insisted that Matt finish his senior year before going off alone, even for such a valuable program. But we agreed—with equal conviction—that

Matt was ready for this kind of intensive study, and without your direction. He needed autonomy. His senior advisor even endorsed the trip."

His words hadn't come out exactly as he'd meant them. He gathered his thoughts while the waiter put plates of the café's special of the night, home-style pot roast, in front of them.

"I usually like this," Sonia said, staring at the steaming food, "but I'm not sure I can eat."

Already slim, Sonia had lost weight in the last several weeks. He'd noticed it, and Dottie had remarked on it, too. He forced himself to pick up his fork. "Please, Sonia, you need to eat, and so do I. Let's drop the subject."

She tightened her mouth, but a second later, she looked up and smiled. For a moment his heart lightened. Her lovely smile gave him hope that the woman he adored was still there, somewhere inside her.

19

March 2002

*T*he short winter days had finally lengthened. What a relief. Aaron hoped the extra light would bring about an internal shift. He and Sonia had done little more than slog through the winter.

He sat at his desk in his office at the firm on a quiet Saturday afternoon, again poring over a stack of aviation accident reports. Others in the Unity Flight Family Group were willing to blindly accept statements by the FBI and other agencies that turned up no signs of sabotage. Aaron was the lone holdout. He clung to his skepticism and resolved to follow his instincts as he sifted through evidence. He owed that much to Matt— and to the others who'd died that day. If the stones he rolled over turned up nothing, then so be it, he'd accept that. But what did it hurt to dig deeper to find more stones?

Hard to believe, but only a few months had passed since the afternoon he'd stood with Cal and stared at the wreckage on the field. He'd closed his eyes and silently promised Matt that he'd find out the truth, no matter how long it took. What had happened to cause the plane to break apart? Yes, the main fuselage remained partially intact, gleaming unnaturally bright under the autumn sun. All around it, unidentifiable objects and pieces of metal and burned fabric lay scattered across the ground, where fire had charred the field. Investigating agencies had already started their work of piecing together the plane—and the facts—by the time he and Cal arrived.

They had seen the early press conferences on local and cable television, although he found them almost too hard to bear. With crossed arms held tightly against her chest, Sonia stubbornly insisted that she had to hear every word of the reports, plus all the speculative chatter from the talking heads debating the tragedy. Dottie had tried to coax her away, but she'd refused to budge from the end of the bed where she could see the TV screen clearly. "I don't know why I can't turn it off," she'd said, "but leave me alone...please. I *need* to watch it."

Aaron rubbed his tired, sore eyes, as if wiping out the memory of those first hours and days. Then he adjusted the desk lamp to cast more light on the pages. Too often, Aaron had seen investigations follow a trail defined by early assumptions and premature conclusions. Things that didn't fit tossed aside and facts molded to fit neat theories. Most of his cases involved events that others considered accidents. But as Artie often pointed out, no one liked to come right out and call them careless events—Artie had even coined the term, "care-less-i-dents."

In the aftermath of many so-called accidents, Aaron, like Artie before him, usually demonstrated that most were avoidable. Sometimes tragedy followed a split-second lapse, like a driver who looked away for an instant, later dazed and shocked that he'd hit a pedestrian. But just as often, the problem went deeper, and detecting the facts hidden behind the obvious had formed the foundation of his career. With the help of engineers and builders, he'd discovered reasons why a fail-safe switch did in fact, fail, or why a roof or stairway collapsed. Immersed in looking for the story beneath the lapses and overlooked details, Aaron sniffed out missing links between causes and effects. Often, it wasn't carelessness at all, but deliberate actions like cutting a corner here to save a few dollars or ignoring a warning sign there and calling it an anomaly.

He closed the file folder and leaned back in his chair. The snow had stopped and the late afternoon light had given way to dusk. He should leave all these files behind and go home. But that morning, he and Sonia shared tense, awkward moments—again—when he'd said he had work to do at the office.

"I still believe they dismissed the possibility of sabotage way too soon," he'd said, leaning against the sink with a mug of coffee in his hand. "Just because it isn't obvious that doesn't mean evidence is lacking—if a person is willing to dig for it. And I am. I downloaded more aviation safety reports and I need to go to the office to review them." He'd stared out the window and watched the March snowfall obscure the view of the trees lining the creek and the fields beyond.

"Today? I arranged my schedule to be home today because I thought you'd be here." Her mouth had tightened in anger, but her eyes looked desperate. "Why didn't you tell me last night?"

Because I feared this reaction. "I'm sorry," he responded, "but Chuck's coming in, too, to work on the Texas case. That aside, I'm not ready to accept that a mechanical failure caused the…accident. Just because investigators saw no sign of an explosion, that doesn't mean it wasn't sabotage."

"And by sabotage, you mean exactly what?"

"Do I have to explain it again?"

"No, no, I guess not." She stared at her feet. "I've tried to understand, Aaron, but with so many agencies looking into this, and ruling out…terro…sabotage…I'm not sure why you're still digging into it."

Slamming his empty mug on the counter, he said, "If our son and all those other people were victims of a plot to sabotage that plane, then I'd like to know about it."

She put her palms together and held them in front of her mouth. "Of course, Aaron, but I'm concerned about you, that's all."

He winced at her now familiar patronizing tone. "I'm in touch with a couple of retired aviation investigators. They've agreed to examine a few overlooked factors."

She picked up his empty cup and turned on the water to rinse it, but then scrubbed the inside of the cup with a soapy sponge so vigorously her knuckles turned white. He could feel her worry, but he'd made a promise to Matt and he intended to keep it. Maybe he didn't have an ear that could appreciate the music his son created, but he damn well knew how to piece together facts.

"These retired guys aren't beholden to anyone," he explained, "or obligated to go along with the results of the investigation. I expect that face-to-face meetings in Washington will prove more productive."

She put the cup upside down in the drainer, but didn't turn to look at him. "This is the biggest storm we've had since Christmas."

"I'm sure it will clear by Monday," he said on his

way out of the room. He grabbed his jacket off the hook and went back into the kitchen to say goodbye. She still stood at the sink, and he rested his hands lightly on her shoulders. "This is something I have to do, Sonia."

She nodded. "I know."

Now in his office with the day ending, Aaron gathered the files and put them in the bottom drawer of the cabinet behind the desk. Then he spent the next couple of hours going over Chuck's notes about a case involving a small pharmaceutical firm accused of hiding unfavorable research data. It was right up their alley. Aaron knew Chuck had pointed that out in order to whet Aaron's appetite for a challenge.

He owed Chuck his attention to the case. And he wanted to avoid more awkward moments with Sonia, even if he didn't understand her. She showed more interest in planning memorials to their son than discovering the real reason he'd been taken from them. He didn't get it.

Grabbing his jacket, he locked up the office behind him. The empty streets were still slick with snow, forcing him to concentrate on the drive home. He let himself into the dark house, with the only sound coming from the television in the den. When he went to the doorway, he found Sonia asleep on the couch—again. He ought to gently shake her and wake her up, but she looked so peaceful. No sense disturbing her. Instead, he grabbed a throw out of the basket and covered her with it.

Ever since winter had set in, they'd taken such divergent paths. When was the last time they'd climbed the stairs together and crawled into bed at the same time? How long had it been since they'd shared more than a friendly, ritualistic kiss? Not like the first weeks after they'd lost Matt. They'd clung together, rarely leaving each other's side.

Glancing down at Sonia, hearing her soft breathing, he recalled the night they'd turned to each other in half-sleep, tasting each other's tears on their lips. They'd made love quickly, desperately communicating their bond of shared grief.

Somehow, that urgency had faded, and stiff formality set in, often reminding Aaron of the first days of their marriage.

He climbed into bed and folded his hands under his head. Why had they taken different paths? Maybe Sonia planted the first seeds the day Matt died when she talked about burying him in the garden and building a monument for the public to see. Then, that evening, just outside the hotel entrance, he and Cal passed a reporter giving an on-camera report. Aaron heard him comment that while sabotage hadn't yet been ruled out, nothing indicated that the crash had been caused by an act of terrorism.

"How do they know?" he'd said to Cal, angry at such foolish speculation. "It's absurd to draw that kind of conclusion this early." His anger built like a wave gathering strength, culminating in that moment. And he'd vowed to find out the truth about his son's death.

20

December 2006

Sonia switched back and forth between two cable news stations and an old made-for TV movie she'd seen a couple of times, determined to stay upright and awake. When sleepiness overtook her, she'd head to bed. No more dozing off in the den. This catch-as-catch-can lifestyle she'd sunk into after coming back from Pearson Pond had begun to embarrass her.

First, she'd call the painter in the morning. Even if she reconnected with Ben—maybe even began planning a future with him—she'd still need to fix up the house before she could sell it. And the den was as good a place to start as any.

She picked at the fraying fabric on the arm of the couch. No wonder she felt off balance. She spent most of her time at home in a room she last painted a sophisticated pale gray. But time had darkened the walls, and now they looked drab and sad, begging for new life, like the whole house had the day she first stood in the living room imagining herself living there.

She and Aaron had poured their new-found passion into the house, discovering each other and reveling in the miracle that they'd fallen in love.

No more ancient history. Move on. Maybe selling the place was the only way to make a fresh start. What was she hanging on to it for, anyway? She wouldn't want to live in it with Ben. No, the house belonged to her old life.

Studying the walls in the den, she settled on replacing the gray with a brighter ivory, with the far wall painted in a butterscotch yellow for contrast. Then she'd hang the paintings she'd bought at various art exhibits at the garden over the last few years. Too distracted to decide where to hang them, she'd stashed them in the attic for safekeeping.

Sonia left the couch and knelt on the rug in front of the shelves. Before she could change her mind, she scooped up a row of paperbacks and spread them out in front of her. She needed two piles, one for the keepers and one for the giveaways.

No lingering allowed. If she let the memories grab hold of her, she'd hear echoes of Aaron teasing her about her gritty murder mysteries. But even as she sorted, little snippets popped into her mind and she couldn't order them back into their hiding places.

She sat back on her heels and recalled the day, only a week or two before Matt was born, when she'd flopped into the easy chair to read. She'd ended up resting the open book across her swollen belly and dozed, opening her eyes when she'd felt Aaron's lips on her forehead. "Having sweet dreams?" he'd asked, holding up the book and pointing to the bloody knife on the cover.

She smiled at the memory of his amused eyes.

"Enough of that," she said out loud. Distracting herself by gathering up a second armful of books, she quickly tossed them into one pile or the other.

She was startled when the doorbell chimed. It

chimed a second time before she got to the door and peered through the high leaded glass window to see Ben standing on the stair. He barely smiled when he saw her face.

She opened the door wide and moved aside as she greeted him. "I didn't expect to see you today. Come on in."

"I'm sorry if I've come at a bad time." He stepped inside but stood close to the door.

"No, not at all. I'm just puttering around, thinning the bookshelves at long last." She held out her arms. "Let me take your coat. Would you like a glass of wine?"

He shook his head. "Not tonight, thanks. I only stopped by to tell you that I'm leaving for Florida. My mother has had a heart attack, and it doesn't look good. No one can say if she'll recover…or not."

She clutched his arm. "I'm so sorry, Ben." The aftermath of her mother's strokes had left her always waiting for the other shoe to drop, so she felt for Ben. She pointed back to the kitchen. "Are you sure you don't want a cup of tea or something?"

He shook his head. "I'm still packing and tying things up here. But I wanted you to know I told the principal at school I won't be back until after the holiday break."

"I see." Selfish relief rippled through her. She'd been saved from having to make a decision about going to Florida with Ben after Christmas.

"I think it's best this way." He looked away. "Besides, you didn't seem ready to go away for the holiday—at least with me."

She lowered her head. "No, I'm afraid you're right.

Things have been so strange for me. I can't explain—"

"No need to," he interrupted. His features softened when he looked into her eyes. "I'll call you from Florida. And then we'll see where we stand when I get back."

"Thanks for understanding," she said, suddenly sure that nothing would change between them. What a coward she was. She'd never be ready to make promises to this wonderful man.

"Please, call and let me know how your mother is doing," she said, hearing the crack in her voice. "I'll be thinking of you, Ben."

He pulled the door open, but quickly turned and kissed her cheek. Then, he walked down to his car with slumped shoulders. Guilt stabbed at her heart. But *wanting* to have something to give to another person wasn't good enough. She closed the door.

Leaving the books in piles on the floor, she quickly turned off the TV and went upstairs to get ready for bed. *Just do the ordinary things. Clean the makeup off your face, smooth on the moisturizer, and go to sleep.* Tomorrow, she'd call the painter and start transforming the house. Ben or no Ben, it was time to start over.

* * *

August 2002

"Are you having an affair with someone in Washington?" Sonia stood with her back to the front door waiting for an answer.

"Good God, no!" Aaron let go of the handle of the suitcase. "Why would you ask such a thing?"

"Because this is your *third* trip to D.C." She

sounded whiny. Worse, she'd blocked their front door to have this conversation, in effect not allowing him to leave.

"I'm not going to quit investigating until I rule out all the possibilities, Sonia, one hundred percent." He sighed. "You've known that from the beginning."

Suddenly shivering, she rubbed her arms, even though they were in midst of a hot spell that had stretched on for days. "All you do lately is pore over the same data again and again."

These circular arguments came more frequently now. And he worried about her, she about him. It got them nowhere.

"It's just that you don't give me much notice about when you're leaving and when you're coming home." She laced her fingers and brought her hands close to her chest, but then quickly dropped her arms and moved to the side. She had to let him leave if he wanted to. She wasn't about to plead with her own husband to stay with her. "I've been waiting to show you sketches of the stone sculptures for the children's garden."

He drew his head back, looking surprised—and puzzled. "What sculptures?"

She slumped against the door. "You see? This is exactly the problem. Dottie and I talked with Marita Perez, a sculptor in Sturgeon Bay. I told you about her weeks ago. We've settled on the pieces, a trio of small kids playing instruments." Frustrated, she thrust her hands toward Aaron. "I've explained all this, but now you look surprised."

"I thought we had settled on a meditation garden as a memorial to Matt," he said impatiently. "You described a quiet, contemplative place."

"And I was under the impression you approved of plans for the children's garden. Everyone loves our garden sculptures." She stared at the slate floor. "And what better way to remember Matt than with pieces designed around a musical theme?"

Tears gathered and she struggled to stop them, but her heart ached seeing Aaron with his suitcase next to him. He'd already abandoned her.

"So many memorials," he said with a sigh. "I don't know. We have the farm sculpture for my dad, and the covered picnic shelters dedicated to your father. And two more for our mothers..."

She'd invested so much passion into those memorials—consulting him every step of the way—and now he *dismissed* them. "Those memorials are beautiful additions to the garden. You *used* to agree."

"It's just that every time I walk through the place," he said, clearly perturbed, "I see one thing after another dedicated to the memory of someone."

"To our parents, the Chapels and Van Casters," she reminded him. "And you helped make the decisions about them. I never shut you out." She nervously rubbed her chest, as if dislodging the pain stuck there. "I've tried to find beautiful ways to pay tribute to the people you and I have loved."

"Can't you understand that I don't want to see the garden turned into one big memorial to...to our son?" His features tightened. "Please, Sonia, let's drop this for now."

"I don't know why or how you've changed so much," she said with a huff, "but I'm not going to argue with you. Just go." She walked past him and into the kitchen, surprised to hear his steps behind her.

"Sonia, please—"

"Besides, you got your way," she interrupted, pivoting around so she could look at him.

His eyes narrowed. "*Way?* What way?"

"I wanted to put Matt's ashes in the garden, but you talked me into burying them in the family plot…you and Dottie and Cal."

"I thought you understood why we wanted Matt buried with the family."

Finishing his sentence, she said, "…and not in a prominent place in the garden."

He gently touched her arm. "But Sonia, you acted like Matt was a celebrity—a public person. It's as if you had a vision of people—strangers—coming to the garden to visit his grave."

She had no response. He was right. But Matt would have become that someday, a celebrity known for his music.

"All I've wanted is to add beautiful things to the garden," she finally said, staring into space. "Things that won't decay and die and be forgotten."

That brought a flicker of surprise in his eyes.

He held the back of his neck with his hand. "I know," he said in a softer voice.

Lately, it seemed that if Aaron wasn't sighing or tightening his mouth, he was running his hand across the back of his neck to ease the tension there. He looked older with his forehead always wrinkled in a frown. He was aging right in front of her eyes.

Apparently, he hadn't thought about her heartache and loneliness when he'd taken off on the wild goose chases that kept him in his office late into the night or on these trips to Washington.

"You may be getting sick of my memorials," she said defensively, "but I don't much like your obsession with finding a terrorist to blame either." She bit her lower lip. "Sometimes it seems like you devote more time to Matt now that he's *dead* than you did when he was alive."

For a second she saw his features sag into painful defeat before he recovered and set his jaw in anger. Maybe she regretted what she said, and maybe she didn't. It wasn't the first time she'd danced around that accusation, just as he'd wished she hadn't guided Matt's music with such intensity. *Music had put him on that plane.* That was Aaron's unspoken message.

Aaron stared at her, opening his mouth as if to speak, but then his jaw went slack.

Her knees weakened, almost buckling beneath her. She turned and yanked the back door open and left while her legs would still carry her. Her anger fueling her, she ran blindly to the footbridge and crossed it into the garden and kept on running across the field.

Finally, her labored breathing slowed her down and she stopped long enough to push wet strands of hair off her sticky forehead. Glancing around her, she puzzled over where to go next. But whenever she missed her dad, she chose the path to the picnic tables by the pond and that's where she headed now. Regardless of what he said now, Aaron had agreed the tables were a fine memorial to her dad.

Missing her father had come and gone in stages, sometimes sneaking up on her without warning. She'd long ago forgiven him for his harsh attitude toward her and his stubborn disapproval of Aaron.

"Bill Van Caster was a big enough person to admit

a mistake—eventually," Aaron had assured her. "And he would have been overjoyed to see you happy."

But these past months, she'd desperately longed for her dad's company. On a hot, dry day like this, she imagined fixing glasses of iced tea and sitting together by the window in her office. Then she'd tell him stories about Matt.

The dry twigs and leaves on the path crunched under her sneakers and as she walked, she gradually stopped rehashing her argument with Aaron. In the distance, geese honked, as if beckoning her to the pond. Just the sound of them distracted her and offered comfort.

If her dad were alive, would he tell her to leave Aaron to his quest, futile or not? Aaron coped by taking off for Washington to meet with the one remaining investigator who still agreed to see him. Maybe she should simply back off.

Until he'd announced this latest Washington trip, she thought they'd reached a truce…sort of. When a couple from the Unity Flight Family Group had come to Lady's River for the weekend, Aaron had joined them for a long walk through the garden to admire its early June blooming.

Sonia found hope in the bright glimmers of the couple she and Aaron had once been, especially when they shared a few light moments of laughter. But now, deeper into the summer, they'd drifted apart again.

She trembled inside imagining her worst fear, life without Aaron. Oh no, no. They *had* to talk. Sonia turned on her heel and broke into a run as she retraced her steps on the path. She needed to get back. It was up to her now to make things right.

With sweat running down her face, she pushed the back door open. The house was silent. *Too late.*

"Aaron? Aaron, are you still here?" she called out, knowing it was futile. She rushed up the stairs, ducking her head into his office. *Empty.* She tried the bedroom next. Finding it empty, too, she lowered herself on the edge of the bed and held her head, damp with sweat, in her hands. She wanted to cry, but her eyes were dry.

She stood and peeled off her clothes and checked the clock before heading to the shower. It was already noon. Defeated or not, she had responsibilities to face. Dottie had expected her much earlier.

An hour later she pulled into her parking place at the garden and slipped into her office, hoping no one would see her and note the time. A few minutes later, though, Dottie knocked lightly on her open door, but didn't wait to be invited in.

"Are you okay?" she asked, walking toward Sonia's desk and taking a seat.

Sonia waved her hand dismissively. "As good as I can be, I guess."

She'd counted on her offhand response to allow for a smooth change of subject. No such luck. Dottie sat silent and impassive.

"We're getting by," Sonia quickly added to fill the silence, "each of us trying to get through the days. You know what I mean."

Dottie raised her eyebrows. "Did Aaron leave for Washington? Cal said something about another trip."

Sonia nodded and tried to look busy by reaching for a pile of files.

"I'm concerned," Dottie said quietly, "and I don't know what to do. I don't want to cross any lines and intrude into things that are none of my business."

Dropping the folders on the desk, Sonia opened her hands in a receptive gesture. "Go ahead. Say what's on your mind."

"It's just that you and Aaron once gained strength from each other—or that's how it appeared. You seemed much closer a few months ago than you do now." She tightened her mouth. "There, I guess that was blunt."

Sonia looked into Dottie's face, now pinched into a troubled expression. "I was about to repeat that we're okay," Sonia said, her voice barely above a whisper, "but that's not true. If you don't mind listening, I need to get something off my mind."

For the next couple of minutes, Sonia found relief in expressing her worries about Aaron's latest trip. Nervously drumming her fingers on her desk, she said, "I hate talking about him behind his back like this, but he won't let go of the sabotage theory. Nothing—and no one—supports it, not even those investigators he contacted earlier. There's only one guy left who will even see him."

She spilled out all her pent up frustrations to Dottie, conscious of repeating things that her sister-in-law already knew. Weeks before, Sonia had passed on the information that the accident had been blamed on a faulty maintenance procedure on the wing attachment structure. It was a combination of a badly designed assembly piece that created friction and weakened the metal to the breaking point. End of story. Aaron stubbornly refused to accept the finding. He insisted that such a small flaw couldn't possibly cause the wing to sever from the fuselage and bring it down.

"So, that's it," she said, noting the apprehension in

her sister-in-law's face. "What is it, Dottie? You look like you're afraid to say anything."

"I am," Dottie said, averting her eyes.

She hadn't expected such a direct answer. "Please, we're friends. You can tell me what's on your mind."

Dottie got up and walked to the window, leaning one shoulder against it. "I've listened to you talk about Aaron, but he has concerns about you, too. He's worried that you haven't touched Matt's room and won't even consider letting *him* begin to sort through Matt's things. He told me that all you think about is the meditation garden and looking for more ways to remember Matt."

Sonia's back stiffened. "But like I told him, these things aren't any different from the kaleidoscope or the fountain near the entrance we dedicated to Rona and my mother."

"Aaron thinks you're trying to keep Matt alive in an unhealthy way," Dottie blurted, her voice rushed and loud.

Sonia pushed the chair back and got to her feet. She moved to confront Dottie face-to-face at the window. "So maybe I am trying to make sure Matt isn't forgotten. But what's unhealthy about that? He was my son—he was special, and how will anyone even know that he lived if we don't create these tangible, visible memorials? People don't remember what they can't see. And I'd rather create beautiful things than coop myself up in my office night after night and chase off to Washington looking for someone to blame."

She turned away and rested her fingertips on the glass. "Like I told Aaron earlier, he shows more interest in why our son died than he showed in his music when he was alive."

"You actually said that?" Dottie asked, looking more shocked than Sonia had ever seen her.

"Well, more or less. Those weren't my exact words."

Dottie shook head. "I don't even know how to respond to such a thing. I can't imagine why those words would come out of your mouth."

Through the reflection in the window, Sonia saw Dottie's distressed face and prepared to defend herself. No need, though, because Dottie hurried to the door.

"Here's what worries me most," Dottie said, as she opened the door. "You and Aaron are facing in different directions."

That's not what Sonia wanted to hear. She'd hoped Dottie would rally around her, maybe speak up and take her side.

"One last thing," Dottie said. "Be careful what you say, especially the accusations you make. You can't take those words back."

Sonia opened her mouth, wanting to justify herself. Apparently, Dottie didn't want to hear it, because she quickly slipped through the door and shut it behind her.

Standing alone in the room, Sonia turned to the window and saw her own reflection. Another ally had walked away, she thought, leaving her to stand alone.

21

October 2003

$\mathcal{A}$aron followed Sonia across the field, feeling like an outsider as he watched her from behind. She listened attentively and nodded her agreement to Clark, an older man who'd lost his brother in the crash. Sonia had mentioned Clark now and then, because he'd been one of the strongest advocates for keeping the Unity Flight Family Group together past the official end of the investigation and the settlement with the airlines. And apparently, the email newsletter and coming together for this second anniversary wasn't enough.

The group had found themselves a new mission. At an informal meeting the evening before, Gary and Jane Carpenter told the group that they'd decided against replanting the field where the plane had gone down. Instead, they were donating fifty acres of their land to the Unity Flight Family Group, their only stipulation being that the land had to be used for something that would benefit the whole community.

Aaron had nearly exploded in frustration when Sonia quickly jumped in, praising the idea and volunteering to serve on the committee. She hadn't hesitated for a second, or asked what he thought. No, she'd charged ahead. Now she and Clark batted around ideas as they walked ahead.

This new project promised to keep Sonia steeped in Matt's death. Aaron was certain of it. And just when he thought they might be recapturing a degree of normalcy. He'd finally reached a place that he could begin letting some pieces of the crash fall into their logical places. He'd inched closer to accepting that he'd never find one individual to blame for Matt's death.

Looking at the group of nearly one hundred trekking to the crash site, Aaron identified with the urge to return to places linked to tragedy and loss. He'd witnessed it often enough. He'd stood on tracks where a train had derailed, releasing toxic chemicals and forcing an entire town to evacuate. He'd listened while hundreds of people in a village in Pakistan gestured wildly as they tried to tell him about the fire in the textile plant that killed their loved ones. He'd seen his share of grief in mourners' eyes.

"They just want you to see, to be a witness," he'd once told Chuck, who tried to hide his uneasiness with needy clients. "Maybe they wouldn't bring these lawsuits at all if they could get enough pairs of eyes to look at the results of deliberate negligence, shortcuts, carelessness, and just ordinary mistakes."

Aaron thought of that when he'd gone to the crash site with the other families during the first anniversary weekend a year before. But he'd only needed to make that walk once. On this second visit, he realized he'd lost his connection to that particular piece of ground, which no longer linked him to Matt. He gained no sense of peace on this field, either. Maybe it helped some of the others, even Sonia, but tramping across the field did nothing for him.

When the group stopped, Sonia turned to him and

took his hand during the moment of silence.

"I wish this made me feel better," she whispered when the ceremony was over. "Clark talks about these rituals bringing closure, but I don't know."

"I hate that word," Aaron mumbled, "or maybe I haven't figured out what it means."

When she cast a look of agreement his way, relief settled in over finding one thing about which they were in total agreement.

Later, on the drive home, his body ached from tension and fatigue, but Sonia's wound-up energy bubbled over in the car.

"Isn't it wonderful that Gary and Jane want their field used for something meaningful?"

Maybe. He had his doubts. Even thinking about it tired him out. "Did Clark or the others have something specific in mind?" he asked, attempting to sound not only polite, but interested, too.

"No, but everyone wants to take time to really think it through."

"That's probably wise."

"By the way, the committee is coming to Lady's River after Thanksgiving," she said. "Turns out, we're a central location. We can meet in the conference room at the garden."

"Who's idea was that?" He hadn't intended to sound so terse.

"As a matter of fact, mine," she shot back.

He kept quiet, but groaned inside.

"Aaron, tell me what's going on with you."

He grabbed the water bottle from the holder next to him and took a few gulps to buy some time and gather his thoughts. "Here's the truth. I don't *want* to go back for another visit to that field. It doesn't make me feel better or *closer* to Matt. I can't even think about closure—it sounds ridiculous to me."

"I understand, Aaron, but this is different. We're going to bring that field to life again."

"Damn it, Sonia, if it was a question of bringing the field to life, Gary and Jane should replant soybeans. This is a memorial. It's about death, not life."

"Well, yes, but it's not only about Matt. All those other families signed on to the project, too."

He sighed, unsure of what to say next, but fixated on one thing. "I'd hoped that maybe we were ready to try to go back to a regular life."

"We never had a *regular* life," she snapped. "You were out of town so much, Matt's music demanded my commitment, and I ran the garden. All those things gave us a full, wonderful life, but there's no *regular* to go back to."

He banged the heel of his hand on the steering wheel. "Okay, regular for us. And since I'm already annoyed as hell, why didn't you talk to me before volunteering to be on that committee? Or inviting the group to Lady's River?"

When he glanced sideways, he saw her staring out the passenger window. Maybe she didn't have a good answer.

"I'd like to help plan something beautiful for that land," she said, still looking out the window at the passing fields. "I have the kind of experience the committee needs." She turned and stretched her arm toward him. "Don't you understand that this kind of project helps me heal and connect to the meaning of Matt's life?"

"I wish…" He wanted to say so much, yet lost the words.

"What? What do you wish?"

He shook his head. "Nothing, it's not important."

Silently, he wished they could remember Matt by keeping him in their hearts instead of finding new ways to memorialize him.

* * *

December 2006

Aaron sorted through the bills and the usual fundraising appeals. Then he saw Dottie's handwriting on an envelope. He couldn't remember the last time she'd sent him a note the old- fashioned way. Since he'd moved to Chicago, he and his sister communicated mostly through emails every couple of weeks. They amicably exchanged superficial facts of their lives. That's what passed for staying in touch.

He'd dashed off an email last week, and added a line about no longer seeing Katherine. With any luck, Dottie would leave it at that and not ask too many questions. He snickered to himself. Wishful thinking. His sister's nosy side was imprinted in her very constitution.

He waited until he got inside his apartment and grabbed a beer from the fridge before sitting at the breakfast bar to open and read the letter.

> *Dear Aaron,*
> *We haven't talked in a long time, but I got your email last week. I've never met Katherine, of course, but nevertheless, I know the breakup must have been difficult.*
> *I've been mulling something over for the last*

couple of days and finally decided to go ahead and write. Cal and I talk about coming to visit you, but it never seems to happen, and now it's been two and a half years since we've seen each other. I've wondered if you stayed away because you were afraid that you might feel awkward bringing Katherine up here to meet us.

Wouldn't this be a good year for you to come up for Christmas? You can relax and do as you please. Sonia and I will be busy with the Light Up the Holidays festival, so the two of you could avoid each other—if that's what you want.

I've missed you. Call me—please.

Love,

Dottie

How odd that her letter came when he'd been thinking about Lady's River—and the past—almost nonstop for weeks. Maybe a visit would be a good break, a chance to think about things, maybe find a new direction. He'd relied on Katherine too much since he moved to Chicago. When he came back from his Lady's River visit maybe he'd be finally ready to piece together a new life—at long last.

He checked his watch. Just a little after nine o'clock, so it wasn't too late to call. He looked up Dottie's cell and punched it in.

She answered on the second ring. "Hey, good to hear your voice, Aaron. I take it you got my letter."

Aaron smiled in response to the warmth in her voice. "That's why I called. I'm considering your invitation."

"Ooh, I hope you'll come up. It's been so long."

Curiosity took over. "I'd like to visit, but what about Sonia and her friend, that man who—"

"Ben," she answered. "He's not here. He's gone to

Florida to tend to his ill mother. Besides, Sonia said that they hadn't made any plans. I took that to mean something more than she spelled out." She paused and he didn't fill the silence.

"I feel like I'm telling tales out of school," Dottie said, "but she doesn't seem that interested in him anymore."

He sat up a little straighter. This news, which logically should be of no importance to him, put him on high alert nonetheless. "Do you think Sonia would mind having me around for the holidays?"

When she didn't answer right away, he jumped in. "That's okay, Dottie. I shouldn't put you on the spot."

"You're not. I'm taking my time because I want to find the right words to explain what concerns me about her. The short version is that Sonia hasn't seemed like herself lately. It's as if she's lost ground."

Dottie didn't need to spell it out. "Yeah, I know what that's like," he said. "I'm off kilter myself. Go ahead, blurt it out."

"I'll be honest with you, Aaron. She hasn't been herself since she came back from Pearson Pond. You know, she insisted on going alone—without Cal or me, or Ben."

"I haven't been the same either," he said quietly. "Seeing Sonia at the memorial dedication threw me off and I couldn't make myself move forward with Katherine. She got tired of it and that's why she ended things with me." He gulped some beer and swallowed hard, surprised by his own frankness with his sister.

"It's just my opinion," Dottie said, "but you and Sonia need to talk."

"But—"

"Hear me out, please," she said. "I'm probably overstepping, but truthfully, I don't care anymore. Let me ask you something, Aaron. Are you really happy down in Chicago without Sonia?"

He rubbed his forehead. "No, but I can't say for sure that has anything to do with Sonia." Even to his ears, he knew his words sounded false. She'd been on his mind constantly.

Dottie groaned. "All I'm saying is that it's time for the two of you to talk. I can't keep my mouth shut about this. Sonia's tried hard these last couple of years to come alive again. Ben was good for her. He's an exceptional guy, by the way, smart, caring, and very sweet. He fell hard for her, and I thought her feelings for him were growing. I don't know what happened between them, but I can guess."

"Can you tell me?" Aaron asked, his heartbeat picking up speed.

"I didn't want to get into it," she said with a laugh in her voice, "but your curiosity proves my point. I'm not saying that you and Sonia should get back together, although, speaking for myself, that's what *I* want."

"Now that was subtle," he quipped.

"As you know, subtly isn't a quality of mine. But here's my real point, Aaron. Stop pretending that you're over Sonia. Either get back together or let each other go, once and for all. Set your hearts free." She followed that with a heavy sigh. "Okay, I've said my piece."

"I guess so." He chuckled nervously. "Honestly, when Katherine ended things with me, she said something along those same lines."

"So, you'll take your big sister's advice and come up and see us, and talk to Sonia?"

"As Sonia herself would say, when you're right, you're right."

Dottie laughed. "I'll—*we'll*—be so happy to see you."

"I've missed *you*, Dottie. And I do want to see Sonia," he said, his voice hoarse. "I admit it. I *miss* her."

"That's what I suspected."

"Okay, I'll settle some things here and let you know when I can drive up. And thanks, Dottie."

"You can thank me with a big hug when you get here."

When they hung up the phone, Aaron went into the bedroom and lifted the shoebox from the bottom drawer of the chest. He kept old photos in the box and a few other personal things, including the letter Sonia wrote in response to one he'd written to her after he'd moved to Chicago. He'd never felt ready to throw it away.

He took it back to the breakfast bar before he read it.

June 15, 2004
Dear Aaron,
Thank you for your letter. I'm sorry I've taken so long to write back. I'm not sure why I let so much time elapse, but it's not for lack of thoughts of you—and driving myself crazy mulling over all our mistakes.
I think I finally understand why certain things about Matt's death continue to haunt me. You never liked to hear me talk about this, but it's true that I never fully resolved the way we brought Matt into this world. But I remember telling my father that I'd committed to bringing the best I had to our marriage, to make it work. I got that resolve from you, Aaron, because of your sense of honor. And we made something fine and lovely together, you and I.

Yet, when another accident took our son away, I lost my sense that our life and his life had been real. That's the true impulse behind the memorials. I had to hang on to the sense that he'd lived at all and made his mark in this world. I had to be certain he'd never be forgotten. So, yes, at times my quest was desperate, but I'm moving past that now.

I've accepted that I can't control the fact that Matt wasn't able to share his gift with the world—to fulfill what I felt certain was his destiny. You were right to insist that we bury Matt in the family cemetery on the land. My initial idea of putting his ashes in the garden and building an elaborate monument was very wrong. With the passage of time, I know the scholarship and meditation garden will be wonderful and complete. Yes, the children's sculptures are lovely, but they stand on their own and not necessarily as a tribute to Matt.

It saddens me that we drifted so far apart after we lost our son, not in the first weeks and months, but later. It was painful to admit that we had so little between us without him. I have to stop, because that thought still leaves me heartbroken—and I'm not sure I'll ever accept the truth of it.

Most of the time, I'm fine, even walking with a light step now and then, when I don't go back too far into my memories of the three of us as a family. And today, the garden is in its June glory—a riot of color and scents, to paraphrase the poets.

And, of course, I'll always really, really like you, too.

S.

Heartbroken. Because they had so little left between them? What had propelled them down a path that convinced them they were nothing without Matt? Especially after they'd found such happiness. He slammed his hand on the table. How the hell had they let that happen? *No, be honest.* He'd *let* it happen.

22

March 2003

Aaron heard the voices even before he got to the open door to the conference room. The sounds of Sonia's new life, he thought cynically.

When he appeared in the doorway, Sonia waved. "Come in, Aaron."

"Are you almost done?" he asked, ignoring her invitation.

"No such luck," Clark said with a laugh as he glanced fondly at Sonia.

"We're ordering pizza soon," Sonia said. "Why don't you join us?"

He shook his head. "I've got some things to take care of. I'll be at home."

"Okay, see you a little later." She frowned, even though she'd tried to sound pleasant. He knew better. She'd used her full power of persuasion to get him involved with the committee. If he got to know the nine other members, he'd like them. But he thought the project was just an excuse for the group to spend more time together.

Sonia's committee met at least one weekend a month and always in Lady's River. Aaron hadn't expected this scattered group of people to become a permanent fixture in their lives. Maybe that suited

Sonia, but it sat poorly with him.

Aaron had come straight from his office to the garden, hoping that the meeting would be over. He'd thought that maybe they could go out to dinner by themselves. An irrational notion. Predictably, the meeting would end with a meal. Aaron admitted he'd been downright rude to those people that meant so much to Sonia.

Restless, with no desire to go home to an empty house just yet, he left the building quickly and walked toward Dottie's house. Glancing back at the garden's main building, the fog blurred all the angles and edges and muted the light coming from the conference room. In the fading daylight, the whole garden lay cloaked in mist.

The damp, chilly air hitting his face cooled the heat of his emotions. He passed the house he grew up in, and wondered what Dottie and Cal and the kids were doing inside all those rooms. They were a family, he thought, not like the two distant people who lived in the old Tudor.

He climbed the hill next to a border of cedars until he reached the knee-high stone wall around the family cemetery. He stopped briefly at his grandparents' and both his parents' graves, wishing he could sit down and hash things over with them.

Matt's stone was off to the left, invisible in the fog. Aaron took a few steps and stopped in front of it. The simple stone showed his name and the year of his birth and death, the only embellishment a small cello carved in a lower corner.

Shoving his hands in the pockets of his jacket, Aaron stared down at the stone. Why had he come up here? He'd come to say goodbye. But that was impossible. Matt had been gone for two years. He groaned softly. A ritual or a ceremony sometimes felt good in the moment, but the feeling never lasted, at least not for him. Turning quickly, he went back down the hill and jogged to his car and drove home.

Rather than turning on the lights and brightening the rooms in the quiet, dark house, he went straight to his office and closed the door. Then he opened the file and took out the letter from the law firm in Chicago confirming the offer made the previous week. The letter included a brochure featuring listings for apartment rentals in downtown high-rises. The color photos were like a PR packet for Chicago, and Aaron admitted the city looked appealing. Between festivals and live music and theater, he could stay busy every night of the week. This small firm had offered him a chance for a fresh start. And maybe he should take it.

He folded his arms on the desk and let his imagination take him away from Lady's River, and more to the point, away from Sonia. Would she care? They'd fallen into a rut with each other, an uncomfortable one at that. Sonia spent one evening after another alone in the den while he hid out behind his office door, each working on their separate projects.

It seemed to him that their slide away from each other had only picked up speed since that second anniversary weekend in the fall. She'd come away determined to immerse herself in the damn committee. Then she'd started talking up the idea of building a band shell in the garden, once again not consulting him. She probably assumed he wouldn't understand anyway.

Lowering his head to rest on his hands, it hit him

that maybe she preferred the company of that Clark guy. His loud guttural sound of frustration pierced the silence in the room. He was so tired.

Lost in a dream somewhere, he felt something jostling his shoulder.

"Aaron, wake up, wake up."

He sat straight up and drew his hands down his cheeks. Then he looked up, surprised to see Sonia's eyes wet with tears. "What's wrong? I didn't hear you come in."

Then he remembered. Out the corner of his eye he saw the rental brochure on the desk. He stood and brushed the papers back into the folder.

"So, the secret is out. You're leaving me."

"No. I don't…" His voice trailed off because he had no answer.

"But it's obvious you're thinking about it." Tears ran freely down her cheeks. "How dare you?"

"Sonia, wait. It isn't like I planned anything. I got an offer from a firm." He pushed the file folder to the far side of the desk.

"That you didn't tell me about?" She stepped back from him. "So, it's happened. It's like my fears materialized."

He gestured helplessly while he tried to gather his thoughts. She rushed out of the office and down the hall into their bedroom. He went after her, but she moved around him to grab her robe off the bathroom door.

"Sonia, please listen to me."

"Why?" she demanded, wiping away her tears. "Nothing will ever again be the same between us."

"But we can talk." He braced his hand on the doorjamb. "I've wanted to talk with you, but you're so busy with the Unity group now, and—"

"Great, bring that up." She waved dismissively. "What a weak excuse to go ahead and do what you've probably been thinking about for a long time."

"That's not true. This just came up. I got a job offer in Chicago." He paused to breathe, finding himself reluctant to explain how a casual conversation with a jury consultant started the ball rolling. He could have stopped it, but didn't.

"And you didn't think to mention it?" She threw the robe over her arms and grabbed a nightgown off the closet shelf. "Since when would a job offer slip your mind?"

He didn't know where to start explaining, but maybe it didn't matter.

"Turns out that without Matt, we have nothing. Our big fear had a kernel of truth, after all." She brushed past him and stood in the hall. "Besides, you'll never forgive me anyway."

"Forgive you for what?"

"For my insistence that we put everything we had into Matt's music and see how far he could go with it." She covered her eyes with her palms. "It's always there, Aaron, whether you say the words out loud or not. You blame the cello, but more to the point, you blame *me* for his death."

"It's *not* about blaming you! But sure, if I go back in time, I'd do anything to keep him off that plane, even wish away his talent."

"And so would I," she screamed. "But that doesn't change anything. You will always link me with the plane crash." She headed to the stairs.

"Where are you going?"

"Down to the den. I'll sleep there."

"Like you already do most of the time," he muttered.

She'd turned her head, so he knew she'd heard the words. But she kept on going.

He followed her, but when she got to the bottom of the stairs, she turned around and put up her hand. "Stay away from me. I can't talk to you right now."

When she disappeared down the hall, he sat on the stairway and held his head in his hands. Seconds later, he jumped at the sound of the slamming door.

* * *

December 2006

Sonia brushed a thick layer of dust off the top of Rona's old trunk, and then bumped it down the attic stairs and into Matt's room. The rusty hinges added to its beat up appearance, but it would hold the things she knew she'd never be able to part with.

For years, she'd steadfastly refused to sort through any of Matt's belongings, prompting Aaron to accuse her of turning their son's room into a shrine. "That isn't healthy," he'd said more than a few times.

Those days were over, though.

The house still smelled of the fresh paint that had begun the rejuvenation of the downstairs, and last Saturday, she'd hauled eight shopping bags of books to the library for their annual sale. A new couch for the den would be delivered later that afternoon. Those had been steps, and now Matt's room was another. Determination to break out of her rut had transformed her.

Two days ago, Dottie had come into her office to tell her that she'd invited Aaron for a holiday visit and he'd said yes. "He's looking forward to talking with you, Sonia."

The statement had sounded perfunctory, like Aaron attempting to be polite. Her body tingled, though, even shook, when she asked, "But is he bringing...um, his friend?" She'd known her name but couldn't remember it.

"He's not seeing Katherine anymore."

"Oh," she'd said to fill in the silence, but the knot in her chest made it nearly impossible to breathe.

Dottie's gaze had darted around the room and she'd thrust her balled fists into the pockets of her blazer.

"What is it?" Sonia asked. "You've never looked so nervous before and you've got me feeling jittery, too."

"Okay. I'll tell you the same thing I told Aaron," Dottie had said matter-of factly. "I think you still have things to settle between you...one way or another." Dottie left before Sonia had a chance to pry more information out of her.

Maybe their meeting in Pearson Pond had thrown him of his center, as it had her. Or, perhaps, like her, he had resolved to live like a so-called normal person again and that included a trip to visit his sister. And what did *'things to settle'* and *'one way or another'* mean? The memory of that conversation with Dottie played over and over in her head as she put the trunk in the middle of Matt's room.

But before she started, she had one more job to get out of the way. She went into the bedroom and grabbed her phone and made a long overdue call to the women's shelter to tell the director that she had bedroom furniture available if they'd like to have it. Ashamed of herself for waiting so long to act, it hurt even worse to know Matt would never have wanted his useful things to go on gathering dust year after year when other people needed this basic furniture. She alone shouldered the blame for clinging to almost everything he owned.

Back in Matt's room, she opened the first of the row of three wooden boxes under the window that held sheet music. She sifted through them, pulling out the music for her favorite Chopin and Mozart pieces. They were destined for the trunk, but the other sheet music could go to the high school music department or to Olivia Morton, who still kept in touch. Then she made a pile of the classical and popular CDs Matt had collected over the years. She'd keep some of those for herself and donate the rest to the library. She'd let Aaron look through them, but he probably wouldn't choose to keep any. He'd always ached to hear the qualities in Matt's music that she and others had enjoyed.

Two special photos sat on a shelf over Matt's desk. One showed Matt with his kindergarten teacher, Karen Baldwin, at her wedding at the garden. Matt held his cello and bow and she had knelt down next to him for the picture. He'd been proud of himself that day for playing at his favorite teacher's wedding—and he hadn't been especially nervous. Sonia had suffered the stage fright for him.

Sonia favored the other photo. She picked it up and held it in her hands and studied the image of Aaron and Matt standing in front of the lions at the Art Institute in Chicago. They wore identical Green Bay Packer hats and their smiles matched, too, as they stared into the camera. Matt looked completely happy, she thought. Not a care in the world. Those Orchestra Hall performances were the best of Matt's career to that point, and the three of them had shared every minute of the excitement.

She touched the glass over the photo, sliding her index finger to touch Matt's face and allowing herself to savor the memories of that weekend. Did Aaron have a copy of this photo? Not knowing the answer to that question, she set it aside to give to him. He should have it. Besides, her most cherished photo was the one she'd insisted on taking a couple of hours later when the two men in her life were all dressed up in their suits.

The prospect of seeing Aaron had stirred up something different from the restless, unsettled feeling that had been with her since coming back from Pearson Pond. And Dottie had spoken bluntly, yet Sonia sensed she'd held something back. A hunch of some kind? Something significant Aaron had said?

Wouldn't it be something if he wanted to come back to me? An excited shiver traveled down her spine and through her. "Stop this," she mumbled to herself, "and keep your hands busy."

Satisfied with the work she'd done in Matt's room, she quickly went into her room and scanned her closet, pulling down older sweaters off the top shelf and yanking slacks she no longer wore off their hangers. She efficiently sorted them into piles to wash or dry clean before they, too, went to the shelter. Then she surveyed the evidence of her morning's work. *Out with the old, and it was about time.*

23

"*I* should have called first," Aaron said, looking into Sonia's surprised face. "I'm sorry."

"Don't be silly," she said, her fingertips nervously touching her face. "I expected to see you at some point." She stepped aside. "Come in, come in."

Aaron walked into the house for the first time in almost three years. On the drive over, fingers of apprehension poked his solar plexus. Could he handle the color and texture of the memories associated with that house? The cello music coming from Matt's room or Matt clomping up and down the stairs. The spicy aromas Sonia created when she fixed one of her stir-fried dishes. Now inside the door, he felt a bittersweet tug at his heart recalling Sonia's baby-talk voice telling little Matt all about the Wreck of the Tudor.

"Don't mind the paint odor," Sonia said with a grin.

Maybe that's what had brought up the memory. During their year of renovating the house, that smell had become constant.

"I had the den and family room painted, and bought a new couch for the den. I'm picking out new wallpaper for the dining room."

"Well, the old place looks good."

She planted her hands on her hips. "Truthfully, I've faced that the whole place is overdue for an update. I've made some plans to replace other furniture and lighten up the atmosphere."

She spoke faster than usual while self-consciously fluffing up her hair. Rather than being pleased to see him, dropping in unannounced had thrown her and made her uncomfortable. Man, he could be so stupid sometimes.

"Really, Sonia, I can leave if I came at a bad time."

Waving him off, she said, "Take off your coat. I'll make us some coffee."

As he slipped out of his jacket and boots, he absorbed the familiarity of the place. The varnish on the woodwork gleamed, and the fireplace still stood like a jewel in the living room. Involuntarily, he glanced upstairs.

Sonia's faced reddened as she followed his gaze.

"Let's go into the kitchen," she said, gesturing for him to follow her.

A wave of dizzying longing surged through him as he walked behind her. They passed the den on the way to the kitchen. The last time he'd looked into that room, he'd stared down at her back as she slept on the couch, facing away from the blue-gray flickers of the television. He'd left her there and climbed the stairs to start clearing things out of his office.

He'd let her slip away.

"Would you like wine instead?"

He eagerly said yes. "I'll bet you have some Lady's Slipper merlot around."

"But of course," she said with a laugh. "Sit down. I'll pour us each a glass."

"It surprised me when Dottie said you were at home today." He watched her graceful hands setting out the glasses and pouring the wine. "I know this is the busiest time at the garden."

"And one of the most beautiful. I don't know if Dottie mentioned it, but tomorrow is the last night of Light Up the Holidays. The designers really outdid themselves." She chuckled softly. "Would you believe we even have an entire gnome village made only with the tiniest lights available." She sat across from him at the table. "Almost everyone calls it a winter fairyland."

All his senses came alive watching her. Her eyes sparkled as she went on about the festival. The scent of the wine added to his heady confusion. He fought the urge to gather her into his arms and kiss her. He wanted to pick up where they'd left off years ago and chat about regular things. He felt like asking her opinion about two opposing strategies for a case. Lover, best friend, sounding board—some things didn't change.

"When did you get in?" she asked suddenly.

"About twenty minutes ago. I went to your office at the garden."

Her eyebrows shot up in surprise. "You did?"

He nodded. He'd never been good at playing it cool. "Like I said, I thought I'd find you there, but Dottie said otherwise." He laughed. "I guess my car steered itself here. The truth is, I couldn't wait to see you."

She flushed and quickly folded her hands and rested them in her lap. "It's good to see you, too, Aaron."

"I need to talk to you, Sonia, tell you some things. But now that I'm here, I don't know where to start."

"Did something happen at the dedication in Pearson Pond?" she asked. "I know I'm being my usual blunt self, but..." She shrugged as her voice trailed off.

"Maybe Dottie told you," he blurted, "but I'm not

seeing Katherine anymore." He smacked his lips. "See? I can be blunt, too. To be honest, she dumped me, sent me packing, as the saying goes." He paused, and finally added, "She had good reasons, too."

Sonia laughed, which wasn't exactly the reaction he'd expected.

"Back to your question about Pearson Pond." He picked up his wine glass, unsure where to begin. "After I got home from the dedication, I was forced to face a few things about myself. For one thing, it turned out that my so-called new life never was a good fit."

Plunking her elbow on the table, Sonia rested her cheek in her palm. "For me, I'd turned the dedication of the pavilion into a rite of passage. I'd convinced myself I'd come home energized, ready to look ahead, move on. All that cliché stuff."

Nodding, he relaxed back in his chair and stretched his long legs out in the empty space next to the table. "I sound like an amateur psychologist, but I think the business about closure is pretty much a crock, at least when it comes to Matt. But..." He closed his eyes. Did he really want to talk about what plagued him?

"But what?" Sonia whispered.

"I thought I could find closure with you—with us. Turned out I was wrong."

She quickly glanced away, as if something in the corner of the room grabbed her attention.

"Am I embarrassing you?" he asked.

She bobbed her head back and forth. "Maybe." With a laugh in her voice, she said, "What are we doing? Following Dottie's orders? She *insisted* we need to talk."

"She said that to you, too, huh?"

She narrowed her eyes in a knowing look. "I suppose she's mentioned Ben, my friend, the man I was seeing."

He nodded.

"Ben called last night to tell me that he's giving up his teaching job to stay in Florida. He needs to look after his mother and he'd like to be closer to his daughter and her family."

She glanced at him, but then tipped her wine glass and absently twirled the stem, sending the red liquid swirling in the glass. "He was good for me, but I didn't have enough to give back. I knew that after Pearson Pond. Truthfully, he let me off the hook."

Watching her fidget with the wine glass and listening to her admission, his chest ached. "Dottie told me he's a good man, Sonia."

"Yes," she said, still looking into her glass. "I wasn't fair to him. He deserves more."

"I said the same thing to Katherine." He spoke in a low voice, hoping to clear the air with these necessary discussions of other people, the two people that didn't get the best of either of them.

"The time we spent together in Pearson Pond," she said, looking directly at him, "stirred something in me. Memories kept demanding my attention, as if they had me in a tight grip. But I fought them." She paused. "Correction—I tried to fight them."

Tangible ripples of relief coursed through him. "I understand. Believe me, I do." She always did express these hard, emotional things so much better than he ever could.

Silence hung there in the room, but the air buzzed around him.

"I haven't been able to stop thinking about you since we met at the pavilion." He slid his hand across the table toward her. "But what do we do now?"

She put her hand on top of his. "I don't know. But we've been sitting here, sharing a glass a wine, and neither of us has mentioned Matt directly. But we got married and divorced because of him."

Before Aaron could respond, she pulled her hand back and quickly got to her feet. "Wait right here. I've got something for you." She disappeared down the hall and he heard the sound of her feet going up the stairs.

When she came back, she was clutching two framed pictures against her chest. "When you left, everything happened so fast that some things were left behind…things you should have. No matter what, I want you to have these."

He took the pictures from her outstretched hand. He instantly felt the dampness in his eyes, and swallowed hard. The first was a photo he'd taken of Matt as a toddler sitting on the boulder down at the river. The second showed him with Matt standing next to the lions at the Art Institute in Chicago.

"The morning after Matt's concert," he said, patting the glass. "I remember that day in vivid color. I walk past those lions often."

Sonia touched his arm lightly. "Remember how I insisted the two of you go back for more pictures when you were dressed up in your suits? But this informal shot ended up as Matt's favorite of the weekend."

"I gave an early morning TV interview a few weeks ago," he said, "and after I left the studio I bought a cup of coffee and sat on the steps thinking about that weekend."

She laughed in surprise. "I saw that interview. I'd turned on the TV to check the weather, and there you were. I saw you as I flipped through the channels."

Odd coincidence, he thought. He wasn't quite sure what to say.

Smiling wistfully, she touched the picture frame. "You should have had these pictures a long time ago."

"Thanks." He nodded in acknowledgment of the gift. "So, what's next, Sonia?"

She folded her arms across her chest and rubbed her upper arms. Was she cold, he wondered, or was that a protective gesture?

"How about if you join us for the employee buffet at the garden tomorrow afternoon before we open for the last night of the festival?" Her eyes sparkled again when she looked at him. "We'll find a job for you. Maybe you can ladle hot cider into cups or pass trays of cookies, like you used to do."

"Sounds good," he said with enough forced enthusiasm to hide his disappointment. He'd hoped they could go out to dinner or that she'd invite him to stay and talk more. But maybe it was too soon. Still, his heart felt heavy when he drained his glass and stood.

"One more thing before you leave," she said, walking towards the front door and then stopping abruptly. She stared at the floor, but he'd already seen her eyes grow wet. "No matter what happens now, my preoccupation with memorials is over. Years ago, I thought I wanted a band shell in the garden, but…no more."

He lightly touched her cheek, but stayed silent.

She lifted her head. "I'm finally over that desperate need to prove to the world that our son lived."

He read in her expression a determination to remain composed. He squared his shoulders. "And I want *you* to know that my hunt for blame is finished. I've accepted mechanical failure caused the crash. Now I spend my time on issues where it's possible to make a difference."

"Like the Safe Play Council?"

"Yes." So, she still understood what drove him.

She opened the door. "I'll see you tomorrow afternoon for the staff buffet."

"I'll report for duty." He grabbed his coat off the hook in the hall. Was it his imagination or was she hustling him out? He kissed her cheek, as he had when he saw her in Pearson Pond. Looking back, that moment of closeness at the dedication, breathing in the scent of her, had started the unraveling of his assumptions about a final, uncomplicated goodbye.

Heading down the walk to his car, he sensed her watching him. When he stood at the driver's side and saw her in the doorway, he wished he could see past her impassive expression and read her thoughts. He waved and she waved back, but then quickly shut the door. He wanted to stay, but she'd made herself clear. Sighing, Aaron drove away.

24

December 2006

So many young people.

Standing at the end of the buffet table, Sonia watched the crew of mostly college-age temporary employees mingle with the regular staff as they came into the garden's main meeting room. The blaze in the stone fireplace at the far end of the room and candles flickering on the tables infused the warm air with a mix of woody scents and the holiday aromas of cranberry and cinnamon. She happily soaked up the laughter and conversation coming from the clusters of people gathering in the room.

Spirits always ran high during the annual employee buffet dinner they held on the last night of the light festival. While the garden stayed open all winter and drew a fair share of visitors during the winter festivals, including an indoor arts and craft show, Light Up the Holidays stood tall and proud as the culmination of a year of special events and programs.

Dottie and Cal greeted each employee at the door, directing them to the table where Aaron handed out cups of hot chocolate and cider. Sonia had chosen to wear a velvet dress, one of her favorites because of its color, a rich, deep green. She stood back and out of the way as caterers carried out soup tureens, chafing dishes, and baskets of hot rolls. The dessert table in the far corner would soon be piled with Christmas cookies and pumpkin bars.

With everyone busy and engaged, except for her, she watched Aaron's relaxed smile as he introduced himself to employees he didn't know or shook hands with those he hadn't seen in years. She saw pleasant surprise register in their faces and reflected in their body language. She wished she could hear his responses to curious queries about what brought him there that night. What *had* brought him back? She'd come close to inviting him to stay the day before, but she needed time to think.

One night over twenty years ago, she'd heard a knock on her apartment door, and there was Aaron standing in the hall. He'd quickly apologized for showing up without calling first, but before she'd even invited him in, he proceeded to list all the good reasons to get married. She'd wanted to say yes then and there, but held back, needing time to be sure.

He'd shown up on her doorstep again, triggering hot, nervous energy and stirring up yearnings for him inside her. These last few days, knowing she'd see him, she'd succumbed to her hope that he'd want to come back to her. Yet Aaron's soft expressions and his hungry eyes had thrown her. That, she realized after she'd closed the door behind him, was the reason she'd hurried him out of the house. Years before she'd listened to the father of her child argue his case for marriage. Yesterday, she'd seen in his posture and stance all the signs that he was about to use his powers of persuasion yet again. But once more, she needed time to sort out her thoughts and feelings in order to be certain a second decision would be as sound as the first.

Shortly after Aaron left, she'd called Dottie at the garden and asked if she and the others could handle the festival on their own that evening. "I need to stay home and take care of a few things," she'd said without elaboration. Dottie had sounded almost too happy when she assured her that she and the staff could manage the evening crowd just fine.

Sonia was jolted back to the present moment when the caterer approached and asked if it was time to start the buffet line.

Nodding, she said, "Go ahead and steer people this way."

"This is quite an undertaking," Aaron said as he moved toward her. He nodded to the line forming near the tables heaped with food. "More employees than ever."

"This evening always makes me think of Rona," she said with a sigh. "She suggested the employee dinner in the first place."

"Matt used to enjoy it, too," he said, smiling.

Not a wistful or sad smile either, she noted.

He stood behind her and to the side as she greeted each person going through the line. She wouldn't see some of the seasonal staff until the spring. Others, especially the students, would likely move on to permanent jobs, although a few might eventually stay on as fulltime employees at the garden. With college behind her, Heather, Cal's oldest daughter, worked fulltime at the garden now, helping it remain a family business.

Later, the dinner officially ended when Dottie stood and clapped her hands to get everyone's attention. "One hour to show time," she called out. "And thanks to all of you for helping to make this another wonderful year at the garden."

The employees scattered and the catering crew cleaned up the buffet table and reset it with a bright red cloth and platters of cookies. Coffee urns and carafes of hot chocolate were set out for visitors.

The next hours sped by, with several hundred visitors passing through, and finally, the festival ended for another year. When she'd said goodbye to the last of the gift shop employees, she went back to the main room where Dottie and Cal stood at the fireplace chatting with Aaron. When she joined them, Aaron offered to help finish closing up.

"Okay, we're outta here," Dottie said, grabbing Cal's arm and steering him toward the door.

Sonia almost laughed out loud at Dottie's ear-to-ear grin.

Until that moment, Sonia had been too busy to focus on her case of nerves, but she and Aaron would soon be alone. She was excited and afraid.

"There's not much left to do," she said. "The maintenance guys will turn off all the lights at midnight."

"Let's walk in the garden," Aaron suggested. "I took a stroll through last night, but I'd like to see the displays one more time."

"Sure. Sounds good," she said.

Aaron got their coats and when they left the building and started down the path, he stopped and pointed to the red and white lights ringing the fountain near the entrance. "It's even more beautiful than it was years ago—and that's saying something."

"It's true. The garden looks like a different place

when it's lit up in winter." She pointed to the lacy spider web formed by golden lights woven in the bare tree branches. "The kids love the spider webs, so we added a few more this year—a little family of spiders."

As they walked, only the sound of their boots crunching on the snow broke the stillness of the empty garden. They soon came to a crossroads where a short path would take them across the small pond to the entrance to the meditation garden. Tiny white ground lights guided the way to the bridge, now outlined in the same subtle lights. Sonia's body buzzed and tingled with energy tinged with apprehension. They were steps away from the snow-covered benches and then they'd see the plaque bearing Matt's name. Sonia let Aaron make the choice to turn in or move on.

As if he'd assumed they were heading to the meditation garden, Aaron stepped on the path leading to it.

"Do you ever wonder what's ahead for the garden—I mean, long term?" Aaron asked, stopping in the middle of the stone bridge.

"You bet. I've given it a lot of thought. I hired Heather last summer because she's a naturalist with a nose for business—I could see her taking over one day. Dottie and I have also talked about creating a land trust or working with an organization to create a nature preserve if and when we or Cal's kids want to bow out. But we want it always available to the public, and a land trust would stave off the developers, pretty much forever." She looked up at Aaron. "Dottie would have checked with you about any final plans."

"I know. I'm glad you've looked into it," Aaron said as they strolled the rest of the way across the bridge.

"We keep coming up with new strategies to keep the place running as a private garden for decades to come," she said, her tone businesslike.

They came to a stop in front of the plaque dedicating the meditation garden to Matt. Aaron brushed the snow off the bronze piece. Then he reached for her gloved hand and held it to his chest. "Matt would be so disappointed in us," Aaron whispered, "and I'd give anything to turn the clock back—"

"Aaron," she interrupted, looking at his profile illuminated by the garden lights, "you know we can't go back."

"Hear me out, Sonia, please."

His pleading tone left her contrite and she lowered her head.

"We don't have Matt. We'll never have Matt again."

She freed her hand and held it to her eyes.

"This needs to be said. I know it hurts, Sonia, but I've been thinking about it all day—and for years, really."

She skimmed tears from her cheeks. "Okay, I'm listening."

"I don't know why it's taken me so long to get this, but I finally do. We're always going to hurt because we lost Matt." He stared at the plaque and reached out as he ran his hand over the lettering. "Nothing is going to fill that hole. Not placing blame or creating memorials. I thought there was something wrong with me—with us—because we didn't wake up one day and feel…I don't know…*over it*."

She made small half-circles in the snow with the toe

of her boot, suddenly fearing what he might say next.

"But the thing is," he said, "being away from you hasn't helped me. And even worse, I know in my heart that our son would never have wanted his death to break us up. He loved us. We were his family and he knew we were a team. He knew all about the garden and how it started." He paused and lifted her chin with his fingers. "Tell me, has being apart helped you?"

She closed her eyes and shook her head.

"These past couple of years in Chicago, I'd walk down to the river and lean on the bridge and think about the boulders and willows down at our river. I'd head down Michigan Avenue and think about you and Matt and Orchestra Hall. I'd see those lions at the Art Institute and well…oh, hell, I don't have to explain it to you. You know what I mean."

He put his hands on her shoulders. "No matter how much I went about my business and claimed I was starting a new life, some part of me felt like a fraud."

She'd been with him right up to that point. "A fraud?"

"I was pretending that I'd done the right thing to make a fresh start without you. But it was never true, not for a minute."

Her heart pounded while she tried to think of words to express her thoughts.

"I'm sorry, maybe I'm rushing things," he said, lowering his arms.

"No, no. I'm just overwhelmed. The thing is, you're echoing what's been going on with me." She chuckled, but stepped back and created space between them. "Besides, when did you get so good at talking about these emotional things?"

Smiling, he reached out to her, but she shook her head. "There's something else."

"Go ahead," he said, "I've had my say."

She peered into his face. "Yesterday I said that we got married and divorced because of Matt. That's what I meant when I said we can't go back. It has to be about us now."

He touched her cheek. "But there came a time when we knew our relationship wasn't only about Matt anymore. That's what we lost after Matt died. We forgot the fun—and joy—we discovered with each other."

Aaron chuckled softly. "Every day something reminds me of how funny you are, and how enthusiastic. Plus, there's that business mind of yours and the way you also appreciate beauty and create it around you." He gestured in all directions in the garden. "Especially here. I miss that. I've missed *you*."

Her stomach fluttered. For the first time in a long time, her heart felt full, complete. "So, does this mean you want to come home?"

Nodding, he said, "I want the two of us to take a chance on each other—just like we did before."

Her fears softened, leaving only lingering apprehension. Besides, someone had to state the obvious. "But, Aaron, really, it may not be easy to fall into a rhythm of living together and making plans for the future. We're different people now. Are you *certain* you want this?"

"I'll do whatever it takes," he said, taking her face in his hands, "to make a new life with you."

She glanced at the plaque with Matt's name on it and out of the corner of her eye, she saw Aaron looking at it, too. "Well, then, let's go."

His lips brushed the corner of her mouth in sweet, teasing kisses that left her breathless.

"I've missed your kisses," she whispered.

"That's a good sign," he said, laughing.

"*I'll say*," she replied, amused at her own flirtatious tone.

"You have no idea how much I've longed to hear you say that."

"We have so much to talk about," she said, "and the rest of our lives to do it."

Slipping her arm through his, they headed away from the garden and down the path toward home.

As they walked, he told her about the offer he'd had to lecture at the law school in Madison, laughing when he added, "I'll be a non-flamboyant Artie Silverman."

She stopped in place. "Wow. I hadn't even thought about what coming back here will mean for your work. Professionally, everything will change for you, but not for me. How can that work?"

He pulled her into his embrace. "I'll call Chuck. I'm sure we can work something out. Whatever I do, I'll stay closer to home. No crisscrossing the country and living out of suitcases anymore. And I look forward to teaching."

She broke their embrace and stepped back. "I'm glad you feel that way. I'd never want you unhappy because you gave up something important to you."

"I know, but you don't need to worry about that."

They walked on in silence and soon they reached the edge of the creek and the house came into full view.

After they crossed the creek, Aaron sighed as he stared at the house. "I just want to stand here and have a look at it."

She clung to his arm while he gazed at the Tudor. It stood serene in its cloak of snow.

"Why don't I make a fire when we go in?" he asked.

"And I'll break out some Lady's Slipper merlot, and you'll feel right at home." Then she let go of him and stepped back, her body alive with energy so electric she could barely contain it.

"What is it?" he asked, as if sensing her excitement.

She stepped back and with arms akimbo, she threw her head back and made a quick full turn in the ankle deep snow. "I'm deliriously happy and afraid all at the same time."

He reached for her and kissed her softly. "Maybe having me back in the house will feel a little odd at first."

"Not *that* odd." Even in the cold air, heat rose in her cheeks over the way she ached for him. "And I'll probably still do the same little things that annoy you," she warned.

He put an index finger on her lips. "Shush. You amused me far more than you ever annoyed me. We'll figure this out, Sonia. I promise I won't let you down," he whispered.

He wrapped his arms around her and held her tight. "You have no idea how much I really, really like you."

"Oh, yeah?" she asked in her best mocking tone. "What do you know? I really like you, too."

They laughed as they linked hands and headed home.

* * *

Virginia McCullough

The River Gazette
January 2, 2007

Spotlight on Lady's River People

We had a hunch something was up in Lady's River when we saw Sonia and Aaron Chapel having lunch at the River's Bend Café a couple of days after Christmas. But, we thought, sometimes a lunch is just a lunch. But yesterday we heard through the grapevine that a small and very private winter wedding has been added to the schedule at Chapel's Botanical Garden. It's a second-time-around story for Sonia and Aaron Chapel. Without going into their private history, let's just say that the entire staff of The River Gazette joins us in wishing them all the best!

Mandy & Amy

Note to Readers

$\mathcal{D}$ear Reader,

Before relocating to Green Bay, Wisconsin, I lived in Asheville, North Carolina, the site of the famous Biltmore Estate. My friend and colleague, Lynda McDaniel, now living in Sebastopol, California, lived near the estate. Lynda introduced me to the yearly pass I could buy that gave me unlimited access to the estate, the winery, the restaurants, but most important of all, the gardens and the estate's trails. For several years, I had the privilege of wandering the estate year round. Those hours spent on the grounds are among my favorite memories of my eight years in a city that offered me many wonderful friendships and experiences. That's why the Biltmore Estate makes a "cameo appearance" in this book.

For a long time, I wanted to write a story in which a couple starts with little more than hope and good will, and only after they marry do they begin to see the possibilities of a rich life with each other and their child. Although admittedly sad, this story also provided me with another opportunity to write about hope, healing, and second chances.

I hope you enjoyed Sonia and Aaron Chapel's story. I welcome your thoughts and comments. You can visit me on Facebook and LinkedIn, and be sure to stop by my Web site, www.virginiamccullough. com, and sign up for my newsletter.

Virginia McCullough
January 2014

About the Author

*R*aised in Chicago by avid readers, it seems inevitable that Virginia would try her hand at writing. She broke into magazine markets when she worked as assistant librarian at the public library in Rockland, Maine. A decade later, she began coauthoring books on medical topics and soon became a ghostwriter/editor for doctors, therapists, business leaders, professional speakers, and many others who had a story to tell.

Virginia has written over 100 books for her clients, including 12 titles for Alan R. Hirsch, MD., a neurologist-psychiatrist and well known smell and taste researcher. Her coauthored books include, *The Oxygen Revolution* (Hatherleigh, third update, 2012), with Paul Harch, MD, a pioneer in the field of hyperbaric medicine; *Option Trading in Your Spare Time* (Sourcebooks) with Wendy Kirkland, an expert in option trading; *52 Ways to Bring More Humor, Hugs, and Hope into Your Life*, with professional speaker, Greg Risberg, MSW, CSP.

In 2011, she and her friend and colleague, Lynda McDaniel, cofounded The Book Catalysts, a book writing coaching service that also offers webinars and tools for writers. Since she likes nothing more than hanging out with other writers, Virginia belongs to the Authors Guild and the Romance Writers of America, along with several of its affiliate chapters. A three-time Golden Heart finalist, Virginia's manuscripts have been chosen as finalists in many contests and she's also won a few.

Virginia has two grown children, and enjoys being a grandmother, too. She currently calls Green Bay, Wisconsin home, but she's lived in six states and the U.S.V.I. When asked about the themes that emerge in her fiction, Virginia says she likes to explore the various ways we create families, plus her books always focus on hope, healing, and plenty of second chances.

Check out Virginia's 2013 release, *Island Healing*, Book 1 of her St. Anne's Island series, available in print and digital editions on amazon.com, and in other formats at Barnes & Noble and Smashwords.com.

Coming soon…

Greta's Grace, a Golden Heart finalist, explores the complex mother-daughter relationship—oh, my—and what happens when a health crisis shakes up everything. This story also has its roots in family, love and loss, and it brings together three generations. It also offers the promise of new directions and enduring love. I used Lake Michigan and the beauty of Door County, Wisconsin to create my fictional lakeside town, Simon's Point. Although not "officially" a series, *Greta's Grace* is the first of three books I've set in Simon's Point. I hope you enjoy the preview.

Greta's Grace

1

I'd wasted too much time longing for what I didn't have and waiting for the tiniest indication that it might be on its way. For years, I'd listened to other women tell amusing mother-daughter stories about shopping adventures or wedding glitches or the challenge of finding a free day to meet for lunch. I struggled to keep my heart free of envy, but I admit that too often I *grudgingly* laughed at these glimpses into other women's lives. They already had what I wanted for

Greta and me.

For so long I nurtured my wish and kept it alive in my heart. Then, in an instant, it no longer mattered. All I wanted was for Greta to get well.

She didn't look sick when I saw her shortly after her diagnosis, leading me to the ridiculous thought that perhaps someone had made a horrible mistake. I'd hurried to the conference room on the oncology floor at the Bayside Medical Center, but stopped to peer through the half-open door and breathed in deeply to collect myself.

She'd tossed aside her boots and sat cross-legged in the middle of a short couch, her elbows resting on her knees. Using her fingers like a pair of scissors, she captured flyaway strands of her long blond hair and tucked them behind her ears. When she looked up and saw me in the doorway, I rushed to hug her.

"Mom, you got here." Greta's slender arms stretched up and loosely circled my neck. "I never saw this coming," she whispered.

"Oh, sweetheart, I don't think we ever see this kind of thing on the horizon." Her cheek felt smooth against my own. But did I imagine it, or were the bones in her shoulders more prominent than ever? My daughter couldn't spare even a single pound on her willowy frame.

When she dropped her arms, I sat in the chair next to the couch and nodded to the older woman across from me. I hadn't expected to see Greta's grandmother-in-law, Ida, who sat with shoulders squared and ankles crossed, her stubby fingers wrapped around the strap of the purse she held firmly in her lap.

"It's nice to see you again, Ida, but—"

"I know. You wish it were a better occasion." After finishing my sentence, she frowned and moved to the edge of the chair. "I'll wait outside, Greta, so you and your mother can talk alone."

I thought it kind of her to understand, but Greta reached across the space between them and gave Ida's knee a quick pat. "Oh no, don't go. I want—I need—everyone here."

Ida didn't reply, but she slid back in the chair.

I'd seen Ida only twice, the second time at Greta and Jake's wedding. They'd had their reception in Simon's Point at the Iverson Café and Bakery, a business Ida had owned for decades and turned into a Wisconsin landmark, thanks to her Swedish pancakes and cinnamon rolls. Theoretically, Ida's pink cheeks and cap of tight gray curls should have made her look like a cheerful and grandmotherly baker, but I found her stiff posture and frown disapproving, even intimidating.

"Where's Jake?" I asked out of curiosity, but also to fill the uneasy silence of waiting to learn what was in store for Greta.

"He's hunting up lunch. I didn't eat this morning and that drives him nuts, especially now." Her silky hair again refused to stay put and she busied her hands trying to make it behave. I glanced at Ida and defensively explained that even as a small child, Greta had often forgotten to eat.

"If anyone had told me, I'd have gladly fixed a container of meat loaf and mashed potatoes."

Ida's gruff tone grated on me, but Greta's expression reflected only fondness and good-natured acceptance of the older woman's quirks.

"I want to get this meeting with the doctor over with

so I can go home," Greta said, a shaky tone seeping into her voice. "I'm sick of this place already."

I understood why. The half-open door was a compromise between preserving privacy and encouraging more air into the hot, stuffy room. Everything had a dull cast, from the matte gray walls to the blue-gray carpet and the matching tweed fabric on the couch and chairs.

Sadly, Greta was destined to spend many hours at the Bayside Medical Center, a square brick building with panoramic views of the Fox River in Green Bay. We already knew that a stubborn flu hadn't caused Greta's on-and-off fevers or the malaise that dragged on through January and into February. Jake first noticed the swelling above Greta's collarbone and from that moment on, worry and waiting took over and consumed every hour of every day.

At first, any news about Greta and her symptoms fell into simple categories, bad and good. When the biopsy led to a diagnosis of Hodgkin's disease, the categories were shaken up, leaving us suspended in despair, while at the same time holding on to reasons for optimism. That explained the dizzying euphoria that rushed through my body when I heard the magic words, Stage I! Even though she had symptoms, the disease itself was confined to one side of her upper body. Only caught up in the terrifying world of cancer could we find ourselves overwhelmed with gratitude that Greta's case fell into the least bad of the bad.

I'd driven over to Green Bay from a hospital in Madison, where, ironically, I'd delivered the keynote at a two-day conference for several hundred cancer patients and survivors, most of whom were women.

Many were nurses, and a few doctors, who'd fought the good fight themselves, also attended. I presented my usual topic, the healing power of women's stories. True, professional speaking isn't exactly show business, but we do live by the ethic that the show must go on. Over the previous days, I'd given my talks, but immediately rushed off to find a quiet place to check my voice mail. I lived with the paradox of desperately wanting to hear some news about my daughter's health while dreading the message itself.

Suddenly, Greta straightened her spine and squared her shoulders, as if remembering one of her signature characteristics, great posture. "Mom? Does Grandma Annie know yet? Have you talked to her?"

"No, not yet," I said with a sigh. "I left her a message, but she's still off on her hiking trip in Costa Rica. She'll be back in a few days."

"She's where?" Ida leaned forward and tapped her index finger against one ear as if checking her hearing aid.

"Costa Rica," Greta said in a slightly raised voice, "the country in Central America. She's on a hiking trip."

Ida's eyes widened in alarm. "My stars! Hiking in a foreign country at her age."

"My mother is what one would call active." I hoped my tone came across as dry but amusing.

Ida shook her head. "Lots of good hiking right here in Wisconsin. No need to fly way down there."

I stifled a snicker, but Greta hooted. "Oh Ida, you are so funny."

Our light interlude ended when Brian, my ex-husband, appeared at the door. Two long strides later he had Greta in his arms.

"Daddy, oh Daddy." She wrapped her arms around him and dug her fingers into the back of his sweater, desperately grabbing at the fabric and hanging on tight. She scooted over to make room for him to sit next to her, and then rested her head on his shoulder.

With one arm draped around her, Brian rested his chin on the top of her head.

Ida stood, but Greta straightened up and quickly spoke. "Don't go."

"I'm sure she isn't going far, honey." Brian raised his free hand in a half wave that could have meant either hello or goodbye, or in that moment, both.

That settled that.

"Jake should be right along." Ida narrowed her eyes at Brian as she gave Greta's hand a quick squeeze before she left.

Brian gently rubbed Greta's shoulder as she talked about the alphabet soup of tests, the CAT scans and the noisy MRI machine that felt like a coffin and the vials of her blood drawn and carried off. I was certain that like me, Brian had heard much of this before, but he let her tell the stories over again without interrupting.

I had talked briefly with Brian a few times over the previous days, but I hadn't seen him since Greta's wedding, not that he'd changed much over the last year. His thick hair had once been the sunny color of Greta's, but before he'd turned forty, it had turned snowy white. That feature alone triggered quick double-takes from women young and old.

Greta inherited her tall, angular stature from Brian, along with his light blue eyes, clear and bright as marbles. Their resemblance was nothing less than startling. I provided the contrast. Short and curvy best described me, not a straight line anywhere. Brian had once said my hair and eyes reminded him of bittersweet chocolate, mouth-watering bittersweet chocolate to be exact, but he'd said those words long ago.

Only the most scrutinizing eyes could see that the slope of Greta's long nose was identical to mine, but then her nose had never been her favorite feature.

"So, like I told you on the phone," Greta said, "today Dr. Hunter is going to explain the treatment team's recommendations." She snuggled deeper into Brian's shoulder. "I'm so scared."

"I know, honey, I know." He cupped her shoulder in his palm and drew her even closer. "So, who is this Dr. Hunter?"

Greta frowned. "My oncologist, Daddy, like I told you on the phone."

"I know, but how do we know he's the best?"

Greta pulled back, her eyebrows lifting in surprise. "Everyone agrees *she's* the best."

"Hunter Passwater," I explained, "but her patients call her Dr. Hunter."

"Thanks for the info, Lindsey, but that tells me exactly nothing." He emphasized his dismissal with a flick of his hand.

"Well hello to you, too," I said, glad I could manage weak sarcasm in response to his rude gesture.

"I'm trying to get some real information here, Lindsey."

"Oh no," Greta said, looking at me, "don't start in on each other or I'll make you both leave."

Brian quickly skimmed away beads of sweat that had formed at his hairline. "It's okay, Greta. We'll be fine."

It was so like him to raise questions about a doctor he hadn't handpicked and doubt anyone else's ability to find the so-called best.

"You two better behave," Greta said. "I don't want you embarrassing me."

Brian looked sheepish, and started to respond, but the door swung wide open and the aromas of garlic and starchy steamed rice filled the room.

"Your favorite—spicy chicken, darlin'." Jake set the containers on the end table next to Greta. "And wonton soup that's still hot." As he tore the plastic wrapping off a fork and spoon, he nodded at Brian and me. "I'm glad you were able to get here."

He lifted the lid off the soup and handed it to her. "Please, please eat."

Brian stayed on the couch, oblivious to the commanding presence of his tall, broad-shouldered son-in-law planted in front of him.

Since the dad showed no sign of giving up his place to the husband, I stood and touched Jake lightly on the shoulder. "We'll leave the two of you alone." I cast a pointed look at Brian as I cocked my head toward the door. He followed me out only when Greta shifted her body—and her attention—away from him and toward Jake.

We walked a few feet down the hallway before he said, "You managed to hustle me out of there pretty fast."

"Anyone could see they needed to be alone, Brian."

"Right, right." He raised his hand and snapped his fingers. "How could I forget? You know everything."

Resting one hand against the wall as if steadying himself, Brian nodded to the glass partition that separated them from the large waiting room. Ida sat in the one overstuffed chair in the room, while Jake's father, Sam, leaned against the wall next to her.

"You won't like this question, but why are *they* here?" Brian asked.

I deliberately let out an audible huff. "Because that's what Greta wanted. They're her family, too, whether you like it or not."

"You really do have an explanation for everything, don't you, Lindsey?" He tightened his mouth in an angry grimace.

I slumped against the wall and a gulping sob came from deep in my throat. "Oh my God, listen to us."

Brian exhaled a tired sigh, and then drew me close to him. "I'm sorry. I didn't intend..." He swallowed hard and tightened his embrace.

I rested my cheek against his chest and breathed in the soapy lemon scent of his wool sweater. His embrace felt strange. Aside from the quick hug we shared at Greta and Jake's wedding, it had been years since I'd felt Brian's arms around me. Until we'd both heard about Greta's illness, we'd spoken only when we had a specific reason and ended our calls after exchanging polite questions about each other's wellbeing.

I tilted my head and looked up into his face. "We can't do this, Brian, we just can't."

He quickly released me, but his hands slid down my arms and he gently held on to my wrists. "I suppose I reached out to console myself as much as to try to comfort you."

"No... I meant that we can't snipe at each other like this."

Brian was about to respond when I spotted a woman

walking toward us, and he followed my gaze down the hall. I knew she was Dr. Hunter, because Greta had described her black hair, worn in a distinctive braided twist sitting like a crown on the top of her head.

She walked toward us with her hand outstretched. "You must be Greta's parents. She mentioned you'd both be here today."

Her palm felt comfortably warm and she held our handshake long enough to communicate concern. And as if I'd been holding my breath, I released all the air in my lungs and the stiff muscles in my neck relaxed.

Glancing through the glass partition, Dr. Hunter raised her hand in silent greeting to Ida and Sam. "Greta's a fortunate young woman," she said, looking back at me. "So many people love and support her."

Brian folded his arms across his chest. "I'd like to talk with you about the protocol. I assume you're recommending a combination of drugs. Correct?" It sounded more like a challenge than a question.

Dr. Hunter cut her eyes to me before focusing on Brian. "First, I'm going to talk with Greta and Jake," she said, her voice kind but firm, "and after that, if it's okay with Greta, I'll be happy to answer your questions." With that, she walked the few feet to the conference room and knocked softly before she entered.

His face pinched, Brian looked like someone had just landed a blow. "Don't start in on me, Lindsey." He puffed out his cheeks and sighed. "I don't mean to act so obnoxious, but I guess it's the best I can do when I'm scared out of my mind."

"I know, I know." I felt as if I were clinging to ropes on a swing, riding up on my impatience over Brian's bluster and bullying, then swinging back and feeling as sorry for him as I did for myself. With no words left, I turned away. Through the glass partition, I caught both Sam and Ida watching at us. Sam quickly shifted his gaze to the window, but Ida, her forehead still wrinkled in a frown, continued staring as I walked into the waiting room to join them.

* * *

Despite the twists and turns, the footpath through the woods was easy to follow. I shivered as I grabbed the collar of my jacket and pulled it tighter around my neck, all the while wishing for a thick scarf to protect me from the damp wind blowing off Lake Michigan. Marianne, the desk clerk at the Iverson Inn, had given me directions to Sam's workshop, so I'd headed down a path behind the café and the tennis courts before it veered off into the woods along the shore.

Rather than going back home to Chicago, I'd followed Greta and Jake to Simon's Point and checked into a room at the inn that Sam and Jake owned together, along with their rental cottages and cabins. Before leaving Green Bay, I'd pulled Greta aside and told her my idea about moving to Simon's Point during her months of treatment. At first she objected, but in a distracted sort of way, arguing that moving would disrupt my life. Her words sounded like a reflex response, and a weak one at that.

I'd also told Greta that I wanted my mother, her beloved Grandma Annie, to be comfortable during what I expected to be extended visits. A place we could really settle into appealed to me more than a room at the Inn, no matter how lovely. When I briefly spoke with Jake he assured me that his dad would be happy to show me one of their cottages.

I shoved my cold hands deeper into my coat pockets. How I could be so poorly prepared for the biting cold of an upper mid-west February? I'd endured raw Chicago winters all my life, after all. But the nature of my work as a professional speaker had led to the habit of dressing for short jaunts between airports or parking lots and hotel check-in desks. Walks in the woods weren't part of my typical day.

The faint sound of piano music filtering through the trees caught me by surprise. As I continued on the path the lilting melody became louder, and more unlikely yet, recognizable. I could match only a handful of classical pieces with their composers, but this Chopin waltz happened to be one of them. Greta had leapt and twirled to its rhythms in ballet class when she was perhaps seven, certainly no more than eight.

The memory flowed through me in one heartbreaking piece. In my mind's eye I saw myself sitting with a dozen or so other mothers in a row of folding chairs, each of us fixing our gaze on our own miniature ballerina in the sea of black leotards and pink tights moving in a wave across the floor. I felt lightheaded as the image sharpened. Even in the woods, I could almost smell the damp and slightly sweaty scents that filled the air in that old dance studio.

When the path took a sharp turn, the workshop appeared. Through the open door I saw Sam bent over a piece of wood stretched across two sawhorses. I froze in place and watched him tap his fingers back and forth over it, as if playing the Chopin piece on a keyboard.

He appeared completely absorbed in the rhythms of the music. If he suddenly saw me, he might be embarrassed and wonder how long I'd been standing there watching him. I made a quick decision to call out to him and when he glanced up I said, "I hate to interrupt a man so deep in concentration. Should I come back later?"

He smiled broadly. "No, no, you're not interrupting." He reached behind him and flipped off the radio, abruptly silencing Chopin. "Jake said you'd be looking for me."

Sam's long narrow face with its high forehead and slightly receding hairline struck me as more pleasant than handsome, but he had the appealing lanky build of a long-distance runner. As I approached him, though, his dark blue eyes threatened to completely disarm me. They communicated such kindness that I had to focus somewhere else. I'd been trying so hard to stay strong, and knew I couldn't handle looking into a face capable of revealing such empathy.

With effort, I kept my voice casual and light. "I can't resist asking what you're going to do with that piece of wood you're, uh, examining so carefully."

Sam tapped the wood a few times. "It's going to be two storage-locker doors in the boat I'm building." In a soft voice, he added. "But that's not important now. Why don't you and I go take a look at one of our cottages? I imagine you want to make your plans."

Sam grabbed his gloves and led the way up another narrow path along a crescent-shaped cove, where the dull gray of Lake Michigan matched the color of the smoky bank of clouds hanging heavy in the afternoon sky. I tried to fall into rhythm behind Sam's sure steps and match the crunch and squeak of his boots as he left footprints ahead of me on the hard-packed snow. But my awkward steps kept me a frustrating half-beat behind.

"I understand why you want to come up here and stay for a while," he said. "Greta must be pleased to know you'll be nearby."

"We didn't talk for long, of course, but she warned me not to disrupt my life too much. She assured me she had many people to help her...blah, blah, blah."

Sam laughed and turned his head halfway around. "Words...those were only words she felt obligated to say."

Since we were talking about Greta, I couldn't be certain Sam was right, but I didn't expect him to understand my daughter's ambivalence about me.

"Before I even see the cottage, Sam, I want you to know that I insist on paying the full seasonal rent. I'll probably stay here all summer. No favors just because."

"I know, I know," Sam interrupted, "just because we're family and our Greta is in trouble, blah, blah, blah."

Sam's mimicking tone amused me and coaxed a smile to my face. I hadn't found much to smile about in the last couple of weeks.

Then I saw it and drew in a quick breath. "Oh my—how lovely it is."

Painted white with cranberry trim on the windows and porch, the square frame cottage looked like a present wrapped in white tissue and tied with red ribbon. And someone's loving hands had tucked it under the protective branches of pines and white birches. "Thank you, Sam, thank you so much."

He glanced down at me, smiling. "I'm kind of partial to the little place myself. I call it the Christmas Cottage..."

Made in the USA
San Bernardino, CA
23 March 2014